GHOST SCHOOL

GHOST SCHOOL

BY

ETH CLIFFORD

ILLUSTRATED BY BOB DOUCET

A
LITTLE APPLE
PAPERBACK

SCHOLASTIC INC.
New York Toronto London Auckland Sydney

ISBN 0-590-35032-3

12 11 10 9 8 7 6 5 4 3 2 8 9/9 0 1 2 3/0

Printed in the U.S.A. 40

First Scholastic printing, October 1998

With much love
for my grandchildren, some of whom are beginning to write stories of their own.

CONTENTS

1

A HAUNTED ADVENTURE

"You want to go *where*?" Elizabeth Summers stared at her twin sister. Carol Summers was grinning. Carol always grinned when she was about to get the twins into trouble.

"You heard me, Elizabeth. The old Lincoln schoolhouse," Carol said. Her dark brown eyes, which looked just like her sister's, were shining. "Come on, Elizabeth," she said in her special please-do-this-with-me voice. "Jeff has a great plan for seeing ghosts."

Jeff Manly lived in the last house on their street and was in the same second-grade class as the twins. He loved ghosts. You never had to guess what Jeff would be on Halloween. He was always a ghost!

In his room, Jeff had a long shelf of ghost books. The scarier they were, the better. He read every kind of ghost book. He even decided to write his own books about ghosts.

Elizabeth knew that Jeff wanted to go to the old schoolhouse. Everyone knew that the schoolhouse was haunted. That was why Jeff wanted to investigate it. He was sure that ghosts lived there. A real writer would go and search for the facts, he said. All the facts . . . But Elizabeth didn't think that it was such a great idea.

"I'm not going to any old haunted schoolhouse at night. You and Jeff can go if you want. But I am positively, absolutely, cross-my-heart-

and-hope-to-die not going," Elizabeth said. "Not ever!"

Then she had an idea. "We can't go anyway, Carol," she said happily. "Grandma Bertha is here."

Grandma Bertha was not their grandmother but their next-door neighbor. Their mom and dad were away at a big business convention. Grandma Bertha was staying with them for the weekend.

"Grandma Bertha?" Carol laughed. Grandma Bertha always turned on the TV really loud and then slept through every program. "She'll never know we went out," Carol said as she zipped up her jacket.

Elizabeth stared at her twin. Why did she always lose arguments with her?

"Listen," Carol said. "We have to go. Jeff is waiting for us right now outside his house."

Carol handed Elizabeth a jacket. "You can't just leave a friend all alone."

Elizabeth knew Carol was right. Jeff and Carol were her best friends. She had to go. She buttoned her jacket and followed Carol down the staircase.

The TV was blasting some news report as the twins sneaked outside. The girls giggled. Grandma Bertha was snoring!

When they reached Jeff's house, the girls could see a shadowy figure standing by an old oak tree.

"What took you so long?" Jeff grumbled. "I thought you weren't going to show up."

Carol didn't answer him. She was curious about the bag in his hand. "What's in the bag?"

"It's just some things we're going to need when we go into the schoolhouse," Jeff told her.

"What kind of things?" Elizabeth asked nervously.

"Things to protect us," Jeff said. He reached into the bag. One by one, he pulled out three masks.

A skeleton mask.

A vampire mask.

A ghoul mask.

"Oooooh. Gross," Carol said. She smiled a wide grin that seemed to stretch from ear

to ear. "I know which one I want. The ghoul mask."

"Which one do you want, Elizabeth?" Jeff asked.

Elizabeth closed her eyes and pointed.

"You picked the vampire," Jeff said. "Great! Now I can be the skeleton." He really wanted the ghoul mask, but the skeleton was next best.

Elizabeth pulled on her mask. "Why do we need these?" she asked.

Jeff slipped his skeleton mask over his head. "Just in case. It might be good to scare the ghosts. You know, instead of them scaring us."

Carol grinned and put on her ghoul mask. "Jeff, you thought of everything."

Jeff reached into his bag and grabbed three flashlights. "I also have these. There is no electricity in the school."

"Isn't the school going to be locked?" Elizabeth asked. She still was looking for a way to get out of going to a dark and haunted schoolhouse.

"The door isn't locked," Jeff said. "I know. I tried it. Why would they lock it, anyway? Nobody is going to break into a place that is haunted."

"Except us," said Carol.

Elizabeth stared at Carol and Jeff.

Her heart began to pound. She had a very uncomfortable, scary thought.

This wasn't just a story in a book. This was going to be a real haunted adventure.

2
EEEKS AND BOOS

When they reached the schoolhouse, all three stopped and looked at the dark, old building.

"Come on. Let's go in," Carol said. She couldn't wait for the adventure to begin!

"Shhh . . . we have to be very quiet," Jeff said. "We don't want to disturb anyone."

"Especially not any ghosts," Elizabeth added.

As they walked up to the large red door, Elizabeth stuck her hands and flashlight deep in her pockets. The autumn wind was blowing and she wasn't sure if the howling she heard was the wind — or something else.

"Hurry up, Jeff!" Carol whispered.

The door creaked when Jeff began to open it. Elizabeth's heart started to pound faster. *Ker-thump! Ker-thump! Ker-thump!*

"Okay," Jeff said. "Follow me."

"We look pretty weird," Elizabeth whispered as they tiptoed down the hall, wearing

their masks and carrying flashlights. Every classroom they passed seemed to be silent and dark. The three walked close together. They kept their eyes wide-open, ready to spot a clue — or a ghost.

Suddenly, Jeff stopped. Carol bumped into him and Elizabeth bumped into Carol.

“What is it?” Carol asked. “What’s the matter?”

“I thought I heard something,” Jeff said.

"Like what?" Carol whispered. She knew she had great hearing. She always did well on those school hearing tests, but she hadn't heard a thing.

"Over there, in that classroom," Jeff said as he pointed to room 222. "Turn off your flash-lights," Jeff said. "We don't want them to know we're here."

Huddled together, they slowly walked to the classroom door. Elizabeth held on to Carol's jacket. She began to whisper, "One plus one is two. Two plus two is four. Four plus four is eight. Eight plus eight is sixteen. . . ."

Jeff turned and stared at her. "Shhh," he said. Then he asked Carol, "What is she saying?"

"Our dad always tells us if we get scared or upset, we should do something really bor-ing," Carol explained. "It helps to calm us down."

"Well, can't she do it quietly?" Jeff asked.

"Sorry," Elizabeth whispered. She moved closer to the door and peeked inside.

"Why, this isn't scary at all," she said, surprised. "It looks just like our classroom."

In three neat rows, just like in their second-grade classroom, was a class. But here all the students were ghosts. In the front of the room was a larger ghost. She was pointing at the blackboard with a stick.

"E-E-E-E-E-K!" the ghost teacher said as she tapped the board. The class repeated the teacher's sound.

"B-O-O-O-O-O!" the teacher said next. Again, the class of ghosts repeated after her. "Very good, class," the teacher said. "But you must learn to elongate your boos. E-LON-GATE." She put her hands together, then slowly stretched her arms apart. "E-LON-GATE. Make the sound last."

When the young ghosts were finished with the sounds, the teacher said, "And now we will have our poetry time. Who would like to go first?"

"Ms. Shriek! Ms. Shriek!" a small ghost in the front row waved her hand up and down. "I know one!"

"Go ahead, Scare. Please share it with the rest of the class," Ms. Shriek said.

"She's just like our teacher, Ms. Cleaver!" Carol whispered.

"Shhh," Elizabeth and Jeff said together and pressed their faces up to the window on the door.

Scare flew to the front of the room. She stood tall and began her poem:

Hickory, dickory, dock
A ghost flew around a clock.
It frightened a mouse
Who ran out of the house
In a terrible state of shock!

All the ghost children laughed. But so did Jeff, Carol, and Elizabeth! At once, all the ghosts turned and stared at the door.

3

SPOOKY LESSONS

"Run!" Carol whispered. They raced away from the door and down the dark hallway.

"That was close!" Jeff said, panting. He looked around the corner and then back at the twins.

"Do you think they saw us?" Carol asked.

Jeff didn't answer. He had already spotted a new classroom to spy on. He motioned for Carol and Elizabeth to come stand next to him. "This is great! I want to find out what else ghosts learn in school," he said.

"Me too," the twins said together.

"Shhh! Not so loud," Jeff warned the twins.

"I know," Elizabeth said. "We have to be very quiet."

"Yes. Silent," Carol agreed. Slowly they tiptoed over to the door and looked through its glass window.

"Now, class," the ghost teacher was saying. "Do you remember that last week we talked about famous ghosts in history?"

"I like the Headless Horseman the best," one ghost called out. "I like the way he carried his head under his arm."

"Look up on the wall!" Jeff whispered.

It was like seeing a movie on TV. A man on a horse galloped by. The horse's hooves went *clop, clop, clop*. But this rider was headless! He carried his head under his arm.

The class clapped and cheered.

GHOSTS

"All right, class, settle down," the ghost teacher said. She was shorter and fatter than the first ghost teacher. "Who can tell me what we learned this evening?"

A few hands waved in the air and the teacher picked one ghost sitting in the third row. "Yes, Fright, please go ahead."

"Fading in and out," Fright said, sitting very straight in her seat. "I can show you, Mrs. Spook."

Mrs. Spook shook her head. "Not right now, Fright."

Fright stood up next to her desk. "But I've been practicing and practicing. All I have to do is—"

"Please sit down!" Mrs. Spook said. Mrs. Spook looked so sternly at Fright that she sat down at once in her seat.

"Mrs. Spook?" a ghost in the back row asked.

"Yes?" Mrs. Spook turned her attention to the student who had called her name.

"What are those creatures doing outside our classroom?" the ghost asked.

Jeff looked at Carol and Carol looked at Elizabeth and Elizabeth looked right at Mrs. Spook!

"Monsters!" the class cried.

"FADE!" Mrs. Spook said sharply. In seconds, everyone disappeared. Almost everyone.

Except for the one ghost who had asked the question. He was staring at the door.

In a moment, an arm appeared out of nowhere. The arm curled around the ghost and yanked him away.

POOF!

He vanished.

"Cool," Jeff said as he peered into the empty classroom. "That was super cool. I wish I knew how to do that!"

"Maybe if we stick around here long enough we can learn," Carol said.

"Who knew that spying on ghosts could be so much fun?" Elizabeth asked, laughing. "And it's educational, too!" she added.

Carol was about to say, "See? I told you so," when a hand reached out and grabbed her shoulder.

It wasn't Jeff's hand.

It wasn't Elizabeth's hand.

Carol froze. Right now, she wished that she could do what the ghost students had done . . . just fade away.

She wanted to fade right out of this haunted hall.

Instead, she did what Elizabeth would have done. She began to add!

"One plus one is two. Two plus two is four. Four plus four is eight. Eight plus eight is sixteen. . . ."

Jeff and Elizabeth didn't turn around to look at Carol. They were too busy looking for the vanished class of ghosts.

But then Jeff heard what Carol was saying.

She was adding!

"Oh, no!" Jeff said. "Not you, too. What's the matter with you?"

"My shoulder," Carol managed to whisper. "Look at my shoulder. There's a hand on it!"

Jeff turned to look.

So did Elizabeth.

They were both frozen with fear!

For the hand on Carol's shoulder belonged to a very big, very scary ghost.

4

A GHOSTLY PROBLEM

"Do you have a hall pass?" the large ghost demanded.

The twins and Jeff stared at him. The ghost didn't wait for an answer. Instead, he asked, "Why are you wearing masks?"

Jeff and Carol both shook their heads. Jeff tried to speak, but his words came out in a squawk that didn't make any sense at all. Then Elizabeth said very quickly, "The class play. We're in the class play."

"And we're late," Jeff added. "We're very late."

"Well, don't let it happen again," the ghost said. And vanished.

"Whew!" Jeff sighed.

"That was great thinking, Elizabeth!" Carol said.

Elizabeth smiled at her twin, but her smile quickly faded when she heard a low moan. There was someone else in the hall with them.

All three spun around, but no one was there!

"I'm up here," a voice said. "Against the ceiling."

When they looked up, they saw another ghost who seemed to be floating back and forth.

"Excuse me, Mr. Ghost, sir," Carol said politely.

"My name is Mr. Haunt. I'm the principal of this school." He sounded quite angry.

"Why are you floating up against the ceiling?" Carol asked. "Is that what ghost principals are supposed to do?" she asked curiously.

"Of course not!" he said sadly. "But you see, I have not been able to touch the ground for some time." The old ghost sighed. "You have no idea how annoying it is, never being able to land anyplace."

Jeff and the twins looked up at him. They felt sorry for him. They wished they could help.

"But there are so many other problems as well." Mr. Haunt sighed again. "I need to find a new school for the students."

"A new school? Don't you like it here?" Elizabeth asked. She was just getting used to the idea of having a ghost school in the neighborhood. And she was beginning to like it, too.

"Oh, dear. Oh, dear," Mr. Haunt said. "First, I need to get down on the ground. I am so tired of flying up here. Do you know how hard it is to sleep when you are floating up here on the ceiling? I haven't slept in days!"

"Maybe we could find a ladder someplace, climb up, and yank him down," Jeff said.

"Or we could climb up on a desk," Carol told him.

"Great idea," Jeff agreed. "Come on. Help me push a desk from a classroom out here."

Jeff and the twins tried to move a desk out into the hall. Working together, they finally moved the desk, inch by inch, to the door of the classroom.

"This'd better go through the door," Carol said. "Pushing this desk is hard."

Elizabeth kept looking around nervously. They were making a lot of noise moving the desk. She hoped that the other ghosts wouldn't get mad. But they were doing this for the principal, so maybe the teachers wouldn't get upset about all the squeaking sounds the desk made as they pushed it.

When the desk was finally in the hall and under the old ghost, Jeff climbed up and tried to reach him. But Jeff was too short!

Jeff thought and thought.

"Can you float down just a little bit?" Jeff asked finally. "Just a little — so I can grab you?"

"If I could float down, I wouldn't need you, would I?" Mr. Haunt said.

Jeff jumped down off the desk.

"It wouldn't have worked, anyway," Carol pointed out. "How do you grab hold of a ghost?"

Then Elizabeth had a wonderful idea. "Think heavy!" she shouted up at the ghost. "Think heavy!"

"That's a whiz of an idea, Elizabeth," Jeff said.

Mr. Haunt stared down at her. And then he sighed. "I've been so upset, I've forgotten how to think."

Elizabeth was disappointed. However could they get him down? Then Carol had an idea.

"Think of bricks!" Carol shouted.

"Yes, a load of bricks in a shopping cart!" Jeff added.

"A shopping cart?" Mr. Haunt asked.

Jeff and the twins looked at each other. Then Elizabeth stepped forward. "It's the wagon you push around in the supermarket," she explained.

"What do you do with the horse?" Mr. Haunt said, looking very confused.

"The horse?" Carol asked, puzzled. "What horse?"

"The horse that pulls the wagon," Mr. Haunt said. He floated back and forth as if he were pacing.

Carol shook her head. “We’ll just have to think of something else. But what?”

“I know!” Elizabeth said. “Think of something very sad,” she shouted up to the principal. “When our mom is sad, she says she is down in the dumps. That’s way down low.”

“I had a wonderful dog once,” Mr. Haunt said. “I sure loved him.” He sounded very sad.

“What happened to him?” Carol asked.

“He ran away. His name was Apparition,” Mr. Haunt told her.

"Apparition? That means ghost!" Jeff whispered. "You had a ghost dog?" Jeff was excited. Imagine having a dog who was a ghost!

"Why of course," Mr. Haunt said. "What other kind of dog can a ghost have?"

"I have a dog named Butch," Jeff said. "He ran away once, too. But he came back."

The principal sighed. "All this talk isn't helping me get down, is it?"

Elizabeth felt sorry for this very tired ghost. "Let's talk about the bricks again. Just think of very heavy, heavy bricks. Lots of them. Pulling you down. And down. And down."

"Heavy, heavy bricks. Lots and lots of heavy bricks," the principal repeated softly. "Pulling me down. And down. And down."

Jeff and the girls stared at Mr. Haunt as he slowly, slowly began to move. It seemed like forever to Jeff and the twins as he inched his way down to the ground. When at last his feet touched the floor, Jeff and the girls grinned.

"Hooray!" they shouted.

"We did it!" Jeff said. "Well, I mean Mr. Haunt did it!"

But the principal didn't say a word. Instead, he just laid down on the floor and began to snore!

"Poor, tired ghost," Elizabeth said. "I hope he remembers to think of heavy things when he wakes up."

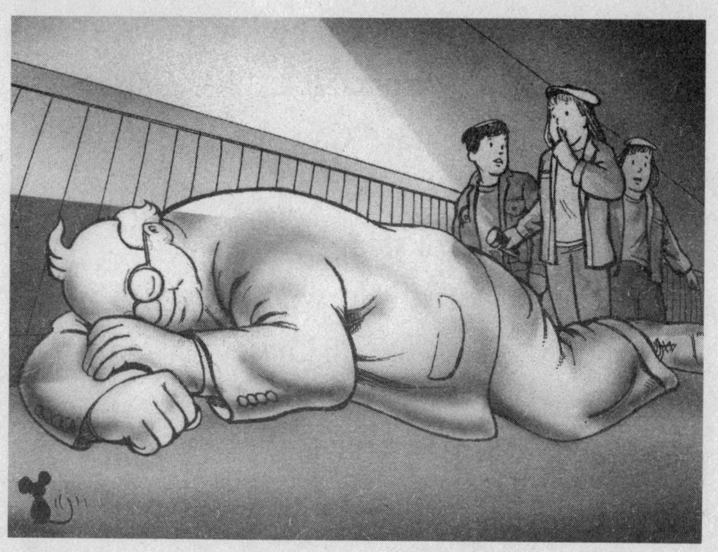

5

IT'S NOT FAIR

Seeing Mr. Haunt sleeping made Elizabeth sleepy, too. She yawned a big, wide yawn that made her cheekbones crack. "It must be awfully late," she said. "Can we just go home now? I'm tired."

"Me too," Carol said.

Jeff wasn't tired. He wanted to see more. "We didn't get to see all the classrooms," he complained.

"You can stay if you want to," Carol told him. "But Elizabeth and I are going home."

"All right," Jeff said. "I guess we should go."

He followed the twins out the door. They walked quickly to the rusted school gate. The twins walked ahead, but Jeff stopped when he saw a sign hanging on the fence.

In red letters, the sign read:

"Oh, no!" Jeff said. Elizabeth and Carol stopped walking. They ran back to Jeff and stared up at the sign, too.

"They can't do that," Elizabeth said.

"Where will the ghosts go? This is their school."

"Where would Ms. Shriek and Mrs. Spook teach? It's not fair," Carol added. She thought of how sad she would be if her school were torn down. "This is what Mr. Haunt was talking about. He has to move the school!"

"We have to do something," Jeff said. "We can't let them do this!"

Elizabeth and Carol agreed. After seeing the ghosts, they felt that it was up to them to save the school.

6
A GHOSTLY SCHOOL PLAN

The three friends sat under the sign and tried to think of an idea for saving the ghost school. The wind blew fallen leaves in little circles on the pavement.

"We can't tell people that this is a school for ghosts," Jeff said. He put his head in his hands. "No one would believe us."

"And parents for sure wouldn't like the idea of a ghost school in the neighborhood," Elizabeth said.

Jeff and Carol looked at each other. Elizabeth was right. No one would want a ghost school in the neighborhood.

"That's it!" Jeff said. He jumped up and stood in front of the twins. He had a great idea. At the same time, Elizabeth and Carol started to grin at each other. They had an idea, too!

"The Frothington House!" they all shouted at the same time.

Jeff beamed. "We all had the same idea. It would be perfect for a ghost school."

"Perfect," both girls agreed.

The Frothington House was once visited by George Washington! The Frothingtons allowed their home to become a schoolhouse in colonial times. Later, it was turned into a historical site. It was the oldest schoolhouse in the whole state.

"No one ever goes there at night," Jeff said. "So the ghosts could still be a secret and be safe."

"Let's go tell Mr. Haunt!" Elizabeth said. She turned and ran toward the school so quickly, Carol and Jeff had to race to catch up with her. But it was Jeff who reached the door first and opened it.

They fixed their masks and put on their flashlights to see down the dark hallway.

The girls didn't need to add or multiply anymore. They weren't scared now because they were too busy thinking of everything they wanted to tell the principal. "Do you think Mr. Haunt is still there?" Carol asked anxiously.

"Maybe we'll be lucky," Elizabeth said.

And they were! For they found the principal, fast asleep. He must have been dreaming of a ton of bricks, because he hadn't moved off the floor.

And he was still snoring.

"I didn't know ghosts could snore," Elizabeth said, smiling.

Jeff tried tapping the principal on the shoulder, but it is very hard to tap a ghost on the shoulder. Jeff's hand went right through the sleeping ghost!

"I don't think this is going to work," Jeff said sadly.

"Maybe you should just whisper in his ear," Carol suggested.

Jeff nodded and leaned closer to the principal. "Ummm, Mr. Haunt?"

Finally, the ghost opened his eyes. "Did you forget something?" he asked sleepily.

"No," Carol said. "We came back because we need to tell you something important."

"If it is something heavier than bricks, I don't want to hear it," the principal said. "I'm very tired. I'm just glad school is over for the night."

"Go ahead. Tell him about the Frothington House, Jeff," Elizabeth said excitedly.

Jeff looked at the sleepy ghost and spoke very slowly. "This building is going to be torn down soon. But we have thought of another place for you and the ghost children to have a school."

The principal opened his eyes wider and sat up. He stared at Jeff and then at Elizabeth and Carol.

"You know of another place? You do, really?" He sounded as if he couldn't believe what he had just heard.

"It is a historical place," Jeff said. "There

are visitors all during the day, but no one ever goes there at night. You would be safe from people finding out about you and the other ghosts. Plus, it is a bigger building."

The principal stood up. His feet were actually on the ground! He smiled at them and then took a tiny book from his coat pocket. "The Frothington House, I believe you said?"

He wrote the name down carefully. Then he nodded at the twins and Jeff, who were grin-

ning. “Thank you. For myself and our whole ghost school!” He shook his head. “We knew we would have to leave this place. It has happened to us before, you know. We have to move every hundred years or so.” He looked all around sadly. “This has been a very good place for us, but it is time to move on.”

“You’ll like the Frothington House,” Elizabeth told him. “We went there on a field trip once.”

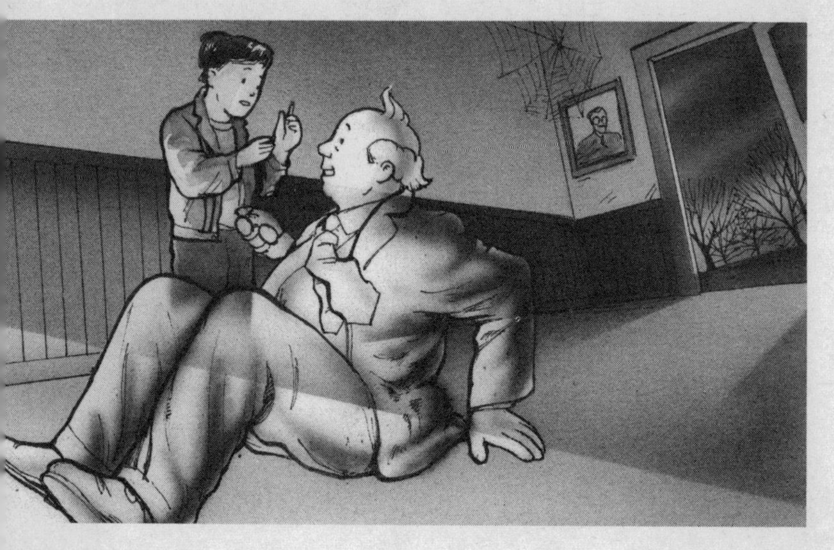

The principal smiled. "I'm sure it will be grand. Thank you, children. You have been a huge help. If you hadn't found another place, our little ghosts would have been lost."

Jeff stood a little straighter and Elizabeth and Carol smiled. They had saved the ghost school!

But Mr. Haunt wasn't smiling.

Had they done something wrong?

7

A GHOSTLY SECRET

Mr. Haunt bent down so that he could whisper to Jeff, Elizabeth, and Carol. He looked very serious.

"You must keep our school a secret," he whispered. "It is very rare that we allow humans inside our schools, especially without a hall pass!"

"I guess our masks didn't fool him," Carol whispered to Elizabeth.

"We won't tell anyone," Jeff said. And Elizabeth and Carol nodded.

"It will be our secret," Elizabeth said.

"We'll never tell," Carol promised.

Mr. Haunt reached inside his vest pocket and took out his pocket watch. He flipped open the top and looked surprised. "It is late. Shouldn't you humans be home by now?"

Elizabeth looked worried. "I forgot all about the time. Do you think Grandma Bertha is still sleeping?" she whispered to Carol.

"She'd better be. Or we'll be in big trouble," Carol agreed.

"Thank you, children. Thank you so much," Mr. Haunt said as he started to fade. "You have saved the ghost school!" And suddenly, he was gone!

Jeff looked at the twins. They were both grinning at him. "We saved the ghost school!" he shouted.

"Yes, we did," Carol agreed. "We really and truly did!"

“This was a great haunted adventure,” said Elizabeth. “I’m really glad that we came to this ghost school tonight.”

“Me too,” Carol said and hugged her twin.

Jeff opened the rusted schoolhouse door. It creaked as it swung open. “We’re lucky we had a ghost school in our town. Too bad we can’t tell anyone!”

“Do you think anyone would believe us, anyway?” Elizabeth asked.

"I don't care," Jeff said. "We know we saw those ghosts and helped them out."

"Who cares what people think?" Carol shouted. "We found the ghosts a new school!"

As the three walked home with their masks on their heads, Mr. Haunt sat high above them in the old oak tree. He waved farewell to the children who had found a new school for his ghost students.

As they walked away, Elizabeth said, "You think he will remember to think heavy thoughts when he gets stuck up on the ceiling again?"

They stopped for a moment to look back at Mr. Haunt in the tree. He was gone!

The twins said good night to Jeff at the oak tree in front of his house and then quickly ran home. Grandma Bertha was fast asleep in her chair and the TV was still on. Quietly the girls tiptoed to their room and crawled into bed.

"It really is too bad we can't tell anyone about our haunted adventure," Elizabeth whispered to her sister.

"It can be our own special secret," Carol said. She reached over to turn out their light, but not before she grinned at her twin. "And maybe one day we can visit our ghost friends."

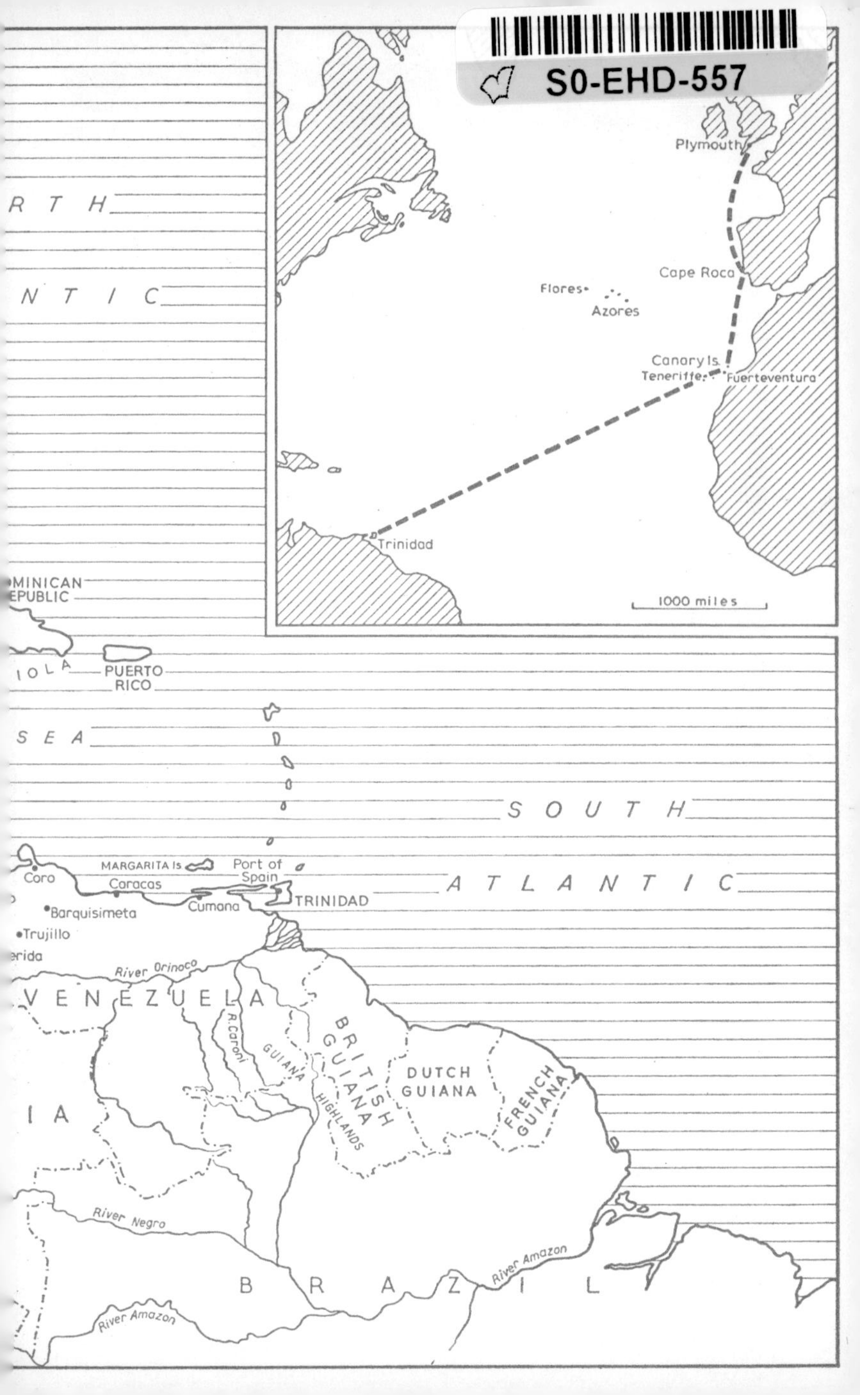

Plymouth
Cape Roca
Flores
Azores
Canary Is.
Teneriffe
Fuerteventura
Trinidad
1000 miles
R T H
N T I C
MINICAN
EPUBLIC
IOLA
PUERTO
RICO
S E A
S O U T H
A T L A N T I C
MARGARITA Is.
Port of
Spain
Coro
Caracas
Cumana
TRINIDAD
Barquisimeta
Trujillo
erida
River Orinoco
V E N E Z U E L A
R. Caroni
GUIANA
HIGHLANDS
BRITISH
GUIANA
DUTCH
GUIANA
FRENCH
GUIANA
I A
River Negro
River Amazon
B R A Z I L
River Amazon

Sir Walter Raleigh

Selected Prose and Poetry

Athlone Press Texts for Schools and Colleges

CHAUCER

The Franklin's Tale

edited by Phyllis Hodgson

RALEIGH

Selected Prose and Poetry

edited by Agnes M. C. Latham

MASSINGER

A New Way to Pay Old Debts

edited by Muriel St Clare Byrne

MILTON

Milton's Dramatic Poems

edited by Geoffrey and Margaret Bullough

WORDSWORTH

A Wordsworth Selection

edited by Edith C. Batho

Sir Walter Raleigh

Selected Prose and Poetry

edited by

AGNES M. C. LATHAM

UNIVERSITY OF LONDON
THE ATHLONE PRESS
1965

Published by
THE ATHLONE PRESS
UNIVERSITY OF LONDON
at 2 *Gower Street London* WC1
Distributed by Constable & Co Ltd
12 *Orange Street London* WC2

Canada
Oxford University Press
Toronto

U.S.A.
Oxford University Press Inc
New York

Printed in Great Britain by
WESTERN PRINTING SERVICES LTD
BRISTOL

CONTENTS

MAPS AND ILLUSTRATIONS

NOTE

Asterisks in the texts indicate the presence of a corresponding note at the end of the volume.

GENERAL INTRODUCTION

SIR Walter Raleigh was born in 1554, into a world of fierce competition and golden opportunities. With supreme self-confidence, he collected the prizes. For himself he collected the favour of Queen Elizabeth I, which was the foundation of his fortunes. For his country he tried to collect no less than two continents, North and South America. His success with Elizabeth was offset by a failure with King James. He was committed to the Tower in 1603, on a not very well substantiated charge of treason. He whiled away the long hours of captivity in writing a history of the world, shrugging off the humiliating present by sitting in judgement upon the past. The point was not lost on James, who found his book 'too saucy in censuring princes'. He also tinkered with metallurgy and chemistry and compounded a potent medicine which won an honourable place in the dubious pharmacopoeia of the day. In 1616 he was released, to open up a gold mine in Spanish America and in 1618 he was beheaded upon a charge of breaking the peace with Spain. By this time he was a national hero, and has remained so ever since; a man accustomed to accept outrageous odds, so that whether he won or lost the results were always sensational.

His father, another Walter Raleigh, was a country gentleman, and young Walter was brought up in Devonshire, involved in a network of cousinship among the gentry of the West. They were ambitious, independent people, with an interest in mining, in seafaring, and in their country's foreign wars. Their proximity to the Continent made them sensitive to the threat of invasion, and Devon and Cornwall were some of the first counties to be asked to supply men for service overseas, because they had shipping available and no problem of transport to the coast. These interests, in mining, seafaring and soldiering abroad, are plainly reflected in Raleigh's career.

Since he was a younger son he had his own way to make. He was given a good education, which included a year at Oriel College, Oxford. He was always going to be interested in books and ideas, but his academic training was strictly non-professional, and he did not take a degree. In 1569 he was seeing active service in France with an English contingent fighting for the Huguenots. In 1575 he was in London, at the Middle Temple, a place which as well as training lawyers put a final polish on young men who wanted a career in the world, and found the universities too remote from it. He looked hopefully for court preferment, till necessity or inclination sent him soldiering again, this time against the Irish rebels. Ireland was a potential danger to Protestant England because it offered an invasion base to her Catholic enemies. In 1580 a small Spanish troop actually landed on the west coast. They did not find the support they had hoped for among the native Irish, and on their unconditional surrender the Lord Deputy ordered every man to be put to the sword. One of the two officers in command that day, to whom this operation was entrusted, was Captain Walter Raleigh. He had seen some ugly fighting in France. He saw worse in Ireland, and he had some hairsbreadth escapes.

It was typical of Raleigh that he was never content to mind his own affairs. He was extremely critical of the conduct of the war, and indeed of the whole policy of the English towards the Irish. He did not conceal his opinions, and since they were lively and intelligent, and the war seemed to be costing more than it was worth, they caught the ear of someone in authority at home. He was recalled in December 1581.

The following year, 1582, was crucial for him. It was the year in which he attracted the attention of the Queen. One account has it that he addressed the Privy Council so cogently on Irish policy that the Queen became curious to see him. No such address appears in the Council minutes. It seems highly probable, however, that it was his report on Ireland which first distinguished him among the crowds that jostled for attention. The tradition that he spread his rich cloak in a puddle so that the Queen need not dirty her shoes supplies another facet of the story. Part at least of the legend has a basis in fact. His clothes were quite fantastically rich and the man who wore them meant to be noticed. But Raleigh was much more than a handsome gallant, ready with a grand gesture. He was an intelligent, forceful, capable man, and the same imagination which dressed him in jewelled doublets, and hung pearls in his ears, could be bent to more serious ends. The Queen, whose personality also expressed itself in silks and gems and grand gestures, was no fool. She did not choose Raleigh for his outside only. There was a fund of unquenchable life in him. His mind was overflowing with schemes and projects. In his company it was impossible to be bored. The long-faced, tight-lipped, pale queen of England must often have been bored.

Once his foot was on the ladder he climbed fast. In the next few years he became Vice-Admiral of Devon and Cornwall, Lieutenant of Cornwall, and Warden of the Stanneries, that is of the Cornish tin mines. He had lucrative monopolies, huge estates in Ireland, and was not squeamish about inheriting the lands of a convicted traitor. You could no more be squeamish at court, than in the French and Irish wars. In 1585 he was knighted and in 1587 he became Captain of the Queen's Guard. Much of the work which accrued with these offices was done by deputies—that was normal procedure—but Raleigh took a genuine interest in anything entrusted to his care. If he bothered to work at all he worked very hard. It was unwise, however, for a courtier to absent himself much from court. There were too many people waiting to step into his shoes should he vacate them for a moment. The young Earl of Essex constituted a threat. He was a nobleman by birth, and Raleigh in comparison was an upstart. Many people thought they were as good as he was and grudged him his success, and he did not go out of his way to conciliate them. He was said to be 'damnable proud'.

In days when much political power was vested in the sovereign, a court was more than a social centre. It was a place where a man's fortune was made or marred, one of the most ruthless, competitive, and nerve-racking places in the world, as well as the most civilized, exciting, and splendid. It bore very hard on those who fought for advancement there, living as it were constantly in the eye of a far from impartial appointments board. It also bore hard on the sovereign, upon whom all its pressures were ultimately concentrated. It was too much for Henry VIII, and he was no weakling. James I succumbed early to senile decay, and Charles I lost his throne and his head. Elizabeth, who did not live in easier times, contrived a long and prosperous reign. We no longer think that this was because she was a vain and rather tiresome woman who happily left the business of government to able ministers. It may be true that she rarely wore the same dress twice. If she gained courage to face a new day by strapping on a new burden of velvet and seed-pearl it was a small means towards a great end.

The Queen needed all the help she could get. She turned to her favourites for emotional support. Without some channel for her natural feelings she could not have carried on the unnatural business of being England's queen. With her first favourite, the Earl of Leicester, she played at having a husband. With Raleigh she played at having a lover. It was not a very satisfactory state of affairs, because it was only play, but Elizabeth was an adept at pretending. The love game that she entered into with Raleigh was the fashionable petrarchan, neo-platonic one, in which a lover serves a superlative mistress, so far beyond him that he can hope for no reward. The convention seemed to fit the real situation like a glove. It transmuted some of its less amiable aspects without seriously falsifying them.

It does not matter whether the Queen was physically

attractive, nor whether she was young. In 1583 she was fifty, a very modish and elegant person, though not in the mode of the twentieth century. What matters was that she was the Queen, the giver of all good things and the focus of all desire. She was also a woman. To call a queen a goddess was an easy bit of gallantry, much easier than to call a king a god. It was a poetical commonplace.

> Praised be Diana's fair and harmless light,
> Praised be the dews wherewith she moists the ground,
> Praised be her beams, the glory of the night,
> Praised be her power, by which all powers abound.
>
> Time wears her not, she doth his chariot guide,
> Mortality below her orb is placed,
> By her the virtue of the stars down slide,
> In her is virtue's perfect image cast.

Many poets praised her publicly, as a public figure. What distinguishes Raleigh is that his verses were private and personal. They were a formalized courtship; though he was courting a woman who could never be won. It followed naturally that few of them appeared in print, and only fragments have survived. They were intended for a very select circle. He was not averse, however, to a fellow-poet seeing his lines. Spenser describes how Raleigh, visiting his Irish estates in 1589, came to Kilcolman and listened to part of *The Faerie Queene*, in return for which he read Spenser some verses of his own.

> His song was all a lamentable lay,
> Of great unkindness, and of usage hard,
> Of Cynthia, the Lady of the Sea,
> Which from her presence faultless him debarred.
> And ever and anon with singults rife,
> He cried out, to make his undersong,
> Ah my love's queen, and goddess of my life,
> Who shall me pity, when thou doest me wrong?

Certainly his estates needed his attention, but equally certainly he would not have been attending to them had there not been some cloud of court disfavour. It was not serious. He took Spenser back with him quite confident of a good reception.

> Right well he sure did plain,
> That could great Cynthia's sore displeasure break
> And move to take him to her grace again.

All seemed to have been smoothed over. But Raleigh, as usual, was playing his luck and it could not hold forever. There was one respect in which the real situation failed to tally with the feigned one, and it was basic. For some time now the perfect platonic lover had been secretly married to Elizabeth Throckmorton, one of the maids of honour. When that became known to the Queen, the whole house of cards would inevitably collapse. She had thought she was being made much of and all the time she was being made a fool. The date of the marriage is uncertain. A French scholar, Pierre Lefranc, has found documentary evidence suggesting that it may have been as early as 1588. We know now, from A. L. Rowse's recent study of the diary of Sir Arthur Throckmorton, Lady Raleigh's brother, that Sir Arthur first heard of the marriage in November 1591 and that in March 1592 his sister gave birth to a son, to whom Essex stood godfather. History has nothing to say of this child, who perhaps died in infancy. In 1593 there was a second son, christened Walter, and in 1604 a third, Carew. Carew was the only one who survived his father.

It was natural enough that Sir Walter should marry—he had waited till he was more than thirty—and natural that he should fear the effect on the Queen. He had the sense, when the scandal was about to break, to try and put a considerable distance between himself and the court. Ireland was not far enough this time. He assumed command of a small squadron bound for Panama to seize Spanish treasure ships. This kind of privateering, directed against the ships and goods of enemy nations, came naturally to a west-countryman, and could be represented as patriotic, though it had its undesirable side in that it tended to draw reprisals. It was a risky business, but with luck the profits could be enormous. Raleigh's ships and their consorts had one of the most spectacular successes in the whole history of Elizabethan commerce-raiding. They took a great carrack, the *Madre de Dios*, loaded with jewels and spices, and brought her to Dartmouth, where the sailors proceeded to hold a kind of wild Bartholomew Fair, in which they traded purloined gems for a fraction of their value. Raleigh was the only person who had any control over them and he was no longer in command. He had been urgently recalled, not this time because the Queen was anxious for his safety or wishful for his company. She would never again invest her emotional capital in Sir Walter Raleigh. He and his wife were sent to the Tower, from whence he was grudgingly released, to ride down to Dartmouth and calm the uproar there and to disentangle the complicated finances of the voyage. Two of the ships had sailed at the Queen's cost and she did not want to see her profits dissipated. So in the end the *Madre de Dios* bought Raleigh a pardon.

He retired to Sherborne, in Dorset, where he had recently acquired a country house. A phase of his life was ended, not wholly to his disadvantage. His successful career as a courtier had brought him a knighthood, a name in the world, influential friends, offices of authority, money and estates, though never enough to satisfy his insatiable appetite for such things. He was now free to attend to the wider interests which had always been pulling him from the Queen's side. His Irish estates cried out for development. The Cornish tinners were fighting an economic depression and he owed them support. He was several times elected to parliament and it was not in his nature to sit there dumb. Above all he wanted.

> To seek new lands for fame, for gold, for glory.

As early as 1584, when his half-brother Sir Humphrey Gilbert was drowned on the way home from Newfoundland,

Raleigh had taken over Gilbert's charter for exploring and settling new lands. The first land he settled was in North America. He called it Virginia in honour of the Queen. He never himself set foot on North American soil, but he nursed his struggling colony as well as he could from home. It was a very costly hobby and success did not come until after Raleigh had regretfully given up and Virgina had been taken over by a joint-stock company. In the 1590's he was free to follow his fancy, and this time it led him south of Panama, to the overseas empire whence the Spanish treasure ships brought back to Europe the sinews of war. The English privateers had for a long time been snapping at their carracks as they negotiated the long voyage home. On an enterprise of this kind Sir Richard Grenville was lost, fighting a crazy rearguard action at the Azores in 1591. Raleigh immortalized the battle in a pamphlet known as *The Last Fight of the Revenge*, his first piece of published prose.

It occurred to him now that he might do better than to seize enemy goods at sea. Much of South America was still unexplored and unexploited. Was not this England's opportunity? The territorial claims of Spain need be no deterrent since England and Spain were at war. Catholic Spain threatened the very existence of Protestant England. Spain straddled the sea-routes to the discouragement of English commerce, and her claim to own both the Americas closed the door to overseas enterprise. Only by the grace of God had England survived the Armada of 1588. There were other armadas preparing and the next encounter might not be so blest. Raleigh believed that the way to avert a peril was to move in to the attack. Having once secured a foothold on the South American continent, the English could push steadily further until they were threatening the main Spanish settlements in Venezucla and Peru; until in fact they had pushed the Spaniards into the sea.

The choice of the country bordering the Orinoco was strategically admirable. The great river ran into the heart of the continent, midway between north and south, breaching the wall of hill and forest. The Spaniards had not as yet established much foothold there, but they were beginning to be interested in the country inland, which was known by its native name of Guiana, Land of Waters. There were persistent rumours that the Inca kings, dislodged from Peru, had fled eastward and ruled a civilized empire in a secret valley guarded by almost impassable mountains. Here a priest-king was annually smeared with gum and rolled in gold dust, before he descended for ritual purification into the waters of a lake. The Spaniards called him El Dorado, the gilded man. The story, which may in the beginning have reflected a genuine religious ceremony of the South American Indians, began to sprout and blossom, as stories will. When Raleigh heard it, El Dorado had become a golden city which the natives called Manoa. It was situated on a great lake among the mountains of Guiana, and its whole nobility were regularly powdered with gold. It had to be in Guiana. That was the last remaining mountain fastness which no explorer had yet penetrated. The Indians could testify to the lake, since the rivers habitually overflowed and lay in wide sheets in the higher valleys. And they could, when pressed, produce objects of wrought gold which were in fact relics of the dispersed Incas or of a similar civilization located in what is now the Republic of Colombia. Spanish pressure was very brutal, and it is not surprising that the natives eventually gave the answers which were required of them, or that the golden city was always said to be somewhere just ahead, always further on, in somebody else's country, deeper and deeper in the interior. In this way the first explorers provoked their own nemesis, and one expedition after another perished miserably in fever-haunted jungles.

Raleigh collected every scrap of information available on the subject of Guiana, both from books and from his many contacts in the west-country ports. He studied the mistakes of the Spanish expeditions and decided that he would do differently. He would win the love of the Indians and he would conceal from them the white man's greed for gold, which had already cost them so dear. That is why we find him patiently courting the Indian chiefs and mastering their political affiliations.

In 1594 he sent out a scouting party and in 1595 he sailed, himself, with what looked like a ridiculously small and amateurish company. Actually their small number served them well. They travelled light in circumstances in which it might have proved impossible to travel any other way. The men complained that they had no change of linen but, as Sir Walter rather wryly observes, their shirts were washed several times a day on their backs by the tropical rain. They were a loyal and close-knit company, sharing hardships and all having a stake in success. Even the gentlemen took their turn at the oars. If the men insisted on stuffing their pockets with minerals that Raleigh had warned them were worthless, he did not interfere. 'I could have afforded them little if I should have denied them the pleasing of their own fancies herein.' He was a good leader. All his life witnesses to his power of charming people and winning their love. The Queen was only one among many who succumbed to his personal magnetism. His written work retains this power to charm.

But there was another side of it. Those who did not sun themselves in his grace were often resentful. Nor did everyone wish to submit and be led, or put much reliance upon schemes which were often to sober eyes fantastic. Where he was not loved he was often hated. After his fall from favour the pack could yap at his heels as they had not dared to do in the years of his glory. He came back from Guiana to present the Queen with a new kingdom and he was mocked as a purveyor of tall tales. The tallest of all he seems genuinely to have believed to be true. He did not claim that he or any of his men had actually seen the golden city, or spoken at first hand with anyone who had, but he was convinced that it existed. Thereby he presented to the English imagination an enduring myth, though to him it was not so much an end in itself as a means to an end. He was aiming to add to an English North America an English South America.

It all came to nothing because it received no support from home and it was not a plan a man could prosecute in his private capacity. Raleigh's aggressive policy was not likely to commend itself to the Queen, whose talents—and she was talented—lay in quite another direction. He had to content himself with seconding the officially sponsored moves in the Spanish war. In 1596 he sailed in command of the Warspite as one of a squadron under Essex which attacked Cadiz, and in 1597 he was again with Essex on the Islands Voyage, an attack on the Azores. The party which had attached itself to Essex, as the rising star, let slip no opportunity of blackening Raleigh and fomenting quarrels between two men who in different circumstances might have been friends. The Elizabethans understood faction and intrigue better than team-work. The Cadiz expedition was injured by faction. The Islands Voyage was ruined by it.

Raleigh did not engineer the downfall of Essex, though it was clearly to his advantage, and he bore much of the odium of it. Essex was his own worst enemy. He thought that if he put it to the test, the country would back him against the Queen. She was elderly, tired, irritable, a constant clog on bright progressive spirits. His friends encouraged him and urged him on to his ruin. The English people were shocked and distressed when in February 1601, after an unsuccessful rising, they watched their late idol mount the scaffold, but they had not raised a finger to help him. They had too much sense. Mourning Essex, they found some satisfaction in cursing Raleigh. He stood by at the execution, it was said, contemptuously puffing out tobacco smoke.

In truth, it must have been a sobering sight for him. He was lucky to be able to immerse himself in the business accruing from his recent appointment as governor of Jersey. Jersey was his last attempt to rule a sub-kingdom. He made himself very busy improving the fortifications and encouraging trade there. Then in March 1603 the old Queen died and his luck died with her. King James VI of Scotland became King James I of England. James, who had thought he had a friend and well-wisher in Essex, was convinced that in Raleigh he had a dangerous and subtle foe. If there was no show of overt hostility, that was the man's cunning. James made no effort to hide his antipathy. Raleigh was relieved of most of the offices and emoluments the Queen had bestowed, while hundreds of unsympathetic eyes watched to see how he would take it. He was said to be 'discontented' and well he might be. From here it was easy to go on and assume he must be plotting something. Soon he was answering a charge of treason, in a climate of opinion in which he could hardly hope to disentangle himself from the web of suspicious circumstance.

The whole question of Raleigh's alleged treason in 1603 is obscure. There were some moderately innocent intrigues afoot involving peace overtures from Spain, to be encouraged by influential English courtiers in return for Spanish gold, and another far less innocent and less rational scheme to replace James by another claimant, Arabella Stuart, and to extort toleration for the English Catholics. None of these was a cause with which Raleigh was likely to identify himself. He had always been opposed to Spain and to catholicism, and notably loyal to the Crown. His trial was conducted with shocking partiality and venom, and his guilt has never been satisfactorily proved. Nor has his innocence, either. His defence, which he conducted himself, has been preserved in contemporary records. It was magnificent, and it swung public opinion right round in his favour. James suspended the death sentence, the shadow of the axe having extorted no damaging confession from anybody, and Raleigh went to the Tower.

The letters which survive from this time are frantic and rather humiliating pleas for pardon, and exaggerated expressions of regard for King James. Raleigh was in an impossible position. He could not be grateful to James for injuring him, but if he were ungrateful it justified the injuries. As always, under adverse circumstances, a new side of his genius displayed itself. Denied active participation in affairs, he gathered round him a library of books in a variety of languages, mostly Latin, and set about writing a history of the world. Always behind his practical, active life there had been a passionate interest in theory. He had failed in the world and was out of the race. What were the conditions of worldly success or failure and was it worth having? It was not, he decided, worth very much; but if by any means at all he could have prized open his prison doors and re-entered that disillusioning world, he would not have hesitated a moment.

James's Queen was on his side, and so was the heir-apparent, young Prince Henry. But by the time Raleigh had completed the first volume of his history the prince had died, so that key was no longer available to release him. The History, published in 1614, enhanced his growing reputation and displeased the King. James's popularity was by now on the wane. Almost everybody had hoped too much from the new reign and after ten years of it almost everybody was disappointed. People began to look back, perhaps a little sentimentally and unrealistically, to earlier days. James had very sensibly inaugurated a new policy of peace with Spain, now visibly tottering under the weight of her American empire and her losses by land and sea. It was the right moment to call a halt. But not everybody saw it like that. It was not an inspiring policy and it contradicted many fixed prejudices. It was possible to argue that this was the very moment to go ahead energetically with the war, and there was increasing pressure on the King to do something about it.

The tall, distinguished, haggard man, who at one time was daily to be seen taking his exercise on the walls of the Tower, limping a little from an old wound he got leading the ships into Cadiz harbour, was a perpetual reminder of how things had been done in Elizabeth's now golden days. He still had the secret of Guiana's wealth, and he was always offering to open a mine, which he said was easily worked and very rich. It was a vulgar bait compared with that 'large, rich and beautiful empire' he had offered Queen Elizabeth. To James, anxiously placating the Spanish ambassador, a somewhat overbearing and unpopular person, it was impossible to offer an empire which encroached upon Spain. And the golden city was receding into mythology. It was there to find but curiously no one had yet found it. So Raleigh offered a single mine, from which he solemnly pledged his word to bring large amounts of gold without giving 'just cause of offence' to Spain. This involved at least *some* recognition of English rights in Guiana, but it was a precarious understanding he had with the King, if indeed it was an understanding at all. Raleigh was used to playing a lone hand, and it is clear he was going to interpret his commission to suit occasions as they arose. He had in mind employing French mercenaries upon whom he could shift the blame for infringing Spanish rights. In the end they never turned up. It was thought at home that he was meditating commerce-raiding, and perhaps he was, but when it came to the point he had other things to think about, including something like mutiny on board. All stood or fell by the mine. When no mine was discovered, and the English had attacked and burnt a Spanish town which they said barred their way to it, Raleigh's fate was sealed.

He had not himself commanded the expedition into the interior. He was barely convalescent after a bad bout of fever and had to stay with the big ships at Trinidad. His trusted second-in-command, Lawrence Keymis, led the party. Keymis wrote back to tell Raleigh that they had stumbled unawares upon the Spanish town, which had been moved from its previous site. Hostilities were unavoidable and Raleigh's young son, Walter, had been killed in the affray. Then why, Raleigh desperately demanded, no mine? We do not know what answer Keymis made to this, the crucial question. Before long he had put himself beyond the reach of further questioning and reproach by taking his own life. Spanish records prove beyond doubt that the town of San Thomé was exactly where it was to be expected. It was a frontier post, put up in 1596, to guard the entrance to the coveted—and imaginary—empire of Guiana. Raleigh adopted Keymis's argument that it had been moved at least twenty miles. It is impossible to say whether he really believed this. He may have deliberately perpetuated what he now guessed to be a falsehood, in order to clear himself of blame, or he may have been offering the King a useful sop for the Spanish ambassador, to make English policy at least look blameless. He may quite simply have trusted Keymis.

It was a dreadful homecoming. Raleigh thought of his wife and his surviving son, of the friends who had encouraged and financed him, of his good name and the cause of England's greatness which he thought he was serving, and he resisted the temptation to stay away and sell his sword to the highest bidder. He still believed he had a gold mine in his pocket. He could still use his pen, in defence of his ideals, and he argued eloquently and desperately for a foreign policy which would grant that Guiana was English and that if anybody was trespassing it was the Spaniards. It was not doctrine which King James had ever approved and he had some reason to feel injured, the more so because Raleigh's dreams of empire, and his personal tragedy, combined to make him a much more sympathetic figure than his sovereign. To mark his non-participation in the whole distasteful affair the King had omitted to seal Raleigh's pardon along with his release. So it was difficult to behead him on a charge of breaking the peace with Spain when he had been convicted of conspiring to promote a peace with Spain. James must have felt that it was all most unfair. So did the London crowd which flocked to Palace Yard, Westminster, to see a great Elizabethan die; but it was not James they were sorry for. Raleigh had made a last minute attempt to escape to France. Nobody begrudged him that. They reserved their contempt for the man who had pretended to help in the venture and then had betrayed him. He was one of the west-country cousins, Sir Lewis Stukely. 'Sir Judas' he was called ever after.

Raleigh rose nobly to his last great occasion, joking a little, to relieve the tension of his nerves, and promising a friend who feared his levity might be misinterpreted that he would be serious enough when the time came. He had had a recurrence of malaria and had only just stopped shivering. He was anxious people should not think he was afraid or fail to hear his defence because his voice was not very strong. In a great and solemn hush he cleared himself as well as he could of the most damaging charges against him. Whatever he had in fact planned to do, he was certain in himself of one thing, he had never in action or intention meant to be disloyal to his country or to tarnish his personal honour. Then, when he had straightened his account in the eyes of men, he recast it before God.

'And now I entreat you all to join with me in prayer, that the great God of Heaven, whom I have grievously offended, being a great sinner for a long time and in many kinds, my whole course a course of vanity, a seafaring man, a soldier, and a courtier—the temptations of the least of these were able to overthrow a good mind and a good man—that God, I say, will forgive me, and that He will receive me into everlasting life. So I take my leave of you all, making my peace with God.'

He is buried near the altar, in the church of St Margaret's, Westminster.

Poems of
Sir Walter Raleigh

POEMS: INTRODUCTION

RALEIGH was a poet in an age when poetry was both a branch of learning and a social asset, and to write and read it was an accomplishment for a gentleman. That does not mean that the poetry was necessarily trivial. Raleigh's is sometimes rather serious. It does mean, in his case, that it is impossible to read all that he wrote. He was too much the gentleman to contemplate a Collected Works. Very little of his verse appeared in print with even so much as his initials subscribed. A few complimentary poems prefixed to the work of friends and an elegy upon Sir Philip Sidney are all he seems to have acknowledged. A group of poems very likely his was printed anonymously in a choice and well-presented anthology called *The Phoenix Nest.* No contributor to *The Phoenix Nest* is actually named, but a few modest initials appear. They do not include W. R. Then there is the affair of the cancel-slips in *England's Helicon.* In this anthology there were originally two poems assigned to S.W.R. The printer has gone to the great trouble and expense of pasting over them little slips which substitute the word 'Ignoto' (unknown). The usual explanation is that Raleigh had complained of the vulgar and unauthorized use of his name and insisted on something being done about it. It might mean, on the other hand, that he had not written the poems. Almost every poem that we ascribe to him presents a similar problem. Some appear in printed texts. Some are found only in the little manuscript collections called commonplace books, which poetry lovers of the sixteenth and seventeenth century liked to compile. It is hard to be sure that any poem is his. If there are several versions available it is hard to know which is nearest to the original. It is hard to know at what date and in what order they were composed.

There is, however, one fragment of verse which is incontestably Raleigh's. Among the papers of his friend Sir Robert Cecil, preserved at Hatfield House, are some lines in Raleigh's hand which he has called 'The Eleventh and Twelfth Books of the Ocean to Cynthia'. The Twelfth Book trails off unfinished. They are the passionate laments of a lover who has offended his mistress. We know from Spenser (General Introduction, pp. 11, 12) that in 1589 Raleigh had written a set of plaintive verses with which he successfully coaxed the Queen to overlook some fault or misunderstanding. It seems likely that in 1592, when he was in serious trouble on account of his marriage, he tried to repeat his former success and composed these despairing lines, perhaps begging Cecil to invent a way of bringing them to the Queen's notice. Since they are still at Hatfield House, it would appear that Cecil found the time unpropitious.

An Eleventh and Twelfth Book presuppose ten previous books, and Raleigh has long been credited with a 'lost poem' of some scope and magnitude. Spenser's Cambridge friend, Gabriel Harvey, knew of it, and regretted that it was not generally available, for the honour of English poetry. Recent criticism has been doubtful of the existence of any very considerable 'lost poem', and it has been suggested that the famous *Cynthia* was no major poem but was perhaps a collection of lyrics, metrically various and of varying length, uniform only in subject matter in that in all of them Raleigh is addressing the Queen.

In spite of these doubts and difficulties, the slender corpus of Raleigh's poetry as we know it carries the stamp of a recognizable personality, sceptical, disillusioned, melancholy. Equally characteristic is the tendency to write about vague and abstract things, such as love, time, sorrow and death. The Eleventh Book of *Cynthia* is a quite extraordinary tissue of abstractions. There is in some of his verse an element of strangeness and as it were of disarray. He does not always write with conventional correctness, but speaks as the feeling moves him. This is most noticeable in *The*

Pilgrimage, a strange poem on any showing, but it is also present in *Cynthia* and in the curious treatment accorded to the ballad of *Walsingham*. The intrusion of what seems like a strong personal emotion into his verses is not a characteristic of the sixteenth century. The poems which are marked by it are startlingly unlike his more orderly and ordinary performances.

The earliest date we can give to a poem is 1576, when Raleigh wrote some lines for Gascoigne's *Steel Glass*. The latest date is 1618, when he wrote in his Bible, the night before he was beheaded, 'Even such is Time'. It turns out to be a verse from a love lyric of happier days, dignified with a devout last couplet.

THE TEXT

The poems in this volume are not all that can be attributed to Raleigh. It is hoped they afford a representative and worthwhile selection.

A source is given for the text of each poem, as it is printed here, but there is no note of other places where it can be found or, for the most part, of the reasons for ascribing it to Raleigh. Where there is considerable difference of opinion whether a poem is his, attention is called to the fact.

Spelling and punctuation are modernized. This raises the problem of elided syllables. On the whole Raleigh seems to like the final -ed in past participles to be elided, though in poetry it could be syllabic, and there are places where the metrical stress would permit either. The reader must exercise a certain amount of metrical tact. Spelling is often helpful, as 'opprest' for 'oppressed'. Sometimes the rhyme gives a clue, as 'taste' rhymed with 'placed'. Where Raleigh himself writes 'th'' for a weak or elided 'the' his spelling has been preserved. To indicate all the significant spellings, however, would have produced a rash of apostrophes. It has seemed preferable to mark by an accent one or two places within the line where the metre halts badly without syllabic

-ed. The spelling of the rhyme words in *Cynthia* suggests that Raleigh did not expect the -ed to be regularly sounded at the end of a line.

Some words in sixteenth-century pronunciation were true rhymes which are so no longer, as 'pierce' pronounced to rhyme with 'hearse'. On the other hand the sixteenth century would accept a rhyme which depended upon an unstressed syllable, as 'companion' rhymed with 'done', 'company' with 'fantasy', 'acceptance' with 'abundance'.

Words in poetry tend to be used with exceptional delicacy; sometimes with great precision, sometimes vaguely for their evocative and associative power, or else with deliberate ambiguity, calling upon more than one possible sense. This makes it hard to explain unfamiliar meanings in a simple marginal gloss. If the annotation were extensive the reader would find that the editor was in fact reading the poems for him. He must again fall back to a great extent upon his own tact and skill, which will inevitably be strained, since the meanings and associations which make the language rich and significant are not always of the present century. An instance is the word 'stomach' in the first poem, which means 'bad temper, pride, irascibility' and these senses improve considerably upon the notion of a physical tongue located in a physical stomach, though that sense is there too. The epithet 'cankered' is equally applicable to a physical stomach and a touchy temper.

A word upon whose ambiguity Raleigh sometimes plays is 'kind'. In 10 he says that in behaving 'unkindly' (i.e. cruelly and unnaturally) the lady is none the less typical of her natural 'kind' (i.e. womankind which *is* cruel to lovers). Another difficult word is 'conceit', which must be thought of in connection with the verb 'to conceive', to form an idea in the mind. We still use 'conceive' and 'conception' much as the Elizabethans did, whereas 'conceit' has narrowed in ordinary speech to 'having a good conceit of oneself'. 'Fancy', with sometimes a more serious weighting than we should give the word, comes near the Elizabethan meaning.

'Passionate' is used in a particularly sixteenth-century way in *The Passionate Shepherd* and *The Passionate Man's Pilgrimage*. It refers to a person suffering under the stress of a strong emotion. No precise emotion is implied in the word. It may be anger (as today), or love (with a much less narrow connotation than today), and very frequently it is sorrow.

However disagreeable it is to have to gloss words in poetry, a poet intends his work to be understood, not to be just a series of pleasant sounds. In addition, an Elizabethan intends it to be more than a series of vaguely evocative words.

Poems of Sir Walter Raleigh

I

Walter Rawely of the Middle Temple, in commendation of the Steel Glass

Sweet were the sauce would please each kind of taste,
The life likewise were pure that never swerved;
For spiteful tongues in cankered stomachs placed,
Deem worst of things which best (percase) deserved.
But what for that? This medicine may suffice; 5
To scorn the rest, and seek to please the wise.

Though sundry minds in sundry sort do deem,
Yet worthiest wights yield praise for every pain:
But envious brains do nought (or light) esteem
Such stately steps as they cannot attain. 10
For whoso reaps renown above the rest,
With heaps of hate shall surely be opprest.

Wherefore to write my censure of this book,
This Glass of Steel unpartially doth show
Abuses all, to such as in it look, 15
From prince to poor, from high estate to low;
As for the verse, who list like trade to try,
I fear me much, shall hardly reach so high.

8 *wights*: persons. An archaic word is used for the sake of alliteration. *pain*: pains taken, care.
18 *hardly*: with difficulty.

2

A Vision upon this Conceit of the Faery Queen

Methought I saw the grave where Laura lay,
Within that temple where the vestal flame*
Was wont to burn, and passing by that way,
To see that buried dust of living fame,
Whose tomb fair love, and fairer virtue kept, 5
All suddenly I saw the Faery Queen;
At whose approach the soul of Petrarch wept,
And from thenceforth those graces* were not seen,
For they this Queen attended, in whose stead
Oblivion laid him down on Laura's hearse: 10
Hereat the hardest stones were seen to bleed,
And groans of buried ghosts the heavens did pierce.
  Where Homer's spright did tremble all for grief,
  And curst th' accéss of that celestial thief.

Conceit: invention, imaginative creation.

The Passionate Shepherd to his Love

By Christopher Marlowe

Come live with me, and be my love,
And we will all the pleasures prove
That valleys, groves, hills and fields,
Woods or steepy mountain yields.

And we will sit upon the rocks, 5
Seeing the shepherds feed their flocks,
By shallow rivers to whose falls
Melodious birds sing madrigals.

And I will make thee beds of roses,
And a thousand fragrant posies, 10
A cap of flowers, and a kirtle
Embroidered all with leaves of myrtle.

A gown made of the finest wool,
Which from our pretty lambs we pull,
Fair lined slippers for the cold, 15
With buckles of the purest gold.

A belt of straw and ivy buds,
With coral clasps and amber studs,
And if these pleasures may thee move,
Come live with me and be my love. 20

The shepherd swains shall dance and sing
For thy delight each May morning;
If these delights thy mind may move,
Then live with me and be my love.

11 *kirtle*: gown.

3

The Nymph's Reply to the Shepherd

If all the world and love were young,
And truth in every shepherd's tongue,
These pretty pleasures might me move,
To live with thee and be thy love.

Time drives the flocks from field to fold, 5
When rivers rage, and rocks grow cold,
And Philomel becometh dumb,
The rest complains of cares to come.

7 *Philomel*: the nightingale.

The flowers do fade, and wanton fields
To wayward winter reckoning yields; 10
A honey tongue, a heart of gall,
Is fancy's spring but sorrow's fall.

Thy gowns, thy shoes, thy beds of roses,
Thy cap, thy kirtle, and thy posies,
Soon break, soon wither, soon forgotten; 15
In folly ripe, in reason rotten.

Thy belt of straw and ivy buds,
Thy coral clasps and amber studs,
All these in me no means can move
To come to thee and be thy love. 20

But could youth last, and love still breed,
Had joys no date nor age no need,
Then these delights my mind might move
To live with thee and be thy love.

10 *wayward*: determined on his own way, not to be gainsaid.
12 *fall*: autumn.

4

Praise to Diana

Praised be Diana's fair and harmless light,
Praised be the dews wherewith she moists the ground;
Praised be her beams, the glory of the night,
Praised be her power, by which all powers abound.

Praised be her nymphs with whom she decks the woods, 5
Praised be her knights, in whom true honour lives,
Praised be that force by which she moves the floods,
Let that Diana shine, which all these gives.

In heaven Queen she is among the spheres,
In aye she mistress-like makes all things pure; 10
Eternity in her oft change she bears,
She beauty is, by her the fair endure.

Time wears her not, she doth his chariot guide,
Mortality below her orb is placed, 15
By her the virtue of the stars down slide,
In her is virtue's perfect image cast.

A knowledge pure it is her worth to know,
With Circes let them dwell that think not so.

10 *In aye*: in eternity.

5

Like to a Hermit Poor

Like to a hermit poor in place obscure,
I mean to spend my days of endless doubt,
To wail such woes as time cannot recure,
Where none but love shall ever find me out.

My food shall be of care and sorrow made, 5
My drink naught else but tears fallen from mine eyes,
And for my light in such obscured shade,
The flames shall serve, which from my heart arise.

A gown of gray my body shall attire,
My staff of broken hope whereon I'll stay, 10
Of late repentance linkt with long desire
The couch is framed whereon my limbs I'll lay;

And at my gate despair shall linger still,
To let in death, when Love and Fortune will.

6

Farewell to the Court

Like truthless dreams, so are my joys expired,
And past return are all my dandled days;
My love misled, and fancy quite retired,
Of all which past, the sorrow only stays.

My lost delights, now clean from sight of land, 5
Have left me all alone in unknown ways;
My mind to woe, my life in fortune's hand,
Of all which past, the sorrow only stays.

As in a country strange without companion,
I only wail the wrong of death's delays, 10
Whose sweet spring spent, whose summer well nigh done,
Of all which past, the sorrow only stays.

Whom care forewarns, ere age and winter cold,
To haste me hence, to find my fortune's fold.

2 *dandled*: indulged, happy.

7

Feed still thyself, thou fondling

Feed still thyself, thou fondling, with belief,
Go hunt thy hope, that never took effect,
Accuse the wrongs that oft have wrought thy grief,
And reckon sure where reason would suspect.

Dwell in the dreams of wish and vain desire, 5
Pursue the faith that flies and seeks to new,
Run after hopes that mock thee with retire,
And look for love where liking never grew.

1 *fondling*: little fool.

Devise conceits to ease thy careful heart,
Trust upon times and days of grace behind, 10
Presume the rights of promise and desert,
And measure love by thy believing mind.

Force thy affects that spite doth daily chase,
Wink at the wrongs with wilful oversight,
See not the soil and stain of thy disgrace, 15
Nor reck disdain, to dote on thy delight.

And when thou seest the end of thy reward,
And these effects ensue of thine assault,
When rashness rues, that reason should regard,
Yet still accuse thy fortune for the fault. 20

And cry O Love! O death! O vain desire!
When thou complain'st the heat, and feeds the fire.

14 *Wink at*: close your eyes to.

8

My first-born love

My first born love unhappily conceived,
Brought forth in pain, and christened with a curse,
Die in your infancy, of life bereaved,
By your cruel nurse.

Restless desire, from my love that proceeded, 5
Leave to be, and seek your heaven by dying,
Since you, O you! your own hope have exceeded,
By too high flying.

And you my words, my heart's faithful expounders,
No more offer your jewel, unesteemed, 10
Since those eyes, my love's life and life's confounders,
Your worth misdeemed.

6 *Leave*: cease, here and elsewhere in this poem.

Love leave to desire, words leave it to utter,
Swell on my thoughts, till you break that contains you,
My complaints in those deaf ears no more mutter, 15
That so disdains you.

And you, careless of me, that without feeling,
With dry eyes, behold my tragedy smiling,
Deck your proud triumphs with your poor slave's yielding
To his own spoiling. 20

But if that wrong, or holy truth despised,
To just revenge the heavens ever moved,
So let her love, and so be still denied,
Who she so loved.

9

Those eyes which set my fancy on a fire

Those eyes which set my fancy on a fire,
Those crisped hairs, which hold my heart in chains,
Those dainty hands, which conquered my desire,
That wit, which of my thoughts doth hold the reins.

Those eyes for clearness do the stars surpass, 5
Those hairs obscure the brightness of the sun,
Those hands more white than ever ivory was,
That wit even to the skies hath glory won.

O eyes that pierce our hearts without remorse,
O hairs of right that wear a royal crown, 10
O hands that conquer more than Caesar's force,
O wit that turns huge kingdoms upside down!

Then love be judge, what heart may thee withstand;
Such eyes, such hair, such wit, and such a hand.

4 *wit*: quickness of wit, intelligence.

10

A Secret Murder

A secret murder hath been done of late,
Unkindness found to be the bloody knife,
And she that did the deed a dame of state,
Fair, gracious, wise, as any beareth life.

To quit herself, this answer did she make, 5
Mistrust (quoth she) hath brought him to his end,
Which makes the man so much himself mistake,
To lay the guilt unto his guiltless friend.

Lady not so, not feared I found my death,
For no desert thus murdered is my mind, 10
And yet before I yield my fainting breath,
I quit the killer, though I blame the kind.

You kill unkind; I die, and yet am true;
For at your sight my wound doth bleed anew.

5 *quit*: acquit. 9 *feared*: mistrusting. 12 *kind*: womankind.

11

Sought by the World

Sought by the world, and hath the world disdained
Is she, my heart, for whom thou dost endure;
Unto whose grace, sith kings have not obtained,
Sweet is thy choice though loss of life be sour.
  Yet to the man, whose youth such pains must prove, 5
  No better end than that which comes by love.

Steer then thy course unto the port of death,
Sith thy hard hap no betterer hap may find,
Where when thou shalt unlade thy latest breath,
Envy herself shall swim to save thy mind,* 10
  Whose body sunk in search to gain that shore,
  Where many a prince had perishéd before.

And yet, my heart, it might have been foreseen,
Sith skilful medicines mend each kind of grief,
Then in my breast full safely hadst thou been, 15
But thou, my heart, wouldst never me believe,
  Who told thee true, when first thou didst aspire,
  Death was the end of every such desire.

8 *sith*: since. *hap*: fortune.

12

What else is hell

What else is hell, but loss of blissful heaven?
What darkness else, but lack of lightsome day?
What else is death, but things of life bereaven?
What winter else, but pleasant spring's decay?

Unrest what else, but fancy's hot desire, 5
Fed with delay and followed with despair?
What else mishap, but longing to aspire,
To strive against earth, water, fire and air?*

Heaven were my state, and happy sunshine day,
And life most blest, to joy one hour's desire; 10
Hap, bliss, and rest, and sweet springtime of May,
Were to behold my fair consuming fire.

But lo! I feel, by absence from your sight,
Mishap, unrest, death, winter, hell, dark night.

13

My Body in the Walls Captived

My body in the walls captived
Feels not the wounds of spiteful envy,
But my thralled mind, of liberty deprived,
Fast fettered in her ancient memory,

Doth naught behold but sorrow's dying face. 5
Such prison erst was so delightful
As it desired no other dwelling place,
But time's effects, and destinies despiteful

Have changed both my keeper and my fare.
Love's fire and beauty's light I then had store, 10
But now close-kept, as captives wonted are,
That food, that heat, that light I find no more.

Despair bolts up my doors, and I alone
Speak to dead walls, but those hear not my moan.

6 *erst*: formerly.

14

The Eleventh Book of the Ocean to Cynthia*

I

Sufficeth it to you, my joys interred,
In simple words that I my woes complain;
You that then died, when first my fancy erred,
Joys under dust that never live again.

If to the living were my muse addressed,* 5
Or did my mind her own spirit still inhold,
Were not my living passion so repressed
As to the dead, the dead did these unfold,

Some sweeter words, some more becoming verse,
Should witness my mishap in higher kind; 10
But my love's wounds, my fancy in the hearse,
The Idea but resting of a wasted mind,

The blossoms fallen, the sap gone from the tree,
The broken monuments of my great desires—
From these so lost what may th'affections be, 15
What heat in cinders of extinguisht fires?

Lost in the mud of those high-flowing streams*
Which through more fairer fields their courses bend,
Slain with self thoughts, amazed in fearful dreams,
Woes without date, discomforts without end; 20

From fruitful trees I gather withered leaves,
And glean the broken ears with miser's hands,
Who sometime did enjoy the weighty sheaves;
I seek fair flowers amid the brinish sand.

All in the shade, even in the fair sun days, 25
Under those healthless trees I sit alone,
Where joyful birds sing neither lovely lays
Nor Philomen* recounts her direful moan.

No feeding flocks,* no shepherd's company,
That might renew my dolorous conceit, 30
While happy then, while love and fantasy,
Confined my thoughts on that fair flock to wait.

No pleasing streams fast to the Ocean wending,
The messengers sometimes of my great woe,

But all on earth as from the cold storms bending 35
Shrink from my thoughts in high heavens and below.

Oh hopeful love, my object and invention!
Oh true desire, the spur of my conceit!
Oh worthiest spirit, my mind's impulsion!
Oh eyes transpersant, my affections bait! 40

Oh princely form, my fancy's adamant,*
Divine conceit, my pain's acceptance,
Oh, all in one, Oh heaven on earth transparent,
The seat of joys and love's abundance!

Out of that mass of miracles, my Muse 45
Gathered those flowers,* to her pure senses pleasing;
Out of her eyes (the store of joys) did choose
Equal delights, my sorrows counterpoising.

Her regal looks my rigorous sighs suppressed,
Small drops of joys sweetened great worlds of woes, 50
One gladsome day a thousand cares redressed.
Whom love defends, what fortune overthrows?

When she did well, what did there else amiss?
When she did ill, what empires could have pleased?
No other power effecting woe or bliss, 55
She gave, she took, she wounded, she appeased.

II

The honour of her love, Love still devising,
Wounding my mind with contrary conceit,
Transferred itself sometime to her aspiring,
Sometime the trumpet of her thought's retreat; 60

To seek new worlds,* for gold, for praise, for glory,
To try desire, to try love severed far,

When I was gone she sent her memory
More strong than were ten thousand ships of war,

To call me back, to leave great honour's thought, 65
To leave my friends, my fortune, my attempt,
To leave the purpose I so long had sought
And hold both cares and comforts in contempt.

Such heat in ice, such fire in frost remained,
Such trust in doubt, such comfort in despair, 70
Much like the gentle lamb, though lately weaned,
Plays with the dug though finds no comfort there.

But as a body violently slain
Retaineth warmth, although the spirit be gone,
And by a power in nature moves again 75
Till it be laid beneath the fatal stone;

Or as the earth, even in cold winter days,
Left for a time of her life-giving sun,
Doth by the power remaining of his rays
Produce some green, though not as it hath done; 80

Or as a wheel forced by the falling stream,
Although the course be turned some other way
Doth for a time go round upon the beam
Till wanting strength to move, it stands at stay;

So my forsaken heart, my withered mind, 85
Widow of all the joys it once possessed,
My hopes clean out of sight, with forcéd wind
To kingdoms strange, to lands far-off addressed,

Alone, forsaken, friendless on the shore,
With many wounds, with death's cold pangs embraced, 90
Writes in the dust, as one that could no more,
Whom love and time and fortune had defaced,

Of things so great, so long, so manifold,
With means so weak, the soul even then departing,
The weal, the woe, the passages of old, 95
And worlds of thoughts described by one last sighing;

As if, when after Phoebus is descended,
And leaves a light much like the past day's dawning,
And every toil and labour wholly ended,
Each living creature draweth to his resting, 100

We should begin by such a parting light*
To write the story of all ages past
And end the same, before the approaching night.

III

And though strong reason hold before mine eyes
The images and forms of worlds past 105
Teaching the cause why all those flames that rise
From forms external, can no longer last,

Than that those seeming beauties hold in prime,
Love's ground, his essence, and his empery,
All slaves to age, and vassals unto time, 110
Of which repentance writes the tragedy.

But this, my heart's desire could not conceive,
Whose love outflew the fastest flying time;
A beauty that can easily deceive
Th'arrest of years, and creeping age outclimb; 115

A spring of beauties, which time ripeth not,
Time that but works on frail mortality,
A sweetness which woes wrongs outwipeth not,
Whom love hath chose for his divinity;

105 *worlds*: pronounced as a dissyllable with a strongly marked r.

A vestal fire that burns but never wasteth, 120
That loseth naught by giving light to all,
That endless shines eachwhere, and endless lasteth,
Blossoms of pride that can nor fade nor fall.

IV

But as the fields, clothéd with leaves and flowers,
The banks of roses, smelling precious sweet, 125
Have but their beauty's date, and timely hours,
And then defaced by winter's cold and sleet,

So far as neither fruit nor form of flower
Stays for a witness what such branches bare,
But as time gave, time did again devour, 130
And changed our rising joy to falling care;

So of affection, which our youth presented,
When she that from the sun reaves power and light,
Did but decline her beams as discontented,
Converting sweetest days to saddest night; 135

All droops, all dies, all trodden under dust,
The person, place, and passages forgotten,
The hardest steel eaten with softest rust,
The firm and solid tree both rent and rotten.

Those thoughts so full of pleasure and content, 140
That in our absence were affection's food,
Are razéd out and from the fancy rent,
In highest grace and heart's dear care that stood,

Are cast for prey to hatred and to scorn,
Our dearest treasures and our heart's true joys. 145
The tokens hung on breast* and kindly worn
Are now elsewhere disposed or held for toys.

133 *reaves*: robs.

And those which then our jealousy removed,
And others for our sakes then valued dear,
The one forgot, the rest are dear beloved, 150
When all of ours doth strange or vile appear.

Those streams seem standing puddles which, before,
We saw our beauties in, so were they clear;
Belphoebe's* course is now observed no more,
That fair resemblance weareth out of date; 155
Our Ocean seas are but tempestuous waves,
And all things base that blessed were of late.

And as a field wherein the stubble stands
Of harvest past, the ploughman's eye offends,
He tills again, or tears them up with hands, 160
And throws to fire as foiled and fruitless ends,

And takes delight another seed to sow;
So doth the mind root up all wonted thought
And scorns the care of our remaining woes.
The sorrows, which themselves for us have wrought, 165

Are burnt to cinders by new-kindled fires,
The ashes are dispersed into the air,
The sighs, the groans of all our past desires
Are clean outworn, as things that never were.

V

But in my mind so is her love inclosed 170
And is thereof not only the best part,
But into it the essence is disposed.
Oh love (the more my woe) to it thou art

Even as the moisture in each plant that grows,
Even as the sun unto the frozen ground, 175

Even as the sweetness to th'incarnate rose,
Even as the centre in each perfect round,

As water to the fish, to men as air,
As heat to fire, as light unto the sun.
Oh love, it is but vain to say *thou were*, 180
Ages and times cannot thy power outrun.

Thou art the soul of that unhappy mind
Which being by nature made an idle thought,
Began even then to take immortal kind
When first her virtues in thy spirits wrought. 185

From thee therefore that mover cannot move,
Because it is become thy cause of being;
Whatever error may obscure that love
Whatever frail effect of mortal living,

Whatever passion from distempered heart, 190
What absence, time, or injuries effect,
What faithless friends, or deep dissembled art
Present, to feed her most unkind suspect.

Yet as the air in deep caves underground
Is strongly drawn, when violent heat hath rent 195
Great clefts therein, till moisture do abound,
And then the same, imprisoned and up-pent,

Breaks out in earthquakes, tearing all asunder,
So in the centre of my cloven heart,
My heart, to whom her beauties were such wounder, 200
Lies the sharp poisoned head of that love's dart;

Which till all break and all dissolve to dust
Thence drawn it cannot be, or therein known.
There, mixed with my heart blood, the fretting rust
The better part hath eaten and outgrown. 205

176 *incarnate*: red.

But what of those, or these, or what of aught
Of that which was, or that which is, to treat?
What I possess is but the same I sought;
My love was false, my labours were deceit.

Nor less than such they are esteemed to be, 210
A fraud bought at the price of many woes,
A guile, whereof the profits unto me—
Could it be thought premeditate for those?

Witness those withered leaves left on the tree,
The sorrow-worren face, the pensive mind, 215
The external shows what may th'internal be;
Cold care hath bitten both the root and vinde.

VI

She is gone, she is lost! She is found, she is ever fair!
Sorrow draws weakly, where love draws not too.
Woe's cries sound nothing but only in love's ear. 220
Do then by dying what life cannot do.

Unfold thy flocks and leave them to the fields
To feed on hills or dales, where likes them best,
Of what the summer or the springtime yields,
For love, and time, hath given thee leave to rest. 225

Thy heart, which was their fold, now in decay
By often storms and winter's many blasts
All torn and rent, becomes misfortune's prey;
False hope, my shepherd's staff, now age hath brast.

My pipe, which love's own hand gave my desire 230
To sing her praises and my woe upon,
Despair hath often threatened to the fire,
As vain to keep now all the rest are gone.

215 *worren*: the original spelling indicates an extra syllable which the metre requires. 217 *vinde*: stalk. 229 *brast*: broken.

Thus home I draw, as death's long night draws on.
Yet every foot, old thoughts turn back mine eyes, 235
Constraint me guides, as old age draws a stone
Against the hill, which over-weighty lies

For feeble arms, or wasted strength to move.
My steps are backward, gazing on my loss,
My mind's affection, and my soul's sole love, 240
Not mixed with fancy's chaff, or fortune's dross.

To God I leave it, who first gave it me,
And I her gave, and she returned again,
As it was hers. So let His mercies be
Of my last comforts the essential mean. 245

But be it so, or not, th'effects are past.
Her love hath end; my woe must ever last.

15

The Twelfth Book, entreating of Sorrow

My day's delights, my springtime joys foredone,
Which in the dawn and rising sun of youth
Had their creation and were first begun,

Do in the evening and the winter sad,
Present my mind, which takes my time's account, 5
The grief remaining of the joy it had.

My times that then ran o'er themselves in these,
And now run out in others' happiness,
Bring unto those new joys and new born days.

So could she not, if she were not the sun, 10
Which sees the birth and burial of all else,
And holds that power with which she first begun;

Leaving each withered body to be torn
By fortune and by times tempestuous,
Which by her virtue once fair fruit have born, 15

Knowing she can renew, and can create
Green from the ground, and flowers even out of stone,
By virtue lasting over time and date;

Leaving us only woe, which like the moss,
Having compassion of unburied bones* 20
Cleaves to mischance and unrepaired loss.

16

As you came from the Holy Land

As you came from the holy land,
  Of Walsingham,
Met you not with my true love
  By the way as you came?

How shall I know your true love 5
  That have met many one
As I went to the holy land
  That have come, that have gone?

She is neither white nor brown*
  But as the heavens fair, 10
There is none hath a form so divine
  In the earth or the air.

Such an one did I meet, good sir,
  Such an angel-like face,
Who like a queen, like a nymph, did appear 15
  By her gait, by her grace.

She hath left me here all alone,
  All alone, as unknown,
Who sometime did me lead with herself,
  And me loved as her own. 20

What's the cause that she leaves you alone,
  And a new way doth take;
Who loved you once as her own
  And her joy did you make?

I have loved her all my youth, 25
  But now old, as you see,
Love likes not the falling fruit
  From the withered tree.

Know that love is a careless child
  And forgets promise past, 30
He is blind, he is deaf when he list
  And in faith never fast.

His desire is a dureless content
  And a trustless joy,
He is won with a world of despair 35
  And is lost with a toy.

Of womenkind such indeed is the love
  Or the word Love abused,
Under which many childish desires
  And conceits are excused. 40

But true Love is a durable fire
  In the mind ever burning;
Never sick, never old, never dead,
  From its self never turning.

17

A Poesie to prove affection is not love

Conceit begotten by the eyes,
Is quickly born, and quickly dies;
For while it seeks our hearts to have,
Meanwhile there reason makes his grave;
  For many things the eyes approve, 5
  Which yet the heart doth seldom love.

For as the seeds in springtime sown
Die in the ground ere they be grown,
Such is conceit, whose rooting fails,
As child that in the cradle quails, 10
  Or else within the mother's womb
  Hath his beginning and his tomb.

Affection follows Fortune's wheels,
And soon is shaken from her heels;
For following beauty or estate, 15
Her liking still is turned to hate.
  For all affections have their change,
  And fancy only loves to range.

Desire himself runs out of breath,
And getting, doth but gain his death; 20
Desire nor reason hath nor rest,
And blind, doth seldom choose the best;
  Desire attained is not desire,
  But as the cinders of the fire.

As ships in ports desired are drowned, 25
As fruit once ripe, then falls to ground,

10 *quails*: dies.

As flies that seek for flames are brought
To cinders by the flames they sought;
  So fond desire when it attains,
  The life expires, the woe remains. 30

And yet some poets fain would prove
Affection to be perfect love,
And that desire is of that kind,
No less a passion of the mind;
  As if wild beasts and men did seek 35
  To like, to love, to choose alike.

18

Nature that washt her hands in milk

Nature that washt her hands in milk
  And had forgot to dry them,
Instead of earth took snow and silk
  At Love's request to try them,
If she a mistress could compose 5
To please Love's fancy out of those.

Her eyes he would should be of light,
  A violet breath and lips of jelly,
Her hair not black, nor over bright,
  And of the softest down her belly, 10
As for her inside, he'd have it
Only of wantonness and wit.

At Love's entreaty, such a one
  Nature made, but with her beauty
She hath framed a heart of stone, 15
  So as Love by ill destiny
Must die for her whom Nature gave him
Because her darling would not save him.

But Time which Nature doth despise,
  And rudely gives her love the lie, 20
Makes hope a fool and sorrow wise,
  His hands doth neither wash nor dry,
But being made of steel and rust,
Turns snow and silk and milk to dust.

The light, the belly, lips and breath, 25
  He dims, discolours and destroys;
With those he feeds, but fills not Death,
  Which sometimes were the food of joys;
Yea Time doth dull each lively wit,
And dries all wantonness with it. 30

Oh cruel Time, which takes in trust
  Our youth, our joys, and all we have,
And pays us but with age and dust,
  Who in the dark and silent grave,
When we have wandered all our ways 35
Shuts up the story of our days.

19

The Lie

Go soul, the body's guest,
  Upon a thankless errand,
Fear not to touch the best,
  The truth shall be thy warrant:
Go, since I needs must die, 5
  And give the world the lie.

Say to the Court it glows
  And shines like rotten wood,*
Say to the Church it shows
  What's good, and doth no good: 10

If Church and Court reply,
  Then give them both the lie.

Tell Potentates they live
  Acting by others action,
Not loved unless thy give, 15
  Not strong but by affection:*
If Potentates reply,
  Give Potentates the lie.

Tell men of high condition,
  That manage the estate, 20
Their purpose is ambition,
  Their practice only hate:
And if they once reply,
  Then give them all the lie.

Tell them that brave it most* 25
  They beg for more by spending,
Who in their greatest cost
  Seek nothing but commending:
And if they make reply,
  Then give them all the lie. 30

Tell zeal it wants devotion,
  Tell love it is but lust,
Tell time it metes but motion,
  Tell flesh it is but dust:
And wish them not reply, 35
  For thou must give the lie.

Tell age it daily wasteth,
  Tell honour how it alters,
Tell beauty how she blasteth,
  Tell favour how it falters: 40
And as they shall reply,
Give every one the lie.

33 *metes*: measures. 39 *blasteth*: withers away.

Tell wit how much it wrangles
  In tickle points of niceness;
Tell wisdom she entangles 45
  Herself in over-wiseness.
And when they shall reply,
  Straight give them both the lie.

Tell physic of her boldness,
  Tell skill it is prevention*; 50
Tell charity of coldness,
  Tell law it is contention:
And as they do reply
  So give them still the lie.

Tell fortune of her blindness, 55
  Tell nature of decay,
Tell friendship of unkindness,
  Tell justice of delay:
And if they will reply,
  Then give them all the lie. 60

Tell arts they have no soundness,
  But vary by esteeming,
Tell schools they want profoundness
  And stand too much on seeming:
If arts and schools reply, 65
  Give arts and schools the lie.

Tell faith it's fled the city,
  Tell how the country erreth,
Tell, manhood shakes off pity,
Tell, virtue least preferreth: 70
And if they do reply
  Spare not to give the lie.

44 *tickle points etc*: trivial and over-fine distinctions.
70 *preferreth*: to prefer is to advance or promote.

So when thou hast, as I
  Commanded thee, done blabbing,*
Although to give the lie 75
  Deserves no less than stabbing,
Stab at thee he that will,
  No stab thy soul can kill.

20

On the Life of Man

What is our life? A play of passion;
Our mirth, the music of division,*
Our mother's wombs the tiring houses* be,
Where we are drest for this short Comedy.*
Heaven the judicious sharp spectator is, 5
That sits and marks still who doth act amiss.
Our graves that hide us from the searching sun,
Are like drawn curtains* when the play is done.
Thus march we playing to our latest rest;
Only we die in earnest. That's no jest. 10

21

The Passionate Man's Pilgrimage

Give me my scallop-shell of quiet,*
My staff of faith to walk upon,
My scrip of joy, immortal diet,
My bottle of salvation;
My gown of glory, hope's true gage, 5
And thus I'll take my pilgrimage.

Blood must be my body's balmer,*
No other balm will there be given,
Whilst my soul, like a white palmer,
Travels to the land of heaven, 10
Over the silver mountains,
Where spring the nectar fountains;
And there I'll kiss
The bowl of bliss,
And drink my eternal fill 15
On every milken hill.
My soul will be adry before,
But after it will ne'er thirst more.

And by the happy blissful way
More peaceful pilgrims I shall see, 20
That have shook off their gowns of clay,
And go apparelled fresh like me.
I'll bring them first
To slake their thirst,
And then to taste those nectar suckets, 25
At the clear wells
Where sweetness dwells,
Drawn up by saints in crystal buckets.

And when our bottles and all we
Are filled with immortality; 30
Then the holy paths we'll travel
Strewed with rubies thick as gravel,
Ceilings of diamonds, sapphire floors,
High walls of coral and pearl bowers.

From thence, to heaven's bribeless hall.* 35
Where no corrupted voices brawl,
No conscience molten into gold,
Nor forged accusers bought and sold,

25 *suckets*: dainties, particularly candied fruits.

No cause deferred, nor vain spent journey,
For there Christ is the King's Attorney; 40
Who pleads for all without degrees,
And He hath angels, but no fees.

When the grand twelve million jury,
Of our sins and sinful fury,*
Gainst our souls black verdicts give, 45
Christ pleads his death, and then we live,
Be thou my speaker, taintless pleader,
Unblotted lawyer, true proceeder,
Thou movest salvation even for alms;
Not with a bribed lawyer's palms. 50

And this is my eternal plea,
To Him that made heaven, earth and sea,
Seeing my flesh must die so soon,
And want a head to dine next noon,
Just at the stroke, when my veins start and spread, 55
Set on my soul an everlasting head.
Then am I ready, like a palmer fit,
To tread those blest paths which before I writ.

42 *angels*: a familiar pun on the word 'angel', which was the name of a coin. 48 *proceeder*: one who takes part in a process, a trial at law. 49 *movest*: a technical legal term, for making a proposal to a court.

22

On the Snuff of a Candle, the night before he died

Cowards fear to die, but courage stout,
Rather than live in snuff, will be put out.

23

Even Such is Time

These Verses following were made by Sir Walter Raleigh the night before he died and left at the Gate House.

Even such is Time which takes in trust
Our youth, our joys, and all we have,
And pays us but with age and dust;
Who in the dark and silent grave
When we have wandered all our ways 5
Shuts up the story of our days.
  And from which earth and grave and dust
  The Lord shall raise me up I trust.

A REPORT OF THE TRVTH OF *the fight about the Iles of* Açores, this last Sommer.

BETVVIXT THE *Reuenge, one of her Maiesties* Shippes,

And an Armada of the King of Spaine.

LONDON
Printed for william Ponsonbie.
1591.

THE LAST FIGHT OF THE REVENGE: INTRODUCTION

THE war between England and Spain under Elizabeth did not begin with a formal declaration. The fact that England had renounced the Pope, and paid no attention to Spain's monopoly of the New World, made war sooner or later inevitable. England was a small country, not very rich, not highly industrialized or densely populated, and it must have looked rather as though David were taking on Goliath. English strategy by sea was very much that of the lightly armed slinger who was careful never to come within grappling distance of his opponent. Her more far-sighted commanders were learning to abandon the time-honoured method whereby ships were a kind of floating castle filled with soldiers, whose aim was to come near enough to an enemy castle to climb aboard and capture it. They manned their ships with seamen and used them for sailing the sea, their aim being to lie in wait for the unwieldy Spanish treasure ships as they wallowed slowly home from the Indies. Thus they seized the wealth with which King Philip kept his armies in the field, robbed the enemy and enriched themselves at one blow. The Queen allowed this as a form of private enterprise, paying for itself out of profits. She even lent royal ships for the purpose. Whether she would have done better (and whether she had the means) to mobilize a really strong naval force and assume undisputed command of the sea, is a subject upon which historians still differ. Raleigh believed in the intelligent application of sea-power, but the Queen was understandably committed to land operations. Since the coasts that lie opposite to England were potential invasion bases, she found it prudent as well as neighbourly to send aid to the Huguenots in France and to the revolted Netherlands. The Spaniards had their own word for England's naval enterprise. They called it piracy.

Commerce raiding worked at first so well that in 1590 King Philip forbade his treasure fleet to sail. It wintered in the West Indies, to the detriment of the ships' timbers. In 1591 two English squadrons were waiting to attack it on the homeward journey. One patrolled the Spanish coast. The other, twelve or more ships, five of them warships, under the command of Lord Thomas Howard in the Defiance, prowled around the track of the carracks further out in the Atlantic. Lord Thomas was a kinsman of Lord Howard of Effingham, Lord High Admiral of England. He first saw sea service in 1588, against the Great Armada. (All Spanish battle fleets were called armadas.) Raleigh had intended to accompany him but the Queen would not permit it. A west country cousin, Sir Richard Grenville, was second in command. He sailed in the Revenge, one of the finest of the Queen's ships, built by Sir John Hawkins, and reckoned a model of what a modern battleship should be. She had been Drake's flagship in '88. But we are told she was an unlucky ship, with a name so proud she challenged fate.

King Philip continued to keep his treasure fleet in port. He had lost the greater part of his armada of 1588 but was hurriedly building new warships to meet and convoy the double cargo, and small, fast frigates to carry the most valuable and least bulky part of it, the gold and silver plate. Events at first seemed to endorse the wisdom of his plan. After six months at sea the English were in poor shape. It was hard to keep ships at all adequately supplied with food and drink if they were long away. The lack of fresh provisions induced scurvy, and the crowded, insanitary quarters meant that other infections were rife. Yet the longer they waited the surer they were of their prey, for the Spanish fleet must sooner or later sail, and not too late, for fear of the autumn storms. The English might well have asked themselves whether they would not, in their turn, fall a prey to the new armada, but they were very ill-informed about its progress. It is hard to imagine how slowly and uncertainly news travelled at this time.

By the end of August 1591 Lord Thomas could keep the sea no longer and retired to Flores, one of the westernmost islands of the group called the Azores, where the East Indian and West Indian fleets were in the habit of watering on the way home. Flores was a small island and he was not likely to meet with much opposition from the inhabitants. He could clean his ships in peace and take in fresh supplies. All the shingle carried for ballast, and by now filthy with the drainage of the decks, had to be shovelled out and fresh ballast taken aboard. At this moment, and only just in time, came news from the secondary squadron that a fleet was bearing down on him, not the unprotected treasure fleet but a well-equipped armada from Spain. Howard hastily ordered his ships to sea. Raleigh says that Captain Middleton 'had no sooner delivered the news than the fleet was in sight', but he must here be speaking loosely, for effect. If what he said had been literally true none of the English could have got away. Signalling at the time was rudimentary and important messages were carried by advice-boats. Actually, all Howard's ships joined him, to windward of the Spaniards, with the exception of Grenville in the Revenge. Grenville left it so late that the Spanish squadrons came up between him and his commander. He could have turned round and gone the other way, but he interpreted this as flinching in the face of the enemy. He therefore pressed straight on into the middle of the Spanish fleet, determined to take his vessel through or die in the attempt.

The battle which followed, in which the Revenge took on the whole of the Spanish fleet single-handed, was as magnificent as it was foolhardy. It displayed to the full the fighting qualities of the English seamen. It did not display the new naval tactics by which England was going to assert her superiority at sea, keeping the enemy at a distance through the calculated use of naval gunfire and never permitting him to grapple, enter, and turn the encounter into a military operation. Grenville carried no soldiers beyond a very few gentlemen volunteers, and more than half his men were sick. The Spaniards naturally pressed hard to board and enter. That was where their superiority lay.

Raleigh claims, in a very grand way, that the guns went on firing until there was no more powder left, and this may well have been what the survivors said, in the excitement of telling their tale. It is plain that the guns had little chance of firing in the mêlée, and there was enough gunpowder left for Grenville to order the Master Gunner to blow up the ship. The rest of the survivors had other ideas and preferred to bargain with the enemy. They agreed to hand over the battered remains of the Revenge in return for their lives. Thus the Spaniards, in the end, could boast that they had captured the Queen's best ship, though at great cost. They could also taunt the English with missing the treasure fleet by a matter of hours, for the day after the fight the carracks reached the Azores. After that the forces of nature, or as the age interpreted it, God's providence, took a hand against King Philip. He had delayed the return of his fleet too long. The Azores was struck by a cyclone of quite exceptional violence. Many Spanish ships were wrecked and along with them the captured Revenge. Sir Richard had died of wounds and was buried at sea. The Spaniards declared he had gone down below to raise up devils from the deep to avenge his defeat.

It was Raleigh who turned this defeat into a minor English epic, or as a great contemporary, Sir Francis Bacon, put it, 'Memorable . . . even beyond credit, and to the Height of some Heroicall Fable'. His account of it, his first published prose, appeared as an anonymous pamphlet in 1591. When Richard Hakluyt reprinted it in his collection of voyages in 1599 he described it as 'penned by the honourable Sir Walter Ralegh Knight'. It reads like government propaganda and it may have been commissioned. Raleigh, however, was quite capable of commissioning himself and assuming all the air of a government spokesman. He drew for his account upon more than one source, some at least semi-official—Godolphin's letter to Killigrew of the Privy Chamber, for instance (they were both west-countrymen), and the examination of the survivors by the Lords of the Privy Council.

We can compare his version of events with the story told by a Dutch merchant, Jan Huyghen van Linschoten, resident at the time in the Azores. Van Linschoten supplies a lively picture of the cyclone and he knows more than Raleigh did about Grenville's last hours. A. L. Rowse has recently had access to a first-hand Spanish report of the affair, and gives some account of it in *Sir Richard Grenville of the Revenge*. Years after the event, Sir William Monson who as a young man had served in the supporting squadron on the Spanish coast, wrote an account of the action very unfavourable to Grenville.

He suggested that Grenville mistook the armada for the Indies treasure fleet and wilfully refused to listen to advice and follow his commander in weighing anchor until too late. With this one stroke he changes the whole character of the affair from a piece of deliberate gallantry to an error in judgement bitterly repented. But if the supply-ship, the George Noble, could escape, so presumably could Grenville. There seems little sign that he repented anything. He engaged in the contest with considerable gusto.

There was, in any case, no need to invent charges against him. The story even as Raleigh tells it displays his foolhardiness as well as his heroism. Raleigh puts a good face on his delay when he describes him staying behind to collect the men who were still ashore, but we are left wondering why this should affect only the Revenge and not the other ships, all of which successfully joined their commander, even the slow sailing Bonaventure with her much depleted crew. The departure was a strategic withdrawal, not a rout. Possibly he constituted himself rearguard because he knew his ship was an exceptionally good sailer, and it may have amused him to cut things fine. It sounds a bit like the story of Drake finishing his game of bowls.

The decision to join his squadron at all costs was sheer bravado. M. Oppenheim, who has edited Monson's account for the Navy Record Society, comments rather sourly, 'Any captain can make a dramatic ending—at the expense of his men—if by insubordination or want of skill he chooses or is forced into an untenable position.' Geoffrey Callender, writing in *History*, July 1919, speaks of 'that swashbuckling propensity that charms our senses while it staggers our sense of wisdom and propriety'; but he thinks there is a place for 'self-immolation, not for honour's sake alone, but self-immolation to compass the enemy's entire discomfiture'.

It would be natural to think that Raleigh was writing in his cousin's defence and slanting the story in his favour. Actually he gives a singularly detached account and is scrupulously fair to everyone involved. The whole case against Grenville is implicit and sometimes explicit in what Raleigh says. He admits that he could have turned aside and saved his ship. 'Notwithstanding, out of the greatness of his mind, he could not be persuaded.' Commenting upon Howard's impulse to plunge with Grenville into the battle, he has some severe and sensible things to say about the responsibility of a naval commander. We are told that Howard, at his return, was accused of cowardice and that Raleigh challenged him to a duel, but there is no trace of ill-feeling in what he says about him in public. Even the dissentient spirits aboard the Revenge, who made a truce with the enemy, are given reasonable arguments, sympathetically reported, and their success with their shipmates is realistically and tolerantly dismissed, 'being no hard matter to dissuade men from death to life'.

The only side to which Raleigh is unfair is to the enemy. The Spaniards, and their allies the Irish rebels, get no quarter whatsoever. The whole tenour of the pamphlet is to blacken the Spaniards, to praise the spirit of the English, to convince them that they are on the winning side in what is going to be a desperate struggle, and to urge them to support an aggressive naval policy. He assures them that what the enemy is claiming as a victory is morally a defeat. Lastly he supplies answers to the Spanish propaganda which was being spread by a renegade Irishman, whose character and antecedents he blackens, after dismissing his arguments. Raleigh is thinking less of praising his cousin than of prosecuting the war.

Such is his skill in telling his tale that he has made *The Last Fight of the Revenge* a pattern of heroism at sea, to be repeated over and over again, in other contests and with other ships and men. It is a true classic—the ship that sacrifices her own chances in order to see the others safe away; the non-combatant who dutifully asks what he shall do and is told 'Save yourself'; the little ship that hovers all night to see what will happen and whether she can help, and in the morning is 'hunted like a hare among many ravenous hounds'; the massive armaments of the enemy; the courtesies of war observed by the sorely bruised victors. Raleigh had an extraordinary capacity for objectifying an English dream. Hence the ease with which Tennyson was able to turn his prose into stirring verse.

The pamphlet was written hot on the heels of the event. Raleigh knew Grenville had died but he did not even know that he had been buried at sea. It is to Van Linschoten that we owe his last words. They are not to be read as the notes of a shorthand reporter present at the time, but they seem to reflect something of the nobility and something of the ferocity of his character. The final malediction is directed at his crew, not at Lord Thomas and his fleet. When Hakluyt published the relevant pages from Van Linschoten's book he omitted the last sentence, preferring like Raleigh to blot no Englishman's honour.

'Here die I, Richard Grenville, with a joyful and quiet mind, for that I have ended my life as a true soldier ought to do, that hath fought for his country, Queen, religion, and honour, whereby my soul most joyful departeth out of this body, and shall always leave behind it an everlasting fame of a valiant and true soldier, that hath done his duty, as he was bound to do. But the others of my company have done as traitors and dogs, for which they shall be reproached all their lives and leave a shameful name forever.'

NOTES ON SHIPS AND NAVAL TACTICS

The largest vessels afloat in the sixteenth century were the great three-masted *carracks* which brought treasure and produce (mainly silver and spices) home from the Indies. Deck rose above deck to give as much storage space as possible. They were slow and clumsy sailers, dangerous in a storm and not easily manoeuvreable in a fight, a sitting target for a well-armed commerce raider.

The new four-masted battleships, the next largest, were called *galleons*. They were built for speed and manoeuvre, rather long and low in the hull, without the high-built overhanging forecastle of the carrack. They were not armed only with cannon in odd corners, firing forward, but carried rows of guns along each side with portholes specially cut to accommodate them, a startling innovation when it was first introduced, and the shape of things to come.

The old battleship, which sufficed when the Mediterranean was the main theatre for naval warfare, was the *galley*, propelled by several banks of oars at which sat the wretched galley-slaves. To become a galley-slave was a fate to be dreaded by a prisoner-of-war. One of the terms upon which the crew of the Revenge surrendered was that they should not be sent to the galleys. Galleys were not a success in the rougher waters of the Atlantic and were obviously unsuited to long voyages.

Conservative spirits hoped to have the best of both worlds in a *galleas*, a ship which combined oars and sail, but instead they seem to have had the worst. Witness the fate of Hugo de Moncado in 1588 to which Raleigh alludes.

Merchant vessels could be lightly armed and were in regular request to carry supplies for a battlefleet. They were known by various names, often deriving from their country or port of origin, which determined their build. Thus *flyboats* were Flemish or Dutch, *argosies* were Venetian or Ragusan. *Hulks* was a very general name for large merchant ships, store boats and transports.

A *bark* was a general term for almost any small ship.

A host of small boats was required to maintain communications between the big vessels. They could go close inshore even when the water was shallow, and their oars made them independent in a calm. Raleigh gives them a number of names, *barges*, *wherries*, *pinnaces* and *cockboats*. His expedition up the Orinoco was undertaken entirely in vessels of shallow draught, using oars. For his own ship on this occasion he has yet another name. He calls it a *galliot*, which was a small, light galley.

Names for different types of ship were not used with great precision. Any big ship might be called a galleon. Methods of calculating tonnage were various and unreliable, and it is hard to assess the size of a ship with any certainty.

Naval tactics in a sailing ship were largely a matter of taking advantage of the wind. A commander tried to *get in the wind* of the enemy, to come up *on his weather bow*, *to keep the weather gauge of him*; that is, he wanted to have the wind behind him. The windward side is the side from which the wind blows. In close fighting the natural tilt of his vessels enabled him to direct his gunfire down into the body of the ship. The enemy, tilted by the wind away from the aggressor, could only fire upwards and damage masts and rigging. This was Grenville's position with regard to the Spanish ships, until they ultimately encircled him, in which case some were in his lee, or to leeward. The side to which the wind blows is called the lee side. To *luff up*, or *spring one's luff*, is to turn a ship head to the wind.

The Spaniards were not trying to sink the Revenge by gunfire, but to *board and enter*, when they would finish the matter with handfighting and possess the ship. In modern usage the word *boarding* means successfully transferring a party of armed men to an enemy ship, but Raleigh says a ship is *aboard* when she is close alongside. To enter, or transfer men, was a subsequent manoeuvre, and since the slope of the ships' sides was steeply inwards it was not at all an easy one. None the less the Spaniards did succeed in entering the maimed Revenge, though they were repelled. In his *History of the World* Raleigh gave it as his opinion that 'twenty men upon the defences are equal to 100 that board and enter'.

The distinction between legal privateering and piracy was obviously narrow and not carefully defined. A sovereign might issue letters of mark to seamen of any nation authorizing them to destroy enemy shipping. Letters of reprisal permitted a man who had been robbed at sea to recoup his loss by seizing goods of equal value from any compatriot of the original offender. Declarations of contraband allowed an English ship to stop and search neutral ships which might be carrying war-material to Spain. What this amounts to is that once you were at sea you could do almost anything. Disputes were settled in the Admiralty Courts, and Raleigh, as Vice-Admiral of Devon and Cornwall, had an ultimate authority there.

A Report of the Truth of the Fight about the Isles of Açores this last Summer, betwixt the Revenge, one of Her Majesty's Ships, and an Armada of the King of Spain

BECAUSE the rumours are diversely spread, as well in England as in the Low Countries and elsewhere, of this late encounter between Her Majesty's ships and the Armada of Spain—and that the Spaniards according to their usual manner fill the world with their vainglorious vaunts, making great appearance of victories, when on the contrary, themselves are most commonly and shamefully beaten and dishonoured, thereby hoping to possess the ignorant multitude by anticipating and forerunning false reports—it is agreeable with all good reason, for manifestation of the truth to overcome falsehood and untruth, that the beginning, continuance and success of this late honourable encounter of Sir Richard Grenville and other Her Majesty's captains with the Armada of Spain, should be truly set down and published without partiality or false imaginations.

And it is no marvel that the Spaniard should seek by false and slanderous pamphlets, advisoes and letters to cover their own loss, and to derogate from others their due honours, especially in this fight, being performed far off; seeing they were not ashamed in the year 1588,* when they purposed the invasion of this land, to publish in sundry languages in print, great victories in words, which they pleaded to have obtained against this realm, and spread the same in a most false sort over all parts of France, Italy and elsewhere; when shortly after it was happily manifested in very deed to all nations, how their navy which they termed

forerunning: forestalling. *advisoes*: official notifications.

invincible, consisting of 240 sail of ships, not only of their own kingdom, but strengthened with the greatest argosies, Portugal carracks, Florentines and huge hulks of other countries, were by thirty of Her Majesty's own ships of war and a few of our own merchants, by the wise, valiant and most advantageous conduction of Lord Charles Howard, High Admiral of England, beaten and shuffled together, even from the Lizard in Cornwall, first to Portland, where they shamefully left Don Pedro de Valdez, with his mighty ship, from Portland to Calais, where they lost Hugo de Moncado, with the galleas of which he was captain, and from Calais driven with squibs from their anchors, were chased out of the sight of England round about Scotland and Ireland. Where for the sympathy of their barbarous religion, hoping to find succour and assistance, a great part of them were crushed against the rocks, and those other that landed, being very many in number, were notwithstanding broken, slain, and taken, and so sent from village to village coupled in halters to be shipped into England. Where Her Majesty of her princely and invincible disposition, disdaining to put them to death, and scorning either to retain or entertain them, were all sent back again to their countries, to witness and recount the worthy achievements of their invincible and dreadful navy.

Of which the number of soldiers, the fearful burden of their ships, the commanders' names of every squadron, with all other their magazines of provisions, were put in print, as an army and navy unresistible and disdaining prevention. With all which so great and terrible an ostentation, they did not in all their sailing round about England, so much as sink or take one ship, bark, pinnace, or cockboat of ours, or ever burnt so much as one sheepcote of this island. Whenas on the contrary, Sir Francis Drake* with only 800

squibs: fireships. See note for 'the year 1588' above.
to entertain: to provide the necessaries of life.
magazines: stores, especially naval and military stores.
disdaining prevention: confident it could not be hindered.

soldiers not long before landed in their Indies, and forced Santiago, Santo Domingo, Cartagena and the forts of Florida. And after that, Sir John Norris* marched from Peniche in Portugal with a handful of soldiers, to the gates of Lisbon, being above forty English miles. Where the Earl of Essex himself and other valiant gentlemen braved the city of Lisbon, encamped at the very gates; from whence after many days' abode, finding neither promised party nor provision to batter, made retreat by land, in despite of all their garrisons, both of horse and foot.

In this sort I have a little digressed from my first purpose, only by the necessary comparison of theirs and our actions, the one covetous of honour without vaunt or ostentation, the other so greedy to purchase the opinion of their own affairs and by false rumours to resist the blasts of their own dishonours, as they will not only not blush to spread all manner of untruths, but even for the least advantage, be it but for the taking of one poor adventurer of the English, will celebrate the victory with bonfires in every town, always spending more in faggots than the purchase was worth they obtained. Whenas we never yet thought it worth the consumption of two billets, when we have taken eight or ten of their Indian ships at one time, and twenty of the Brazil fleet.* Such is the difference between true valour and ostentation, and between honourable actions and frivolous vainglorious vaunts. But now to return to my first purpose.

The Lord Thomas Howard with six of Her Majesty's ships, six victuallers of London, the Bark Ralegh,* and two or three pinnaces, riding at anchor near unto Flores, one of the westerly islands of the Azores, the last of August in the afternoon, had intelligence by one Captain Middleton of the approach of the Spanish Armada. Which Middleton, being in a very good sailer, had kept them company three days before, of good purpose, both to discover their forces

adventurer: anyone who risked (ventured) his money and goods in the hope of profit.

victuallers: ships carrying provisions.

the more, as also to give advice to my Lord Thomas of their approach. He had no sooner delivered the news but the fleet was in sight. Many of our ship's companies were on shore in the island, some providing ballast for their ships, others filling of water and refreshing themselves from the land with such things as they could either for money or by force recover. By reason whereof our ships being all pestered and rummaging, everything out of order, very light for want of ballast. And that which was most to our disadvantage, the one half part of the men of every ship sick and utterly unserviceable. For in the Revenge there were ninety diseased, in the Bonaventure not so many in health as could handle her mainsail. For had not twenty men been taken out of a bark of Sir George Carey's,* his being commanded to be sunk and those appointed to her, she had hardly ever recovered England. The rest for the most part were in little better state.

The names of Her Majesty's ships were these, as followeth: the Defiance, which was Admiral, the Revenge, Vice-Admiral, the Bonaventure commanded by Captain Cross, the Lion by George Fenner, the Foresight by Master Thomas Vavasour, and the Crane by Duffield. The Foresight and the Crane being but small ships, only the others were of the middle size. The rest, besides the Bark Ralegh, commanded by Captain Thynne, were victuallers and of small force or none.

The Spanish fleet having shrouded their approach* by reason of the island, were now soon at hand as our ships had scarce time to weigh their anchors, but some of them were driven to let slip their cables and set sail. Sir Richard Grenville was the last weighed, to recover the men that were upon the island, which otherwise had been lost. The Lord Thomas with the rest very hardly recovered the wind, which Sir Richard Grenville not being able to do, was persuaded

pestered and rummaging: disordered and in process of putting things straight. To rummage is to clear out and re-stow ship's stores.

Admiral: the chief ship. The commanding officer is called the General.

by the Master and others to cut his mainsail and cast about, and to trust to the sailing of the ship, for the squadron of Seville were on his weather bow. But Sir Richard utterly refused to turn from the enemy, alleging that he would rather choose to die than to dishonour himself, his country, and Her Majesty's ship, persuading his company that he would pass through the two squadrons in despite of them, and enforce those of Seville to give him way. Which he performed upon divers of the foremost, who as the mariners term it sprang their luff and fell under the lee of the Revenge. But the other course had been the better, and might right well have been answered in so great an impossibility of prevailing. Notwithstanding, out of the greatness of his mind, he could not be persuaded.

In the meanwhile as he attended those which were nearest him, the great San Philip being in the wind of him and coming towards him, becalmed his sails in such sort as the ships could neither make way nor feel the helm, so huge and high carged was the Spanish ship, being of a thousand and five hundred tons. Who after laid the Revenge aboard. When he was thus bereft of his sails, the ships that were under his lee luffing up, also laid him aboard, of which the next was the Admiral of the Biscayans, a very mighty and puissant ship commanded by Bertendona.* The said Philip carried three tier of ordnance on a side and eleven pieces in every tier. She shot eight forthright out of her chase, besides those of her stern ports.

After the Revenge was entangled with this Philip, four others boarded her, two on her larboard and two on her starboard. The fight thus beginning at three of the clock in the afternoon, continued very terrible all that evening. But the great San Philip having received the lower tier of the

the Master: the ship's master, in charge of navigation.
on his weather bow: to windward of him.
high carged: built up high above the water.
chase: the guns that lie furthest forward were called 'chase pieces'.
larboard: now called port, to avoid confusion with starboard.

Revenge, discharged with crossbarshot, shifted her self with all diligence from her sides, utterly misliking her first entertainment. Some say that the ship foundered, but we cannot report it for truth unless we were assured. The Spanish ships were filled with companies of soldiers, in some two hundred besides the mariners, in some five, in others eight hundred. In ours there were none at all, beside the mariners, but the servants of the commanders and some few voluntary gentlemen only. After many interchanged volleys of great ordnance and small shot, the Spaniards deliberated to enter the Revenge and made divers attempts, hoping to force her by the multitudes of their armed soldiers and musketeers, but were still repulsed again and again, and at all times beaten back into their own ships or into the seas. In the beginning of the fight, the George Noble of London, having received some shot through her by the armadas, fell under the lee of the Revenge and asked Sir Richard what he would command him, being but one of the victuallers and of small force. Sir Richard bid him save himself and leave him to his fortune.

After the fight had thus without intermission continued while the day lasted and some hours of the night, many of our men were slain and hurt, and one of the great galleons of the armada and the Admiral of the hulks both sunk, and in many other of the Spanish ships great slaughter was made. Some write that Sir Richard was very dangerously hurt almost in the beginning of the fight, and lay speechless for a time ere he recovered. But two of the Revenge's own company brought home in a ship of Lyme from the islands, examined by some of the Lords and others, affirmed that he was never so wounded as that he forsook the upper deck till an hour before midnight, and then being shot into the body with a musket as he was a-dressing, was again shot into the

crossbarshot: cannon balls with a bar through the middle, protruding at either end, and very damaging to masts and rigging.
the Lords: of the Privy Council.
a-dressing: having his wounds dressed.

head, and withal his surgeon wounded to death. This agreeth also with an examination taken by Sir Francis Godolphin* of the 4 other mariners of the same ship, being returned, which examination the said Sir Francis sent unto Master William Killigrew* of her Majesty's Privy Chamber.

But to return to the fight, the Spanish ships which attempted to board the Revenge, as they were wounded and beaten off, so always others came in their places, she having never less than two mighty galleons by her sides and aboard her. So that ere the morning, from three of the clock the day before, there had fifteen several armadas assailed her; and all so ill approved their entertainment, as they were by the break of day far more willing to hearken to a composition than hastily to make any more assaults or entries. But as the day increased, so our men decreased: and as the light grew more and more, by so much more grew our discomforts. For none appeared in sight but enemies, saving one small ship called the Pilgrim, commanded by Jacob Whiddon, who hovered all night to see the success; but in the morning bearing with the Revenge, was hunted like a hare among many ravenous hounds, but escaped.

All the powder of the Revenge to the last barrel was now spent, all her pikes broken, forty of her best men slain, and the most part of the rest hurt. In the beginning of the fight she had but one hundred free from sickness, and fourscore and ten sick, laid in hold upon the ballast. A small troop to man such a ship, and a weak garrison to resist so mighty an army. By those hundred all was sustained, the volleys, boardings and enterings of fifteen ships of war besides those which beat her at large. On the contrary, the Spanish were always supplied with soldiers brought from every squadron, all manner of arms and powder at will. Unto ours there remained no comfort at all, no hope, no supply either of

a composition: terms of peace.
to see the success: to see what would happen. Cp. p. 190, l. 28.
bearing with: keeping company with.
beat her at large: directed their fire on her from a distance.

ships, men, or weapons; the masts all beaten overboard, all her tackle cut assunder, her upper work altogether razed, and in effect evened she was with the water, but the very foundation or bottom of a ship, nothing being left overhead either for flight or defence.

Sir Richard finding himself in this distress, and unable any longer to make resistance, having endured in this fifteen hours fight the assault of fifteen several armadas all by turns aboard him, and by estimation eight hundred shot of great artillery, besides many assaults and entries. And that himself and the ship must need be possessed by the enemy, who were now all cast in a ring round about him, the Revenge not able to move one way or other but as she was moved by the waves and billow of the sea, commanded the Master Gunner, whom he knew to be a most resolute man, to split and sink the ship, that thereby nothing might remain of glory or victory to the Spaniards, seeing in so many hours fight, and with so great a navy they were not able to take her, having had fifteen hours time, fifteen thousand men, and fifty and three sail of men of war to perform it withal. And persuaded the company, or as many as he could induce, to yield themselves unto God, and to the mercy of none else, but as they had like valiant resolute men repulsed so many enemies, they should not now shorten the honour of their nation by prolonging their own lives for a few hours or a few days.

The Master Gunner readily condescended and divers others, but the Captain and the Master were of another opinion and besought Sir Richard to have care of them, alleging that the Spaniard would be as ready to entertain a composition as they were willing to offer the same, and that there being divers sufficient and valiant men yet living, and whose wounds were not mortal, they might do their country and prince acceptable service hereafter. And (that where Sir Richard had alleged that the Spaniards should never glory to have taken one ship of Her Majesty's, seeing they

upper work: forecastle, quarter-deck and poop.

had so long and so notably defended themselves) they answered that the ship had six foot water in hold, three shot under water which were so weakly stopped as with the first working of the sea she must needs sink, and was besides so crushed and bruised as she could never be removed out of the place.

And as the matter was thus in dispute and Sir Richard refusing to hearken to any of those reasons, the Master of the Revenge (while the Captain won unto him the greater party) was convoyed aboard the General, Don Alonso Bazan.* Who finding none over hasty to enter the Revenge again, doubting lest Sir Richard would have blown them up and himself, and perceiving by the report of the Master of the Revenge his dangerous disposition, yielded that all their lives should be saved, the company sent for England, and the better sort to pay such reasonable ransom as their estate would bear, and in the mean season to be free from galley or imprisonment. To this he so much the rather condescended as well, as I have said, for fear of further loss and mischief to themselves, as also for the desire he had to recover Sir Richard Grenville, whom for his notable valour he seemed greatly to honour and admire.

When this answer was returned, and that safety of life was promised, the common sort being now at the end of their peril, the most drew back from Sir Richard and the Master Gunner, being no hard matter to dissuade men from death to life. The Master Gunner finding himself and Sir Richard thus prevented and mastered by the greater number, would have slain himself with a sword had he not been by force withheld and locked into his cabin. Then the General sent many boats aboard the Revenge, and divers of our men, fearing Sir Richard's disposition, stole away aboard the General and other ships. Sir Richard thus overmatched, was sent unto by Alonso Bazan to remove out of the Revenge, the ship being marvellous unsavoury, filled with blood and bodies of dead and wounded men like a slaughterhouse. Sir Richard answered that he might do with his body what he list, for he esteemed it not, and as he was carried out of the ship he swooned, and reviving again desired the company to pray for him. The General used Sir Richard with all humanity, and left nothing unattempted that tended to his recovery, highly commending his valour and worthiness, and greatly bewailed the danger wherein he was, being unto them a rare spectacle and a resolution seldom approved to see one ship turn toward so many enemies, to endure the charge and boarding of so many huge armadas, and to resist and repel the assaults and entries of so many soldiers. All which and more is confirmed by a Spanish captain of the same armada, and a present actor in the fight, who being severed from the rest in a storm, was by the Lion of London, a small ship, taken and is now prisoner in London.

The General Commander of the armada was Don Alonso Bazan, brother to the Marquess of Santa Cruz. The Admiral of the Biscayan squadron was Bertendona. Of the squadron of Seville, Marcos de Aramburu. The hulks and flyboats were commanded by Luis Cuitino. There were slain and drowned in this fight well near two thousand of the enemies and two especial commanders, Don Luis de Saint John and Don George de Prunaria de Mallaga, as the Spanish captain confesseth, besides divers others of special account, whereof as yet report is not made.

The Admiral of the hulks and the Ascension of Seville were both sunk by the side of the Revenge, one other recovered the road of Saint Michaels and sunk also there, a fourth ran herself with the shore to save her men. Sir Richard died as it is said the second or third day aboard the General, and was by them greatly bewailed. What became of his body, whether it were buried in the sea or on the land we know not. The comfort that remaineth to his friends is that he hath ended his life honourably in respect of the

approved: demonstrated.
road: a convenient place for ships to anchor off-shore.
Saint Michaels: one of the larger islands of the Azores.

reputation won to his nation and country, and of the fame to his posterity, and that being dead he hath not outlived his own honour.

For the rest of Her Majesty's ships that entered not so far into the fight as the Revenge, the reasons and causes were these. There were of them but six in all, whereof two but small ships; the Revenge engaged past recovery; the island of Flores was on the one side, fifty-three sail of the Spanish, divided into squadrons on the other, all as full filled with soldiers as they could contain. Almost the one half of our men sick and not able to serve; the ships grown foul, unrummaged, and scarcely able to bear any sail for want of ballast, having been six months at the sea before. If all the rest had entered, all had been lost. For the very hugeness of the Spanish fleet, if no other violence had been offered, would have crushed them between them into shivers. Of which the dishonour and loss to the Queen had been far greater than the spoil or harm that the enemy could any way have received.

Notwithstanding it is very true that the Lord Thomas would have entered between the squadrons, but the rest would not condescend; and the Master of his own ship offered to leap into the sea, rather than to conduct that—Her Majesty's ship—and the rest, to be a prey to the enemy, where there was no hope nor possibility either of defence or victory. Which also in my opinion had ill-sorted or answered the discretion and trust of a General, to commit himself and his charge to an assured destruction, without hope or any likelihood of prevailing, thereby to diminish the strength of Her Majesty's navy and to enrich the pride and glory of the enemy. The Foresight of the Queen's, commanded by Master Thomas Vavasour, performed a very great fight, and stayed two hours as near the Revenge as the weather would permit him, not forsaking the fight till he was like to be encompassed by the squadrons, and with great difficulty cleared himself. The rest gave divers volleys of shot, and entered as far as the place permitted and their own necessities, to keep the weather gauge of the enemy, until they were parted by night.

A few days after the fight was ended, and the English prisoners dispersed into the Spanish and India ships, there arose so great a storm from the west and northwest that all the fleet was dispersed, as well the Indian fleet which were then come unto them as the rest of the armada that attended their arrival, of which 14 sail together with the Revenge, and in her two hundred Spaniards, were cast away upon the isle of Saint Michaels. So it pleased them to honour the burial of that renowned ship the Revenge, not suffering her to perish alone, for the great honour she achieved in her life time. On the rest of the islands there were cast away in this storm, 15 or 16 more of the ships of war, and of a hundred and odd sail of the India fleet, expected this year in Spain, what in this tempest and what before in the bay of Mexico and about the Bermudas there were seventy and odd consumed and lost, with those taken by our ships of London, besides one very rich Indian ship, which set herself on fire, being boarded by the Pilgrim, and five taken by Master Watts* his ships of London, between the Havana and Cape Saint Antonio.

The 4 of this month of November, we received letters from Terceira, affirming that there are 3000 bodies of men remaining in that island, saved out of the perished ships, and that by the Spaniards' own confession, there are 10000 cast away in this storm, besides those that are perished between the islands and the main. Thus it hath pleased God to fight for us and to defend the justice of our cause against the ambitious and bloody pretences of the Spaniard, who seeking to devour all nations are themselves devoured. A manifest testimony how unjust and displeasing their attempts are in the sight of God, who hath pleased to witness

pleased them: this can only mean the powers above, unless it refers ironically to the Spaniards.

Watts his ships: an obsolete possessive case.

the main: the mainland.

by the success of their affairs his mislike of their bloody and injurious designs, purposed and practised against all Christian princes, over whom they seek unlawful and ungodly rule and empery.

One day or two before this wreck happened to the Spanish fleet, whenas some of our prisoners desired to be set on shore upon the islands, hoping to be from thence transported into England, which liberty was formerly by the General promised, one Maurice Fitz John,* son of Old John of Desmond, a notable traitor, cousin german to the late Earl of Desmond, was sent to the English from ship to ship, to persuade them to serve the King of Spain. The arguments he used to induce them were these. The increase of pay which he promised to be trebled, advancement to the better sort, and the exercise of the true Catholic religion and safety of their souls to all. For the first, even the beggarly and unnatural behaviour of those English and Irish rebels, that served the King in that present action, was sufficient to answer that first argument of rich pay.* For so poor and beggarly they were, as for want of apparel they stripped their poor countrymen-prisoners out of their ragged garments, worn to nothing by six months' service, and spared not to despoil them even of their bloody shirts from their wounded bodies and the very shoes from their feet, a notable testimony of their rich entertainment and great wages. The second reason was hope of advancement if they served well and would continue faithful to the King. But what man can be so blockishly ignorant ever to expect place or honour from a foreign king, having no other argument or persuasion than his own disloyalty, to be unnatural to his own country that bred him, to his parents that begat him, and rebellious to his true prince, to whose obedience he is bound by oath, by nature, and by religion. No, they are only assured to be employed in all desperate enterprises, to be held in scorn and disdain ever among those whom they serve. And that ever traitor was either trusted or advanced I could never yet read, neither can I at this time remember any example.

And no man could have less become the place of an orator for such a purpose than this Maurice of Desmond. For the Earl his cousin being one of the greatest subjects in that kingdom of Ireland, having almost whole countries in his possession, so many goodly manors, castles, and lordships, the Count Palatine of Kerry, five hundred gentlemen of his own name and family to follow him, besides others. All of which he possessed in peace for three or four hundred years, was in less than three years after his adhering to the Spaniards and rebellion, beaten from all his holds, not so many as ten gentlemen of his name left living, himself taken and beheaded by a soldier of his own nation, and his land given by a parliament to Her Majesty and possessed by the English. His other cousin, Sir John of Desmond, taken by Master John Zouch and his body hanged over the gates of his native city to be devoured by ravens. The third brother, Sir James, hanged, drawn and quartered in the same place. If he had withal vaunted of this success of his own house, no doubt the argument would have moved much, and wrought great effect, which because he for that present forgot, I thought it good to remember in his behalf.

For matter of religion it would require a particular volume if I should set down how irreligiously they cover their greedy and ambitious pretences with that veil of piety. But sure I am, that there is no kingdom or commonwealth in all Europe, but if they be reformed, they then invade it for religion's sake. If it be as they term Catholic, they pretend title, as if the Kings of Castile were the natural heirs of all the world. And so between both, no kingdom is unsought. Where they dare not with their own forces to invade, they basely entertain the traitors and vagabonds of all nations, seeking by those and by their runagate Jesuits,* to win parts, and have by that mean ruined many noble houses and others in this land, and have extinguished both their lives and families. What good, honour, or fortune ever man yet by them achieved is yet unheard of or unwritten.

pretend title: lay claim to. *parts*: bodies of adherents.

And if our English Papists do but look into Portugal, against whom they have no pretence of religion, how the nobility are put to death, imprisoned, their rich men made a prey, and all sorts of people captived, they shall find that the obedience even of the Turk is easy and a liberty in respect of the slavery and tyranny of Spain. What they have done in Sicily, in Naples, Milan, and in the Low Countries! Who hath there been spared for religion at all? And it cometh to my remembrance of a certain burgher of Antwerp, whose house being entered by a company of Spanish soldiers when they first sacked the city, he besought them to spare him and his goods, being a good Catholic and one of their own party and faction. The Spaniards answered that they knew him to be of a good conscience for himself, but his money, plate, jewels, and goods were all heretical, and therefore good prize. So they abused and tormented the foolish Fleming, who hoped that an *Agnus Dei* had been a sufficient target against all force of that holy and charitable nation.

Neither have they at any time as they protest invaded the kingdoms of the Indies and Peru and elsewhere, but only led thereunto, rather, to reduce the people to Christianity, than for either gold or empery. Whenas in one only island called Hispaniola they have wasted thirty hundred thousand of the natural people, besides many millions else in other places of the Indies, a poor and harmless people created of God, and might have been won to his knowledge as many of them were, and almost as many as ever were persuaded thereunto. The story whereof is at large written by a bishop of their own nation, called Bartholomew de las Casas,* and translated into English and many other languages, entitled *The Spanish Cruelties*.

Who would therefore repose trust in such a nation of ravenous strangers, and especially in those Spaniards which

Agnus Dei: a holy medal with a representation of the Lamb of God.
target: shield.
Hispaniola: Haiti and San Domingo. *natural*: native.

more greedily thirst after English blood than after the lives of any other people of Europe, for the many overthrows and dishonours they have received at our hands, whose weakness we have discovered to the world, and whose forces at home, abroad, in Europe, in India, by sea and land, we have even with handfuls of men and ships overthrown and dishonoured. Let not therefore any Englishman of what religion soever have other opinion of the Spaniards, but that those whom he seeketh to win of our nation, he esteemeth base and traitorous, unworthy persons, or unconstant fools. And that he useth his pretence of religion for no other purpose but to bewitch us from the obedience of our natural prince, thereby hoping in time to bring us to slavery and subjection, and then none shall be unto them so odious and disdained as the traitors themselves, who have sold their country to a stranger and forsaken their faith and obedience contrary to nature or religion; and contrary to that human and general honour, not only of Christians, but of heathen and irreligious nations, who have always sustained what labour soever, and embraced even death itself, for their country, prince or commonwealth.

To conclude, it hath ever to this day pleased God to prosper and defend Her Majesty, to break the purposes of malicious enemies, of foresworn traitors, and of unjust practices and invasions. She hath ever been honoured of the worthiest kings, served by faithful subjects, and shall by the favour of God resist, repel, and confound all whatsoever attempts against her sacred person or kingdom. In the meantime, let the Spaniard and traitor vaunt of their success, and we her true and obedient vassals guided by the shining light of her virtues shall always love her, serve her, and obey her to the end of our lives.

practices: plots.

THE DISCOVERIE OF THE LARGE RICH, AND BEVVTIFVL EMPYRE OF GVIANA, WITH

a relation of the great and Golden Citie of Manoa (*which the Spanyards call* El *Dorado*) And of the Prouinces of *Emeria*, *Arromaia*. *Amapaia*, and other Countries, with their riuers, adioyning.

Performed in the yeare 1595. by Sir *W. Ralegh* Knight, Captaine of her *Maiesties Guard*, *Lo. Warden* of the Stanneries, and her Highnesse Lieutenant generall of the Countie of Cornewall.

Imprinted at London by Robert Robinson.

1596.

THE DISCOVERY OF GUIANA: INTRODUCTION

THE Spanish possessions in the New World were divided into two great Viceroyalties. The Viceroyalty of New Spain included Mexico, and its neighbours north of the isthmus of Panama, which are now part of the United States. The Viceroyalty of Peru included the whole of South America, with the exception of Brazil, which was Portuguese and came under Spain with the union of the crowns in 1580, and parts of Venezuela and Guiana, not then fully explored and colonized. The business of ruling these huge kingdoms overseas (which were the personal property of the Kings of Spain) was onerous and complicated and demanded a genius for organization. The English had for some time been harassing the long lines of communication at sea, and occasionally making raids on the mainland, but as Raleigh saw it the situation required something more. It required a land-base, in the form of a permanent English settlement, which could put a different and more effective pressure on Spain.

The Discovery of Guiana, published in 1596, hot on the heels of the events it relates, is a piece of propaganda, by which Raleigh was trying to sell this idea. The place he selected for his colony was the as yet unexploited territory between the Orinoco and the Amazon. He does not use the word 'discovery' in its modern sense, which would imply that he was the first in the field. He knew that the Spaniards had, in that sense, been the 'discoverers' of Guiana. Indeed, their exploits far surpass his. But they had the advantage of working from colonial bases, exactly the advantage Raleigh was determined to secure for England, and they were accustomed to tropical conditions. As he uses it, the word is equivalent to 'exploration and description of Guiana'.

He is at great pains to supply topographical and ethnographical data, in particular to chart the course of the rivers which give access to the interior. He is also interested in the character and affiliations of the native chiefs, since they constituted an important part of his strategic plan. He intended to exploit their enmity towards the Spaniards and towards the indigenous invaders of Guiana, supposed remnants of Inca tribes, whom he calls Epuremei. The kindness lavished upon the chiefs of the Orinoco was not to be extended to the rulers of Guiana unless they co-operated cheerfully in their own spoliation. Raleigh's expedition hardly entered Guiana proper, largely because the season was too far advanced and the swollen rivers imperilled his return. He prowled round the borders, gathered information, and tried to secure a base from which to operate.

The ancient civilization of the Incas, imagined to be still in existence in the mountains of Guiana, had been concentrated in the high Andes. With no knowledge of the wheel, the plough, or the keystone-arch in building, the people of the Incas had none the less attained some outstanding skills, notably in textiles, pottery and metal work. They had built great bastions without the use of mortar, made cultivation terraces and irrigation ditches, and flung narrow suspension bridges across giddy mountain chasms. They had no written language and no money, but they had a remarkable gift for numbers and an elaborate system of accounting. The government was highly centralized. When, therefore, the Spaniards destroyed the small ruling class (to whom the name Inca properly applied) the mass of the people accepted it as a change of government and did not oppose it as a national disaster.

Francisco Pizzaro, a Spanish adventurer, conquered the empire of the Incas in less than two years, between January 1531 and November 1533. He found Huascar and Atabalipa, the sons of Huayna Capac, at war in a divided empire. A similar civilization, among the Aztecs of Mexico under Montezuma, was destroyed by Hernando Cortez.

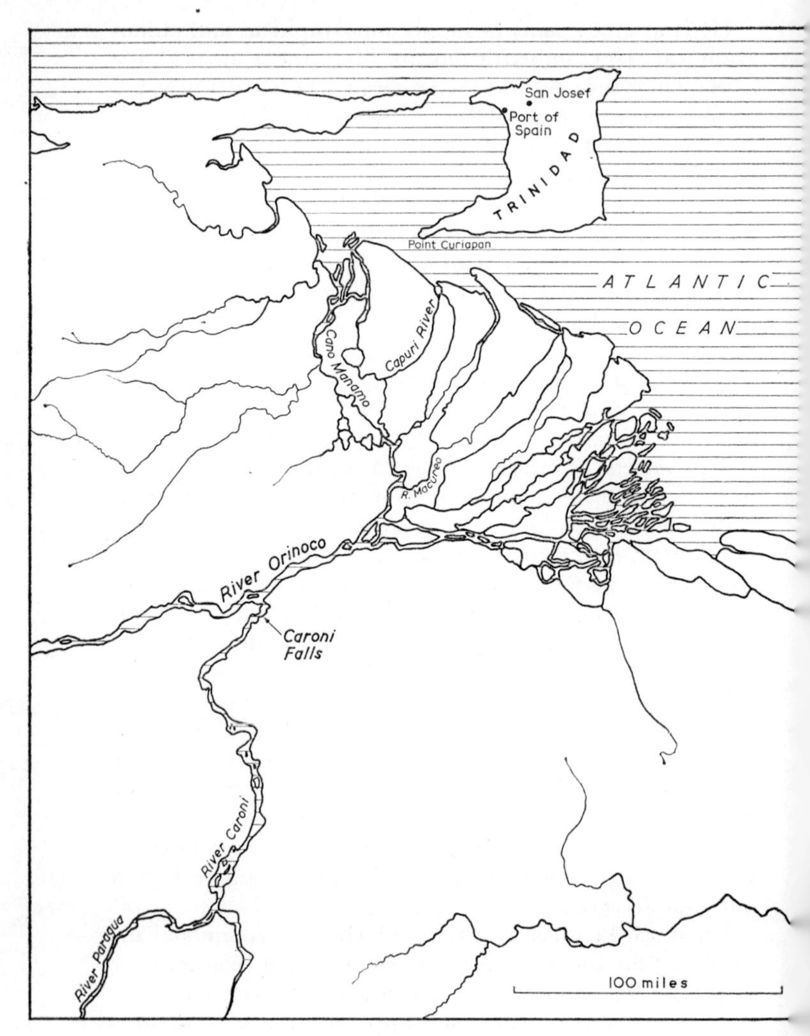

The Orinoco Basin

The Spanish Conquistadors were men of extraordinary courage and endurance, but they proved hard masters. They were willing to fight and to explore, but not to settle down to tilling the land and working the mines in a tropical climate. They therefore used the native Indians as forced labour; and conceiving a great antipathy to their heathen and often repulsively savage ways, they tended to treat them as something less than animals. In the early sixteenth century, Bartholomew de las Casas, a missionary priest, protested eloquently against the inhumanity he saw around him, but it proved impossible to solve the problem of how to be fair both to the foreign settlers and to the native population. The Indians suffered miserably and in some of the islands the native population was wiped out altogether, to be replaced by imported negro slaves. Needless to say, the cruelty and treachery were not all on one side, nor did other nations behave much better than the Spaniards.

Raleigh had some advanced ideas about colonial administration. He managed the chiefs with a mixture of shrewdness and cordiality which would do credit to a District Officer. He was at home in their simple and heroic world, and at the same time he was intellectually and technically ahead of them, and therefore in control. He does not show any contempt for 'lesser breeds', warmly praises the wisdom of old chief Topiawari, and describes native customs with admirable detachment. He thought the cannibals barbarous, especially when they traded their own kin into slavery, but it is not clear that he objected to slavery as such. There is perhaps a trace of civilized surprise when he discovers what the Orenoqueponi hoped to gain from an invasion of Guiana. Chief Topiawari, he says, 'complained very sadly (as if it had been a matter of great consequence) that whereas they were wont to have ten or twelve wives, they were now inforced to content themselves with three or four, and that the lords of the Epuremei had fifty or a hundred. And in truth, they war more for women than for gold or dominion.' Like a good anthropologist he goes on to seek and supply a reason for this odd behaviour. 'For the lords of countries desire many children of their own bodies, to increase their races and kindreds, for in those consist their greatest trust and strength.' In another place he points out that war had seriously depopulated the country. It was not, of course, to his advantage to display his allies at their most primitive.

In *The Discovery of Guiana* he shows no missionary fervour whatsoever, and does not instance the number of souls to be saved as an inducement towards entering the country. He notes at one point that it would have been a tactical error for his company to have helped themselves to Indian grave-furniture because 'if we should have grieved them in their religion at the first, before they had been taught better, and have digged up their graves, we had lost all'. There is however another document, (MS Sloane 1133 in the British Museum printed by Schomburgk and Harlow) which, whether he actually drew it up or not, is plainly inspired by him, and here the rescue of the Indians from heathendom is made a prime motive for the annexation of Guiana. It was perhaps the work of Lawrence Keymis, whose account of the second Guiana voyage shows a similar zeal for promoting a stable government and a sound protestant religion. It sets out in a very thorough and orderly way, though without Raleigh's customary fire, what is to be hoped for from colonizing the country and how best to set about it. It makes it plain that Guiana is to be invaded with the help of native troops from the borders, but it is to be as mild a conquest as possible, since the Guianians in their turn will be required to invade the Spanish settlements west of them.

Beneath the high-minded theory and some unexceptionable practice, there are sinister undertones. Guiana would not be recommended as a country still unrifled were there not some attraction in rifling it. From the first page to the last Raleigh plays upon the lust for gold. How the influx of quantities of bullion would affect the economy of Europe he never pauses to consider. Gold is valued for its rarity. The

Queen and her advisers were probably acting wisely when they declined to assume the burden of disputed territory overseas. Individuals might do as they pleased. If Guiana yielded gold, sooner or later someone would go and get it. But that, Raleigh objected, would be to ruin all. He was not promoting a vulgar gold-rush. He was laying the foundations of a colonial empire. Already he had spent more on Guiana than he had got out of it. He was enough of a realist to see that he must make it attractive to the ordinary merchant-adventurer, but always behind the short term advantages his eyes were fixed upon his colonial dream. 'If Her Majesty undertake the enterprize. . . .'

It is impossible not to recognize and admire the inherent brilliance and farsightedness of Raleigh's plan. Whether it was feasible is another matter. He was selling it. The buyer must look out for himself. He would not be told downright lies. Raleigh mentions Berrio's assertion that his men had actually been in Manoa, but gives reasons for doubting it. He repeats without comment the story of Juan Martines, who claimed that it had taken from noon till night to walk across the city. It is not really hard to distinguish his statements of fact, which are reliable, from his hopes, which are boundless. He has been thought gullible because he believed in the Amazons and the Ewaipanoma, the men whose heads were below their shoulders. He also believed in armadillos, pink herons, the effect of arrow-poison, and oysters growing on trees. He had seen them. In a country whose observed flora and fauna were so curious, fables might become fact. He does not claim to have seen an Amazon or an Ewaipanoma, but he was impressed by the way persistent local beliefs corroborated ancient records. For the servant of a Virgin Queen it would have been agreeable to meet an Amazon.

Throughout the accounts of mountains glittering with the promise of gold ore, parkland bright with birds and flowers, centenarian chiefs, and women 'as well-favoured as ever I saw any', one detects in the narrator something like a will to be deceived, which is more dangerous than any deceit he may have deliberately practised on his reader. Raleigh had lost his heart to the great, rich and beautiful empire of Guiana.

That is why a book which, in so far as it is a factual record, maintains a highly creditable level of accuracy, is also a work of imagination and has borne imaginative fruit. Two names will suffice here, since they are of the greatest. Shakespeare makes Othello fascinate Desdemona by stories of

> the Cannibals that each other eat
> The Anthropophagi, and men whose heads
> Do grow beneath their shoulders.
>
> (I. iii. 143)

In *The Tempest* old Gonzalo calms his companions' fears of the strange sights on Prospero's island by reminding them that such wonders are a commonplace since people took to voyaging.

> Faith, sir, you need not fear. When we were boys
> Who would believe that there were mountaineers
> Dew-lapp'd like bulls, whose throats had hanging at 'em
> Wallets of flesh? or that there were such men
> Whose heads stood in their breasts? which now we find
> Each putter-out of five for one will bring us
> Good warrant of.
>
> (III. iii. 43)

Gonzalo is as willing to believe in the curious physique of the Ewaipanoma as in the goitres which disfigure the inhabitants of some alpine regions, an indubitable fact, strange only to the stay-at-home. The 'putter-out of five for one' was an adventurer who gambled in marine insurance, depositing a certain sum which was to be returned to him fivefold in the event of his safe return.

Raleigh had something to offer for Milton, too; a model of the Garden of Eden, a secret, shining, uncorrupted world, buttressed by crags and forests, where people walked naked and unashamed, trees bore 'blossoms, leaves, ripe fruit and green at one time', and 'the deer came down feeding by the water's side, as if they had been used to a keeper's call'. In Book XI of *Paradise Lost*, Adam sees in a vision the whole world, even to its uttermost bounds,

> Rich Mexico, the seat of Montezume,
> And Cuzco in Peru, the richer seat
> Of Atabalipa, and yet unspoiled
> Guiana, whose great City Geryon's sons
> Call El Dorado.

A more recent book inspired by the forests of Guiana, though at first hand and not through Raleigh's account of them, is W. H. Hudson's haunting *Green Mansions*. And if anyone believes there is still a secret city in South America, which has eluded modern surveyors, he had better read the tragic story of Colonel Fawcett.

Raleigh apologizes to his two sponsors, Cecil and Howard, for the imperfections of his work, in which he says he has 'studied neither phrase, form, nor fashion', and this means perhaps more than the conventional diffidence of a sixteenth-century author. He must have begun to write almost as soon as he arrived home, indeed he may have begun while still at sea, and the mixture of haste, informality and enthusiasm gives his prose something of the quality of good talk. The dedicatory letter is in a noticeably higher strain. Here he piles up the rhythmic, balanced phrases in a way quite foreign to the norms of modern prose, which aims at clarity and practical good sense and avoids ornament of any kind.

> I did therefore even in the winter of my life, undertake these travels, fitter for bodies less blasted with misfortunes, for men of greater ability, and for minds of better encouragement, that thereby if it were possible I might recover but the moderation of excess, and the least taste of the greatest plenty formerly possessed. If I had known other way to win, if I had imagined how greater adventures might have regained, if I could conceive what further means I might yet use, but even to appease so powerful a displeasure, I would not doubt but for one year more to hold my soul in my teeth till it were performed.

There is a much wider gulf nowadays between practical prose, which tends to be grey, unemphatic and unimaginative, and highly coloured kinds of 'literary' prose, so afraid of cliché that the reader is hammered almost unconscious by perpetual surprises. Raleigh can easily modulate from his high style to his middle style, and has no fear that a vivid colloquial phrase will be too low. The grand passage above ends with 'hold my soul in my teeth' and is all the better for it. Is the grandeur perhaps excessive for the occasion? Raleigh writes as he feels, and he felt passionately about his disgrace and his desire for reinstatement. Elsewhere, we find him giving life and colour to the sober subject of military defence, when he writes 'the woods are so thick 200 miles together upon the rivers of such entrance, as a mouse cannot sit in a boat unhit from the bank'. His pleasure in coloured language is shown in the way he preserves the actual idiom used by Chief Topiawari.

> There came down into the large valley of Guiana a nation from so far off as the sun slept (for such were his own words) . . . those that had slain and rooted out so many of all the ancient people as there were leaves in the wood upon all the trees. . . . After he had answered thus far he desired leave to depart, saying that he had far to go and that he was old and weak and was every day called for by death, which was also his own phrase.

He savours delightedly the Queen's native titles, *Ezrabeta Cassipuna Acarewana*, and doubtless hopes that she will share his delight. There is a moment when his sense of the picturesque produces the very accents of the modern journalism of travel more than three hundred years before its time. 'Now', he observes, as the party turns homeward, '. . . it is time to leave Guiana to the sun, whom they worship, and steer away towards the north.'

So much of *The Discovery of Guiana* is narrative and descriptive that it has a kind of natural directness and simplicity of expression. After the long unrewarding toil, the gnawing stomachs and the dark suspicion that the native pilot is deliberately leading the party astray, it is enough to say without any kind of elaboration 'at last about one o'clock after midnight we saw a light, and rowing towards it, we heard the dogs of the village'. But Raleigh has led up to this simple climax with the art of the born story-teller, and the reader releases his breath as the men must have relaxed at their oars. The actual experience, the adventure, in the modern sense of the word, runs in a vivid thread through *The Discovery of Guiana*, with the names of the adventurers duly recorded, comrades, chieftains, river pilots, all who served staunchly and well.

Another thread is descriptive. It varies from the rather dry listing of tribes and rivers to evocations of 'the most beautiful country that ever mine eyes beheld'. Even the river names are a joy to Raleigh, as he makes a net of them to capture and define his new-found land. They had their strictly practical value, they were the equivalent of arterial roads, but there is a sense of glory about 'the Rio Grande, which is one of the great rivers of the world'. The tribes are real people to him. He had met them, watched their drinking bouts, enquired how they worked gold, and learnt their funeral customs. With obvious relish, the champion of tobacco reports of one tribe that

> in the excessive taking of it they exceed all nations, and notwithstanding the moistness of the air in which they live, the hardness of their diet, and the great labours they suffer to hunt, fish and fowl for their living, in all my life either in the Indies or in Europe did I never behold a more goodly and better favoured people, or a more manly.

A similar enthusiasm goes into the description of the Amazons and the headless Ewaipanoma—who, it is to be noted, have no mercantile or strategic significance at all—and into the accounts of the conquistadores. The reality and something of the meaning of their exploits come to life when Raleigh notes that 'at a port called Morequito in Guiana there lieth at this day a great anchor of Ordaz's ship, and this port is some 300 miles within the land, upon the great river of Orinoco'. One finds oneself wondering if it is still there.

Just as he had an unerring sense of what was heroic in *The Last Fight of the Revenge*, Raleigh shows in *The Discovery of Guiana* a sensitivity to the romance of faraway places and strange peoples, a romance grounded, as the heroism is, in fact. His description of the labyrinth of waterways at the mouth of the Orinoco, and of the great savannas, which he was seeing for the first time, is geographically accurate, but it is more than that. It is emotionally coloured too. After the close heat and the entangled boughs, that had to be hacked with swords, the grasslands open out like the country of a dream.

> I never saw a more beautiful country, nor more lively prospects, hills so raised here and there over valleys, the river winding into divers branches, the plains adjoining without bush or stubble, all fair green grass, the ground of hard sand easy to march on either for horse or foot, the deer crossing in every path, the birds towards evening singing in every tree with a thousand several tunes, cranes and herons of white, crimson, and carnation perching in the river's side, the air fresh with a gentle easterly wind, and every stone that we stooped to take up promised either gold or silver by his complexion.

This is not the truly fantastic world of Manoa the Golden. (There Raleigh's romanticism betrayed him, for the story told by Juan Martines reeks of fiction. Or is he using it to betray other romantics?) Nor is it the commercial world of spices, drugs and dyestuffs. It is the archetypal New World, fresh and bright and innocent as the day it was created.

The reader must ask himself how far Raleigh was honest in his recommendation of Guiana. It is rewarding to categorize the different classes to whom he was recommending it and the different means he employs, as well as the different ways he deals with his English comrades, with the native Indians and with the Spaniards. There is nothing naïve about his techniques of leadership and of propaganda.

His account may be hastily written and not too well organized, but it is the record of a highly efficient expedition by a man who had nothing to learn about the arts of salesmanship.

Guiana remains largely unexploited. The Pilgrim Fathers at one time thought of going south but eventually and wisely they decided to colonize North America, where there were no earlier settlers to oppose them. Even there Raleigh's vaulting imagination had been before them. 'I shall yet live,' he said, 'to see it an English nation'. The Orinoco country, which he actually traversed, is now part of Venezuela. The British claims were discussed at length in 1898 in the course of a boundary dispute. It was then decided that exploration and colonization were two different things, and that none of Raleigh's expeditions established any kind of settlement. The existence, further south, of three modern Guianas, British, French and Dutch, reflects the colonial rivalries of the seventeenth century. Raleigh knew the French and Dutch were in the race.

British Guiana exports sugar, rice, bauxite and timber. Gold and diamonds have been mined but not in very large quantities. The flooded rivers, like those which so sorely hampered Raleigh's party, still interfere with cultivation and transport. Venezuelan Guiana has developed her mineral resources to more purpose. At the end of the last century, the mine at El Callao could claim the world's largest output of gold. North American companies have recently turned their attention to the rich deposits of iron in the Guiana Highlands, and the bed of the Orinoco has been dredged to allow ocean-going vessels to come further inland. At Puerto Ordaz, where the Caroni river joins the Orinoco, there is now a great steel plant, powered by a hydro-electric dam.

The Discovery of Guiana: The Epistle Dedicatory

To the right honourable my singular good Lord and kinsman, Charles Howard,* Knight of the Garter, Baron, and Councillor, and of the Admirals of England the most renowned. And to the right honorable Sir Robert Cecil,* Knight, Councillor in Her Highness' Privy Councils.

For your honours' many honourable and friendly parts, I have hitherto only returned promises; and now for answer of both your adventures, I have sent you a bundle of papers which I have divided between your Lordship and Sir Robert Cecil in these two respects chiefly. First for that it is reason that wasteful factors, when they have consumed such stocks as they had in trust, do yield some colour for the same in their account; secondly for that I am assured that whatsoever shall be done or written by me shall need a double protection and defence. The trial that I had of both your loves, when I was left of all but of malice and revenge,* makes me still presume that you will be pleased (knowing what little power I had to perform aught, and the great advantage of forewarned enemies) to answer that out of knowledge which others shall but object out of malice. In my more happy times as I did especially honour you both, so I found that your loves sought me out in the darkest shadow of adversity, and that the same affection which accompanied my better fortune, soared not away from me in my many miseries. All which though I cannot requite, yet I shall ever acknowledge. And the great debt which I

adventures: money invested in the voyage.
factors: agents who trade with their employer's money.
colour: appearance of justification.

have no power to pay, I can do no more for a time but confess to be due.

It is true that as my errors were great, so they have yielded very grievous effects, and if aught might have been deserved in former times to have counterpoised any part of offences, the fruit thereof (as it seemeth) was long before fallen from the tree, and the dead stock only remained. I did therefore even in the winter of my life, undertake these travels, fitter for bodies less blasted with misfortunes, for men of greater ability, and for minds of better encouragement, that thereby if it were possible I might recover but the moderation of excess, and the least taste of the greatest plenty formerly possessed. If I had known other way to win, if I had imagined how greater adventures might have regained, if I could conceive what further means I might yet use, but even to appease so powerful a displeasure, I would not doubt but for one year more to hold fast my soul in my teeth till it were performed.

Of that little remain I had I have wasted in effect all herein, I have undergone many constructions, I have been accompanied with many sorrows, with labour, hunger, heat, sickness, and peril. It appeareth notwithstanding that I made no other bravado of going to sea than was meant, and that I was neither hidden in Cornwall or elsewhere, as was supposed. They have grossly belied me, that forejudged that I would rather become a servant to the Spanish King than return, and the rest were much mistaken, who would have persuaded that I was too easeful and sensual to undertake a journey of so great travail. But if what I have done receive the gracious construction of a painful pilgrimage, and purchase the least remission, I shall think all too little, and that there were wanting to the rest many miseries. But if both the times past, the present, and what may be in the future, do all by one grain of gall continue in an eternal distaste, I do not then know whether I should bewail myself either for my

constructions: interpretations, in the first instance misinterpretations.
painful: laborious, painstaking.

too much travail and expense, or condemn myself for doing less than that which can deserve nothing. From myself I have deserved no thanks, for I am returned a beggar and withered; but that I might have bettered my poor estate, it shall appear by the following discourse, if I had not only respected Her Majesty's future honour and riches. It became not the former fortune in which I once lived to go journeys of picorie, and it had sorted ill with the offices of honour, which by Her Majesty's grace I hold this day in England, to run from cape to cape, and from place to place, for the pillage of ordinary prizes.

Many years since, I had knowledge by relation, of that mighty, rich, and beautiful empire of Guiana, and of that great and golden city, which the Spaniards call El Dorado, and the naturals Manoa; which city was conquered, re-edified, and enlarged by a younger son of Huayna Capac, Emperor of Peru, at such time as Francisco Pizzaro* and others conquered the said empire from his two elder brethren, Huascar and Atabalipa, both then contending for the same, the one being favoured by the Oreiones of Cuzco, the other by the people of Caximalca. I sent my servant Jacob Whiddon* the year before, to get knowledge of the passages, and I had some light from Captain Parker,* sometime my servant, and now attending on your Lordship, that such a place there was to the southward of the great bay of Charvas, or Guanipa. But I found that it was 600 miles further off than they supposed, and many other impediments to them unknown and unheard. After I had displanted Don Antonio de Berrio, who was upon the same enterprize, leaving my ships at Trinidad, at the port called Curiapan, I wandered 400 miles* into the said country by land and river. The particulars I will leave to the following discourse.

The country hath more quantity of gold by manifold, than the best parts of the Indies or Peru. All the most of the kings of the borders are already become Her Majesty's

picorie: roving and robbing. *passages*: routes, ways in and out.

vassals; and seem to desire nothing more than Her Majesty's protection and the return of the English nation. It hath another ground and assurance of riches and glory than the voyages of the West Indies, and an easier way to invade the best parts thereof, than by the common course. The King of Spain is not so impoverished by taking three or four port towns in America as we suppose, neither are the riches of Peru or Nueva Espania so left by the sea-side, as it can be easily washed away with a great flood or spring-tide, or left dry upon the sands on a low ebb. The port towns are few and poor in respect of the rest within the land, and are of little defence, and are only rich when the fleets are to receive the treasure for Spain. And we might think the Spaniards very simple, having so many horses and slaves, if they could not* upon two days warning carry all the gold they have into the land, and far enough from the reach of our footmen, especially the Indies being (as it is for the most part) so mountainous, so full of woods, rivers, and marshes.

In the port towns of the province of Venezeula, as Cumaná, Coro and Santiago (whereof Coro and Santiago were taken by Captain Preston* and Cumaná and San Josef by us) we found not the value of one riall of plate in either. But the cities of Barquisimeto, Valencia, San Sebastian, Corora, Santa Lucia, Alleguna, Maracaibo, and Truxillo are not so easily invaded.* Neither doth the burning of those on the coast impoverish the King of Spain any one ducat; and if we sack Rio de la Hacha, Santa Marta, and Cartagena, which are the ports of Nuevo Reyno and Popayán,* there are besides within the land, which are indeed rich and populous, the towns and cities of Merida, La Grita, San Cristóbal, the great cities of Pamplona, Santa Fé de Bogotá, Tunja and Muzo where the emeralds are found, the

Peru or Nueva Espania: the two viceroyalties, of Peru and New Spain.

riall of plate: a Spanish silver coin.

Nueva Reyno: the New Kingdom of Granada, modern Colombia, of which Popayán, which Raleigh uses as the name of a district, is the capital.

towns and cities of Mariquita, Velez, La Villa de Leiva, La Palma, Honda, Angostura, the great city of Tymana, Tocayma, Sant Aguila, Pasto, Santiago, the great city of Popayán itself, Los Remedios, and the rest. If we take the ports and villages within the bay of Uraba in the kingdom or rivers of Dariena and Caribana, the cities and towns of San Juan de Rodas, Cáceres, of Antioquia, Caramante, Cali, and Ançerma have gold enough to pay the King part, and are not easily invaded by the way of the ocean; or if Nombre de Dios and Panama be taken in the province of Castillo de Oro, and the villages upon the rivers of Zinu and Chagres, Peru hath besides those and besides the magnificent cities of Quito and Lima, so many islands, ports, cities, and mines, as if I should name them with the rest, it would seem incredible to the reader. Of all which because I have written a particular treatise of the West Indies,* I will omit their repetition at this time, seeing that in the said treatise I have anatomized the rest of the sea towns as well of Nicaragua, Yucatán, Nueva Espania, and the islands, as those of the inland, and by what means they may be best invaded, as far as any mean judgement can comprehend.

But I hope it shall appear that there is a way found to answer every man's longing, a better Indies for Her Majesty than the King of Spain hath any, which if it shall please Her Highness to undertake, I shall most willingly end the rest of my days in following the same. If it be left to the spoil and sackage of common persons, if the love and service of so many nations be despised, so great riches, and so mighty an empire refused, I hope Her Majesty will yet take my humble desire and my labour therein in gracious part, which if it had not been in respect of Her Highness future honour and riches, I could have laid hands [on] and ransomed many of the kings and *Cassiqui* of the country, and have had a reasonable proportion of gold for their redemption. But I have chosen rather to bear the burden of poverty than reproach,

the bay of Uraba: the gulf of Darien.
Castillo de Oro: the isthmus of Panama. *mean*: average.

and rather to endure a second travail and the chances thereof, than to have defaced an enterprise of so great assurance, until I knew whether it pleased God to put a disposition in her princely and royal heart either to follow or foreslow the same.

I will therefore leave it to His ordinance that hath only power in all things, and do humbly pray that your honours will excuse such errors as without the defence of art overrun in every part the following discourse, in which I have neither studied phrase, form, nor fashion, and that you will be pleased to esteem me as your own (though over dearly bought) and I shall ever remain ready to do you all honour and service.

W. R.

The Discovery of Guiana

ON Thursday the 6 of February in the year 1595, we departed Engand, and the Sunday following had sight of the North Cape of Spain, the wind for the most part continuing prosperous. We passed in sight of the Burlings and the Rock, and so onwards for the Canaries, and fell with Fuente Ventura the 17 of the same month, where we spent two or three days, and relieved our companies with some fresh meat. From thence we coasted by the Grand Canary, and so to Teneriffe, and stayed there for the Lion's Whelp, your Lordship's ship, and for Captain Amyas Preston and the rest. But when after seven or eight days we found them not, we departed and directed our course for Trinidad with mine own ship, and a small bark of Captain Cross's only (for we had before lost sight of a small gallego on the coast of Spain, which came with us from Plymouth). We arrived at

foreslow: neglect.
the Burlings: islands off the coast of Portugal.
the Rock: Cape Roca near Lisbon.

Trinidad the 22 of March, casting anchor at Point Curiapan, which the Spaniards call Punto de Gallo, which is situate in 8 degrees* or thereabouts. We abode there four or five days, and in all that time we came not to the speech of any Indian or Spaniard. On the coast we saw a fire, as we sailed from the point Carao towards Curiapan, but for fear of the Spaniards none durst come to speak with us. I myself coasted it in my barge close aboard the shore and landed in every cove, the better to know the island, while the ships kept the channel. From Curiapan after a few days we turned up northeast to recover that place which the Spaniards call Puerto de los Hispanioles, and the inhabitants Conquerabia, and as before (revictualling my barge) I left the ships and kept by the shore, the better to come to speech with some of the inhabitants and also to understand the rivers, watering places and ports of the island which (as it is rudely done) my purpose is to send your Lordship* after a few days.

From Curiapan I came to a port and seat of Indians called Parico, where we found a fresh-water river, but saw no people. From thence I rowed to another port, called by the naturals Piche, and by the Spaniards Tierra de Brea. In the way between both were divers little brooks of fresh water, and one salt river that had store of oysters upon the branches of the trees,* and were very salt and well tasted. All their oysters grow upon those boughs and sprays and not on the ground. The like is commonly seen in the West Indies and elsewhere. This tree is described by Andrew Thevet* in his *French Antarctique*, and the form figured in his book as a plant very strange, and by Pliny in his XII book of his *Natural History*.* But in this island, as also in Guiana, there are very many of them.

At this point called Tierra de Brea or Piche there is that abundance of stone pitch,* that all the ships of the world may be therewith laden from thence, and we made trial of

Curiapan: Point Icacos.
Puerto de los Hispanioles: Port of Spain, the capital of Trinidad.
figured: illustrated.

it in trimming our ships to be most excellent good, and melteth not with the sun as the pitch of Norway, and therefore for ships trading the south parts very profitable. From thence we went to the mountain foot called Annaperima, and so passing the river Carone on which the Spanish city was seated, we met with our ships at Puerto de los Hispanioles or Conquerabia.

This island of Trinidad hath the form of a sheep-hook, and is but narrow; the north part is very mountainous, the soil is very excellent and will bear sugar, ginger, or any other commodity that the Indies yield. It hath store of deer, wild porks, fruits, fish and fowl. It hath also for bread sufficient *Mais*, *Cassavi*,* and of those roots and fruits which are common everywhere in the West Indies. It hath divers beasts which the Indies have not. The Spaniards confessed that they found grains of gold in some of the rivers, but they having a purpose to enter Guiana (the magazine of all rich metals) cared not to spend time in the search thereof any further. This island is called by the people thereof Cairi, and in it are divers nations. Those about Parico are called Iaio; those at Punto Carao are the Arwacas, and between Carao and Curiapan they are called Salvaios; between Carao and Punto Galera are the Nepoios, and those about the Spanish city term themselves Carinepagotos. Of the rest of the nations and of other ports and rivers I leave to speak here, being impertinent to my purpose, and mean to describe them as they are situate in the particular plot and description of the island, three parts whereof I coasted with my barge, that I might the better describe it.

Meeting with the ships at Puerto de los Hispanioles, we found at the landing place a company of Spaniards who kept a guard at the descent, and they offering a sign of peace I sent Captain Whiddon to speak with them, whom afterward to my great grief I left buried in the said island after my return from Guiana, being a man most honest and

trimming: caulking. *Annaperima*: Naparima.
nations: tribes. *leave*: omit. *plot*: map or plan.

valiant. The Spaniards seemed to be desirous to trade with us and to enter into terms of peace, more for doubt of their own strength than for aught else, and in the end upon pledge some of them came aboard. The same evening there stole also aboard us in a small *Canoa* two Indians, the one of them being a *Cassique* or Lord of the people called Cantyman, who had the year before been with Captain Whiddon, and was of his acquaintance. By this Cantyman we understood what strength the Spaniards had, how far it was to their city, and of Don Antonio de Berrio the Governor, who was said to be slain in his second attempt of Guiana, but was not.

While we remained at Puerto de los Hispanioles some Spaniards came aboard us to buy linen of the company, and such other things as they wanted, and also to view our ships and company, all which I entertained kindly and feasted after our manner. By means whereof I learned of one and another as much of the estate of Guiana as I could, or as they knew, for those poor soldiers having been many years without wine, a few draughts made them merry, in which mood they vaunted of Guiana and of the riches thereof, and all what they knew of the ways and passages, myself seeming to purpose nothing less than the entrance or discovery thereof, but bred in them an opinion that I was bound only for the relief of those English which I had planted in Virginia,* whereof the bruit was come among them, which I had performed in my return if extremity of weather had not forced me from the said coast.

I found occasions of staying in this place for two causes. The one was to be revenged of Berrio, who the year before betrayed eight of Captain Whiddon's men and took them, while he departed from them to seek the Elizabeth Bonaventure, which arrived at Trinidad the day before from the East Indies; in whose absence Berrio sent a *Canoa* aboard the pinnace, only with Indians and dogs, inviting the company

upon pledge: that no harm was intended.
bruit: rumour.

to go with them into the woods to kill a deer, who like wise men in the absence of their Captain followed the Indians, but were no sooner one arquebus shot from the shore, but Berrio's soldiers lying in ambush had them all, notwithstanding that he had given his word to Captain Whiddon that they should take water and wood safely. The other cause of my stay was for that by discourse with the Spaniards I daily learned more and more of Guiana, of the rivers and passages, and of the enterprise of Berrio, by what means or fault he failed, and how he meant to prosecute the same.

While we thus spent the time I was assured by another *Cassique* of the north side of the island that Berrio had sent to Margarita and to Cumaná for soldiers, meaning to have given me a *Cassado* at parting, if it had been possible. For although he had given order through all the island that no Indian should come aboard to trade with me upon pain of hanging and quartering (having executed two of them for the same which I afterwards found) yet every night there came some with most lamentable complaints of his cruelty, how he had divided the island and given to every soldier a part, that he made the ancient *Cassiqui* which were lords of the country to be their slaves, that he kept them in chains, and dropped their naked bodies with burning bacon, and such other torments, which I found afterwards to be true. For in the city, after I entered the same, there were five of the lords or little kings (which they call *Cassiqui* in the West Indies) in one chain almost dead of famine and wasted with torments. These are called in their own language *Acarewana*, and now of late since English, French, and Spanish are come among them, they call themselves *Capitaynes*, because they perceive that the chiefest of every ship is called by that name. Those five *Capitaynes* in the chain were called Wannawanare, Carroaori, Maquarima, Tarroopanama, and Aterima. So as both to be revenged of the former wrong, as also considering that to enter Guiana by small boats, to

like wise men: ironically said. *arquebus*: musket.
a Cassado: a mortal blow, a finishing stroke (Spanish).

depart 400 or 500 miles from my ships, and to leave a garrison in my back interessed in the same enterprize, who also daily expected supplies out of Spain, I should have savoured very much of the ass; and therefore taking a time of most advantage, I set upon the Corp du Guard* in the evening, and having put them to the sword, sent Captain Calfield onwards with 60 soldiers, and myself followed with 40 more, and so took their new city, which they called Saint Joseph, by break of day. They abode not any fight after a few shot, and all being dismissed but only Berrio and his companion,* I brought them with me aboard, and at the instance of the Indians I set their new city of Saint Josephs on fire.

The same day arrived Captain George Gifford with your Lordships's ship, and Captain Keymis* whom I lost on the coast of Spain, with the gallego, and in them divers gentlemen and others, which to our little army was a great comfort and supply.

We then hastened away towards our purposed discovery, and first I called all the Captains of the island together that were enemies to the Spaniards, for there were some which Berrio had brought out of other countries and planted there to eat out and waste those that were natural of the place, and by my Indian interpreter,* which I carried out of England, I made them understand that I was the servant of a Queen, who was the great *Cassique* of the North, and a virgin, and had more *Cassiqui* under her than there were trees in their island. That she was an enemy to the *Castellani* in respect of their tyranny and oppression, and that she delivered all such nations about her as were by them oppressed, and having freed all the coast of the northern world from their servitude had sent me to free them also, and withal to defend the country of Guiana from their invasion and conquest. I showed them Her Majesty's picture, which

interessed: concerned.

Castellani: a general name for Spaniards, deriving from the fact that the Indies were first possessed by Isabella of Castile and immigration was for a time confined to Castilians.

they so admired and honoured as it had been easy to have brought them idolatrous thereof.

The like and a more large discourse I made to the rest of the nations both in my passing to Guiana, and to those of the borders, so as in that part of the world Her Majesty is very famous and admirable, whom they now call *Ezrabeta Cassipuna Acarewana*, which is as much as 'Elizabeth, the great princess, or greatest commander'. This done we left Puerto de los Hispanioles, and returned to Curiapan, and having Berrio my prisoner I gathered from him as much of Guiana as he knew.

This Berrio is a gentleman well descended, and had long served the Spanish King in Milan, Naples, the Low Countries and elsewhere, very valiant and liberal, and a gentleman of great assuredness and of a great heart. I used him according to his estate and worth in all things I could, according to the small means I had.

I sent Captain Whiddon the year before to get what knowledge he could of Guiana, and the end of my journey at this time was to discover and enter the same, but my intelligence was far from truth, for the country is situate above 600 English miles further from the sea than I was made believe it had been, which afterward understanding to be true by Berrio, I kept it from the knowledge of my company, who else would never have been brought to attempt the same. Of which 600 miles I passed 400 leaving my ships* so far from me at anchor in the sea, which was more of desire to perform that discovery than of reason, especially having such poor and weak vessels to transport ourselves in; for in the bottom of an old gallego which I caused to be fashioned like a galley, and in one barge, two wherries, and a ship's boat of the Lion's Whelp, we carried 100 persons and their victuals for a month in the same, being all driven to lie in the rain and weather, in the open air, in the burning sun, and upon the hard boards, and to dress our meat, and to carry all manner of furniture in them,

Acarewana: see above, p. 111.

wherewith they were so pestered and unsavoury, that what with the victuals being most fish,* with the wet clothes of so many men thrust together and the heat of the sun, I will undertake there was never any prison in England that could be found more unsavoury and loathsome, especially to myself, who had for many years before been dieted and cared for in a sort far differing.

If Captain Preston had not been persuaded that he should have come too late to Trinidad to have found us there (for the month was expired which I promised to tarry for him there ere he could recover the coast of Spain) but that it had pleased God he might have joined with us, and that we had entered the country but some ten days sooner ere the rivers were overflown, we had adventured either to have gone to the great city of Manoa, or at least taken so many of the other cities and towns nearer at hand as would have made a royal return. But it pleased not God so much to favour me at this time. If it shall be my lot to prosecute the same, I shall willingly spend my life therein, and if any else shall be enabled thereunto, and conquer the same, I assure him thus much, he shall perform more than ever was done in Mexico by Cortez, or in Peru by Pizzaro, whereof the one conquered the empire of Montezuma, the other of Huascar and Atabalipa, and whatsoever prince shall possess it, that prince shall be lord of more gold and of a more beautiful empire and of more cities and people, than either the King of Spain or the Great Turk.

But because there may arise many doubts, and how this empire of Guiana is become so populous, and adorned with so many great cities, towns, temples, and treasures, I thought good to make it known that the Emperor now reigning* is descended from those magnificent princes of Peru, of whose large territories, of whose policies, conquests, edifices, and riches Pedro de Cieza,* Francisco Lopez,* and others have written large discourses. For when Francisco Pizzaro, Diego Almagro and others conquered the said empire of Peru, and

return: profit.

had put to death Atabalipa, son to Huayna Capac, which Atabalipa had formerly caused his eldest brother Huascar to be slain, one of the younger sons of Huayna Capac fled out of Peru, and took with him many thousands of those soldiers of the empire called Oreiones, and with those and many others which followed him, he vanquished all that tract and valley of America which is situate between the great rivers of Amazon and Baraguan, otherwise called Orinoco and Marañon.

The empire of Guiana is directly east from Peru towards the sea, and lieth under the equinoctial line, and it hath more abundance of gold than any part of Peru, and as many or more great cities than ever Peru had when it flourished most. It is governed by the same laws, and the Emperor and people observe the same religion, and the same form and policies in government as was used in Peru, not differing in any part. And as I have been assured by such of the Spaniards as have seen Manoa, the imperial city of Guiana, which the Spaniards call El Dorado, that for the greatness, for the riches, and for the excellent seat, it far exceedeth any of the world, at least of so much of the world as is known to the Spanish nation. It is founded upon a lake of salt water* of 200 leagues long, like unto *Mare Caspiun*. And if we compare it to that of Peru, and but read the report of Francisco Lopez and others, it will seem more than credible, and because we may judge of the one by the other, I thought good to insert part of the 120th chapter of Lopez in his *General History of the Indies*, wherein he describeth the court and magnificence of Huayna Capac, ancestor to the Emperor of Guiana, whose very words are these.

[*Raleigh quotes the original Spanish, here omitted, and then translates.*]

'All the vessels of his house, table, and kitchen were of gold and silver, and the meanest of silver and copper for strength and hardness of the metal. He had in his wardrobe

leagues: a league is about three and a half miles. *Mare Caspiun*: the Caspian Sea. *wardrobe*: private treasury.

hollow statues of gold which seemed giants, and the figures in proportion and bigness of all the beasts, birds, trees and herbs that the earth bringeth forth; and of all the fishes that the sea or waters of his kingdom breedeth. He had also ropes, budgets, chests and troughs of gold and silver, heaps of billets of gold that seemed wood, marked out to burn. Finally there was nothing in his country whereof he had not the counterfeit in gold. Yea and they say, the Incas had a garden of pleasure in an island near Puna, where they went to recreate themselves, when they would take the air of the sea, which had all kind of garden herbs, flowers and trees of gold and silver, an invention and magnificence till then never seen. Besides all this, he had an infinite quantity of silver and gold unwrought in Cuzco which was lost by the death of Huascar, for the Indians hid it, seeing that the Spaniards took it and sent it into Spain.'

And in the 117th chapter, Francisco Pizzaro caused the gold and silver of Atabalipa to be weighed, after he had taken it, which Lopez setteth down in these words following. [*As before Raleigh begins with the original text in Spanish.*] 'They found fifty and two thousand marks of good silver, and one million and three hundred twenty and six thousand and five hundred pesoes of gold.'

Now although these reports may seem strange, yet if we consider the many millions which are daily brought out of Peru into Spain, we may easily believe the same, for we find that by the abundant treasure of that country the Spanish King vexeth all the princes of Europe, and is become in a few years from a poor King of Castile the greatest monarch of this part of the world, and likely every day to increase, if other princes foreslow the good occasions offered, and suffer him to add this empire to the rest, which by far exceedeth all the rest. If his gold now endanger us, he will then be unresistible. Such of the Spaniards as afterward endeavoured the conquest thereof (whereof there have been many as shall be declared hereafter) thought that this Inca

budgets: bags.

(of whom this Emperor now living is descended) took this way to the River of Amazons by that branch which is called Papamene, for by that way followed Orellana* (by the commandment of the Marquess Pizzaro in the year 1542) whose name the river also beareth this day, which is also by others called Marañon, although Andrew Thevet doth affirm that between Marañon and Amazon there are 120 leagues. But sure it is that those rivers have one head and beginning, and that Marañon which Thevet describeth is but a branch of Amazon or Orellana, of which I will speak more in another place. It was also attempted by Diego Ordaz,* but whether before Orellana or after I know not. But it is now little less than 70 years since that Ordaz, a knight of the Order of Saint Iago, attempted the same; and it was in the year 1542 that Orellana discovered the River of Amazons; but the first that ever saw Manoa was Johannes Martines,* Master of the Munition to Ordaz. At a port called Morequito in Guiana there lieth at this day a great anchor of Ordaz's ship, and this port is some 300 miles within the land, upon the great river of Orinoco.

I rested at this port four days; twenty days after I left the ships at Curiapan. The relation of this Martines (who was the first that discovered Manoa) his success and end, is to be seen in the Chancery of Saint Juan de Puerto Rico, whereof Berrio had a copy, which appeared to be the greatest encouragement as well to Berrio as to others that formerly attempted the discovery and conquest. Orellana after he failed of the discovery of Guiana by the said River of Amazons, passed into Spain, and there obtained a patent of the King for the invasion and conquest, but died by sea about the islands, and his fleet being severed by tempest, the action for that time proceeded not. Diego Ordaz followed the enterprize and departed Spain with 600 soldiers and 30 horse, who arriving on the coast of Guiana was slain in a mutiny with the most part of such as favoured him, as also of the rebellious part, in so much as his ships perished and few or none returned, neither was it certainly known what became of the said Ordaz, until Berrio found the anchor of his ship in the river of Orinoco; but it was supposed, and so it is written by Lopez, that he perished on the seas, and of other writers diversely conceived and reported. And hereof it came that Martines entered so far within the land and arrived at that city of Inca the Emperor, for it chanced that while Ordaz with his army rested at the port of Morequito (who was either the first or second that attempted Guiana), by some negligence the whole store of powder provided for the service was set on fire, and Martines having the chief charge was condemned by the General Ordaz to be executed forthwith. Martines being much favoured by the soldiers had all the mean possible procured for his life, but it could not be obtained in any other sort than this: that he should be set into a *Canoa* alone, without any victual, only with his arms, and so turned loose into the great river.

But it pleased God that the *Canoa* was carried down the stream, and that certain of the Guianians met it the same evening, and having not at any time seen any Christian, nor any man of that colour, they carried Martines into the land to be wondered at, and so from town to town, until he came to the great city of Manoa, the seat and residence of Inca the Emperor. The Emperor, after he had beheld him, knew him to be a Christian (for it was not long before that his brethren Huascar and Atabalipa were vanquished by the Spaniards in Peru) and caused him to be lodged in his palace and well entertained. He lived 7 months in Manoa, but not suffered to wander into the country anywhere. He was also brought thither all the way blindfold, led by the Indians, until he came to the entrance of Manoa itself, and was 14 or 15 days in the passage. He avowed at his death that he entered the city at noon, and then they uncovered his face, and that he travelled all that day until night through the city, and the next day from sun rising to sun setting, ere he came to the palace of Inca.

After that Martines had lived 7 months in Manoa, and began to understand the language of the country, Inca asked him whether he desired to return into his own country, or would willingly abide with him. But Martines not desirous to stay, obtained the favour of Inca to depart, with whom he sent divers Guianians to conduct him to the river of Orinoco all laden with as much gold as they could carry, which he gave to Martines at his departure. But when he was arrived near the river's side, the borderers which are called Orenoqueponi robbed him and his Guianians of all the treasure (the borderers being at that time at wars with Inca, and not conquered) save only of two great bottles of gourds, which were filled with beads of gold curiously wrought, which those Orenoqueponi thought had been no other thing than his drink or meat or grain for food, with which Martines had liberty to pass. And so in *Canoas* he fell down by the river of Orinoco to Trinidad, and from thence to Margarita, and so to Saint Juan de Puerto Rico, where remaining a long time for passage into Spain he died. In the time of his extreme sickness, and when he was without hope of life, receiving the sacrament at the hands of his confessor, he delivered these things, with the relation of his travels, and also called for his *Calabaza* or gourds of the gold beads which he gave to the church and friars to be prayed for.

This Martines was he that christened the city of Manoa by the name of El Dorado, and as Berrio informed me upon this occasion. Those Guianians and also the borderers, and all others in that tract which I have seen, are marvellous great drunkards, in which vice I think no nation can compare with them. And at the times of their solemn feasts when the Emperor carouseth with his captains, tributaries and governors, the manner is thus. All those that pledge him are first stripped naked, and their bodies anointed all over with a kind of white *Balsamum* (by them called *Curcai*) of which there is great plenty and yet very dear amongst them, and it is of all other the most precious, whereof we have had good experience. When they are anointed all over, certain

of gourds: made of gourds.
solemn: ceremonious. *Balsamum*: a vegetable oil.

servants of the Emperor having prepared gold made into fine powder blow it through hollow canes upon their naked bodies, until they be all shining from the foot to the head, and in this sort they sit drinking by twenties and hundreds and continue in drunkenness sometimes six or seven days together. The same is also confirmed by a letter written into Spain which was intercepted, which Master Robert Dudley* told me he had seen. Upon this sight, and for the abundance of gold which he saw in the city, the images of gold in their temples, the plates, armours, and shields of gold which they use in the wars, he called it El Dorado.

[*Here Raleigh gives a brief account of the explorations and conquests of Pedro Ursua, Lope de Aguirre, Geronimo de Ortal, Pedro de Silva, Diego Fernando de Serpa, and Gonzalez Ximenes de Quesada, whose niece Berrio married.* 'It seemeth to me', *he writes,* 'that this empire is reserved for Her Majesty and the English nation, by reason of the hard success which all these and other Spaniards found in attempting the same.']

How all these rivers cross and encounter, how the country lieth and is bordered, the passage of Ximenes, and of Berrio, mine own discovery, and the way I entered, with all the rest of the nations and rivers, your Lordship shall receive in a large chart or map,* which I have not yet finished, and which I shall most humbly pray your Lordship to secrete, and not to suffer it to pass your own hands; for by a draught thereof all may be prevented by other nations. For I know it is this very year sought by the French, although by the way that they now take I fear it not much. It was also told me ere I departed England that Villiers, the Admiral, was in preparation for the planting of Amazon, to which river the French have made divers voyages and returned much gold and other rarities. I spoke with a captain of a French ship that came from thence, his ship riding in Falmouth, the same year that my ships came first from Virginia.* There was another this year in Helford that also came from thence, and had been 14 months at an anchor in Amazon, which were both very rich.

[*Raleigh does not think that an expedition could reach Guiana by way of the Amazon, though Guianian gold has been dispersed among the tribes that way.*]

Undoubtedly those that trade Amazon return much gold, which (as is aforesaid) cometh by trade from Guiana, by some branch of a river that falleth from the country into Amazon, and either it is by the river which passeth by the nations called Tisnados, or by Carepuna. I made enquiry amongst the most ancient and best travelled of the Orenoqueponi, and I had knowledge of all the rivers between Orinoco and Amazon, and was very desirous to understand the truth of those warlike women,* because of some it is believed, of others not. And though I digress from my purpose, yet I will set down what hath been delivered me for truth of those women, and I spake with a *Cassique* or Lord of the people that told me he had been in the river, and beyond it also.

The nations of these women are on the south side of the river in the provinces of Topago, and their chiefest strengths and retreats are in the islands situate on the south side of the entrance, some 60 leagues within the mouth of the said river. The memories of the like women are very ancient as well in Africa as in Asia. In Africa those that had Medusa for Queen; others in Scythia near the rivers of Tanais and Thermadon. We find also that Lampedo and Marthesia were Queens of the Amazons. In many histories they are verified to have been, and in divers ages and provinces. But they which are not far from Guiana do accompany with men but once in a year, and for the time of one month, which I gather by their relation to be in April. At that time all the kings of the borders assemble, and the queens of the Amazons, and after the queens have chosen, the rest cast lots for their valentines. This one month, they feast, dance, and drink of their wines in abundance, and the moon being done, they all depart to their own provinces. If they conceive and be delivered of a son, they return him to the

valentines: chosen lovers.

father; if of a daughter they nourish it, and retain it, and as many as have daughters send unto the begetters a present, all being desirous to increase their own sex and kind. But that they cut off the right dug of the breast I do not find to be true. It was further told me, that if in the wars they took any prisoners, that they used to accompany with those also at what time soever, but in the end for certain they put them to death. For they are said to be very cruel and bloodthirsty, especially to such as offer to invade their territories. These Amazons have likewise great store of these plates of gold, which they recover by exchange chiefly for a kind of green stones,* which the Spaniards call *Piedras Hijadas*, and we use for spleen stones, and for the disease of the stone we also esteem them. Of these I saw divers in Guiana, and commonly every King or *Cassique* hath one, which their wives for the most part wear, and they esteem them as great jewels.

[*There follows a description of Berrio's most recent attempt to enter Guiana, starting from New Granada and finishing at Trinidad, an immensely long and difficult journey*.]

Berrio affirmed that there fell an hundred rivers into Orinoco from the north and south, whereof the least was as big as Rio Grande that passeth between Popayán and Nuevo Reyno de Granada (Rio Grande being esteemed one of the renowned rivers in all the West Indies, and numbered among the great rivers of the world). But he knew not the names of any of these, but Caroni only, neither from what nations they descended, neither to what provinces they led, for he had no means to discourse with the inhabitants at any time. Neither was he curious in these things, being utterly unlearned,* and not knowing the east from the west. But of all these I got some knowledge, and of many more, partly by mine own travel and the rest by conference. Of some one I learned one, of others the rest, having with me an Indian that spake many languages, and that of Guiana naturally.

Piedras Hijadas: literally 'loin stones' considered efficacious against diseases in that region.

Rio Grande: the Magdalena.

I sought out all the aged men, and such as were greatest travellers, and by the one and the other I came to understand the situations, the rivers, the kingdoms from the east sea to the borders of Peru, and from Orinoco southward as far as Amazon or Marañon, and the regions of Maria Tamball,* and of all the Kings of provinces, and Captains of towns and villages, how they stood in terms of peace or war, and which were friends or enemies the one with the other, without which there can be neither entrance nor conquest in those parts, nor elsewhere. For by the dissension between Huascar and Atabalipa, Pizzaro conquered Peru, and by the hatred that the Traxcallians bore to Montezuma, Cortez was victorious over Mexico, without which both the one and the other had failed of their enterprize and of the great honour and riches which they attained unto.

[*Berrio in Trinidad incurred the jealousy of Francisco de Vides, Governor of Cumaná, since Vides also had designs on Guiana and even, for the matter of that, on Trinidad. With encouragement from Vides, the Caçique Morequito, who at first had appeared friendly, set upon a small party of Berrio's people and killed them all, including a friar. Berrio exacted vengeance, and Raleigh rarely mentions this Caçique without recalling his end, so that it becomes a kind of epic formula, Morequito-whom-Berrio-slew. Raleigh says Berrio told him that the party, who all perished except one, had actually been in Manoa and were on their way back, but adds, 'I could not be assured thereof by the Lord which now governeth the province of Morequito, for he told me that they got all the gold they had in other towns on this side Manoa, there being many very great and rich, and (as he said) built like the towns of Christians with many rooms.'*]

Now Berrio, for executing of Morequito and other cruelties, spoils, and slaughters done in Arromaia, hath lost the love of the Orenoqueponi and of all the borderers, and dare not send any of his soldiers any farther into the land than to Carapana, which he calleth the port of Guiana. But from thence by the help of Carapana he had trade farther into the country, and always appointed 10 Spaniards to reside in Carapana's town; by whose favour and by being conducted by his people, those ten searched the country thereabouts as well for mines as for other trades and commodities.

They have also gotten a nephew of Morequito, whom they have christened and named Don Juan, of whom they have great hope, endeavouring by all means to establish him in the said province. Among many other trades those Spaniards used in *Canoas* to pass to the rivers of Barema, Pawroma, and Dissequebe, which are on the south side of the mouth of Orinoco, and there buy women and children from the Cannibals, which are of that barbarous nature as they will for 3 or 4 hatchets sell the sons and daughters of their own brethren and sisters, and for somewhat more even their own daughters. Hereof the Spaniards make great profit, for buying a maid of 12 or 13 years for three or four hatchets, they sell them again at Margarita in the West Indies for 50 and 100 pesoes, which is so many crowns.

The master of my ship, John Douglas, took one of the *Canoas* which came laden from thence with people to be sold, and the most of them escaped, yet of those he brought, there was one as well favoured and as well shaped as ever I saw any in England, and afterward I saw many of them which but for their tawny colour may be compared to any of Europe. They also trade in those rivers for bread of *Cassavi*, of which they buy an hundred pound weight for a knife, and sell it at Margarita for ten pesoes. They also recover great store of cotton, Brazil wood, and those beds which they call *Hamacas* or Brazil beds, wherein in hot countries all the Spaniards use to lie commonly, and in no other, neither did we ourselves while we were there. By means of which trades, for ransom of divers of the Guianians and for exchange of hatchets and knives, Berrio recovered some store of gold plates, eagles of gold, and images of men and divers birds, and dispatched his Campmaster for Spain* with all that he had gathered, therewith to levy soldiers and by the show thereof to draw others to the love of the enterprize. And having sent divers images as well of men as

Brazil wood: a red dye-stuff.

beasts, birds and fishes so curiously wrought in gold, doubted not but to persuade the King to yield to him some further help, especially for that this land hath never been sacked, the mines never wrought, and in the Indies their works were well spent,* and the gold drawn out with great labour and charge. He also dispatched messengers to his son in Nuevo Reyno to levy all the forces he could, and to come down the river of Orinoco to Emeria, the province of Carapana, to meet him. He had also sent to Santiago de León on the coast of the Caracas to buy horses and mules. After I had thus learned of his proceedings past and purposed, I told him that I had resolved to see Guiana, and that it was the end of my journey, and the cause of my coming to Trinidad, as it was indeed (and for that purpose I sent Jacob Whiddon the year before to get intelligence, with whom Berrio himself had speech at that time, and remembered how inquisitive Jacob Whiddon was of his proceedings and of the country of Guiana). Berrio was stricken into a great melancholy and sadness, and used all the arguments he could to dissuade me, and also assured the gentlemen of my company that it would be labour lost, and that they should suffer many miseries if they proceeded. And first he delivered that I could not enter any of the rivers with any bark or pinnace, nor hardly with any ship's boat, it was so low, sandy, and full of flats, and that his companies were daily grounded in their *Canoas* which drew but twelve inches water. He further said that none of the country would come to speak with us, but would all fly, and if we followed them to their dwellings they would burn their own towns, and besides that the way was long, the winter at hand, and that the rivers beginning once to swell, it was impossible to stem the current, and that we could not in those small boats by any means carry victual for half the time, and that (which indeed most discouraged my company) the kings and lords of all the borders and of Guiana had decreed that none of them should trade with any Christians for gold, because the

well spent: almost exhausted.

same would be their own overthrow, and that for the love of gold the Christians meant to conquer and dispossess them of all together.

Many and the most of these I found to be true, but yet I resolving to make trial of all whatsoever happened, directed Captain George Gifford, my vice-admiral, to take the Lion's Whelp, and Captain Calfield his bark, to turn to the eastward, against the breeze what they could possibly,* to recover the mouth of a river called Capuri, whose entrance I had before sent Captain Whiddon and John Douglas, the master, to discover, who found some nine foot water or better upon the flood, and five at low water, to whom I had given instructions that they should anchor at the edge of the shoal, and upon the best of the flood to thrust over, which shoal John Douglas buoyed and beaconed for them before. But they laboured in vain, for neither could they turn it up altogether so far to the east, neither did the flood continue so long, but the water fell ere they could have passed the sands, as we after found by a second experience. So as now we must either give over our enterprize, or leaving our ships at adventure 400 mile behind us, to run up in our ships' boats, one barge, and two wherries. But being doubtful how to carry victuals for so long a time in such baubles, or any strength of men, especially for that Berrio assured us that his son must be by that time come down with many soldiers, I sent away one King, master of the Lion's Whelp, with his ship's boat, to try another branch of a river in the bottom of the bay of Guanipa, which was called Amana, to prove if there were water to be found for either of the small ships to enter. But when he came to the mouth of Amana, he found it as the rest, but stayed not to discover it thoroughly, because he was assured by an Indian, his guide, that the Cannibals of Guanipa would assail them with many *Canoas*, and that they shot poisoned arrows, so as if he hasted not back they should all be lost.

Capuri: Rio Capure.
at adventure: to take their chance.
the flood: high tide.
Amana: the Boca Manamo.

In the meantime fearing the worst I caused all the carpenters we had to cut down a gallego boat, which we meant to cast off, and to fit her with banks to row on, and in all things to prepare her the best they could, so as she might be brought to draw but five foot, for so much we had on the bar of Capuri at low water. And doubting of King's return I sent John Douglas again in my long barge, as well to relieve him as also to make a perfect search in the bottom of that bay. For it hath been held for infallible that whatsoever ship or boat shall fall therein can never disembogue again, by reason of the violent current which setteth into the said bay, as also for that the breeze and easterly wind bloweth directly into the same; of which opinion I have heard John Hampton of Plymouth, one of the greatest experience of England, and divers others besides that have traded Trinidad.

I sent with John Douglas an old *Cassique* of Trinidad for a pilot, who told us that we could not return again by the bay or gulf, but that he knew a by-branch which ran within the land to the eastward, and that he thought by it we might fall into Capuri, and so return in four days. John Douglas searched those rivers and found four goodly entrances, whereof the least was as big as the Thames at Woolwich, but in the bay thitherward it was shoal and but six foot water, so as we were now without hope of any ship or bark to pass over, and therefore resolved to go on with the boats, and the bottom of the gallego, in which we thrust 60 men. In the Lion's Whelp's boat and wherry we carried 20. Captain Calfield in his wherry carried ten more, and in my barge other ten, which made up a hundred. We had no other means but to carry victual for a month in the same, and also to lodge therein as we could, and to boil and dress our meat. Captain Gifford had with him Master Edward Porter, Captain Eynos, and eight more in his wherry with all their victual, weapons and provisions. Captain Calfield had with

banks: benches.
disembogue: to come out of the mouth of the river.

him my cousin Butshead Gorges and eight more. In the galley, of gentlemen and officers myself had Captain Thynne, my cousin John Grenville, my nephew John Gilbert, Captain Whiddon, Captain Keymis, Edward Hancocke, Captain Clarke, Lieutenant Hughes, Thomas Upton, Captain Facy, Jerome Ferrar, Anthony Wells, William Connock, and about 50 more.*

We could not learn of Berrio any other way to enter but in branches so far to the windward as it was impossible for us to recover. For we had as much sea to cross over in our wherries as between Dover and Calais, and in a great billow, the wind and current being both very strong, so as we were driven to go in those small boats directly before the wind into the bottom of the bay of Guanipa, and from thence to enter the mouth of some one of those rivers which John Douglas had last discovered; and had with us for pilot an Indian of Barema, a river to the south of Orinoco, between that and Amazon, whose *Canoas* we had formerly taken as he was going from the said Barema, laden with *Cassavi* bread to sell at Margarita. This Arwacan promised to bring me into the great river of Orinoco, but indeed of that which we entered he was utterly ignorant, for he had not seen it in twelve years before, at which time he was very young and of no judgement, and if God had not sent us another help, we might have wandered a whole year in that labyrinth of rivers, ere we had found any way either out or in, especially after we were past the ebbing and flowing, which was in four days.

For I know all the earth doth not yield the like confluence of streams and branches, the one crossing the other so many times, and all so fair and large, and so like one to another, as no man can tell which to take. And if we went by the sun or compass hoping thereby to go directly one way or other, yet that way we were also carried in a circle amongst multitudes of islands and every island so bordered with high trees, as no man could see any further than the breadth of the river or length of the breach. But thus* it chanced that entering into a river (which because it had no name we called the River of the Red Cross, ourselves being the first Christians that ever came therein), the 22 of May as we were rowing up the same, we espied a small *Canoa* with three Indians, which (by the swiftness of my barge, rowing with eight oars) I overtook ere they could cross the river. The rest of the people on the banks shadowed under the thick wood gazed on with a doubtful conceit what might befall those three which we had taken. But when they perceived that we offered them no violence, neither entered their *Canoa* with any of ours, nor took out of the *Canoa* any of theirs, they then began to show themselves on the bank's side, and offered to traffic with us for such things as they had, and as we drew near they all stayed, and we came with our barge to the mouth of a little creek which came from their town into the great river.

As we abode there a while, our Indian pilot called Ferdinando would needs go ashore to their village to fetch some fruits, and to drink of their artificial wines, and also to see the place, and to know the Lord of it against another time, and took with him a brother of his which he had with him in the journey. When they came to the village of these people, the Lord of the island offered to lay hands on them, purposing to have slain them both, yielding for reason that this Indian of ours had brought a strange nation into their territory to spoil and destroy them. But the pilot being quick and of a disposed body slipped their fingers and ran into the woods, and his brother being the better footman of the two recovered the creek's mouth where we stayed in our barge, crying out that his brother was slain. With that we set hands on one of them that was next us, a very old man, and brought him into the barge, assuring him that if we had not our pilot again, we would presently cut off his head. This old man being resolved that he should pay the loss of the other, cried out to those in the woods to save

River of the Red Cross: Caño Manamo. *conceit*: notion.
artificial: skilfully made. *presently*: without delay.

Ferdinando our pilot, but they followed him notwithstanding, and hunted after him upon the foot with their deer-dogs, and with so main a cry that all the woods echoed with the shout they made; but at last this poor chased Indian recovered the river side and got upon a tree, and as we were coasting, leaped down and swam to the barge half dead with fear. But our good hap was, that we kept the other old Indian, which we handfasted to redeem our pilot withal, for being natural of those rivers, we assured ourselves he knew the way better than any stranger could, and indeed, but for this chance I think we had never found the way either to Guiana or back to our ships. For Ferdinando after a few days knew nothing at all, nor which way to turn, yea and many times the old man himself was in great doubt which river to take. Those people which dwell in these broken islands and drowned lands are generally called Tivitivas; there are of them two sorts, the one called Ciawani, and the other Waraweete.

The great river of Orinoco or Baraguan hath nine branches which fall out on the north side of his own main mouth. On the south side it hath seven other fallings into the sea, so it disembogueth by 16 arms in all, between islands and broken ground, but the islands are very great, many of them as big as the Isle of Wight and bigger, and many less. From the first branch on the north to the last of the south it is at least 100 leagues, so as the river's mouth is no less than 300 miles wide at his entrance into the sea, which I take to be far bigger than that of Amazon. All those that inhabit in the mouth of this river upon the several north branches are these Tivitivas, of which there are two chief lords which have continual wars one with the other. The islands which lie on the right hand are called Pallamos, and the land on the left Hororotomaka, and the river by which John Douglas returned within the land from Amana to Capuri they call Macuri.

These Tivitivas are a very goodly people and very

handfasted: engaged.

valiant, and have the most manly speech and most deliberate that ever I heard of what nation soever. In the summer they have houses on the ground as in other places. In the winter they dwell upon the trees, where they build very artificial towns and villages, as it is written in the Spanish story of the West Indies that those people do in the low lands near the gulf of Uraba. For between May and September the river of Orinoco riseth thirty foot upright, and then are those islands overflown twenty foot high above the level of the ground, saving some few raised grounds in the middle of them. And for this cause they are enforced to live in this manner. They never eat of anything that is set or sown, and as at home they use neither planting nor other manurance, so when they come abroad they refuse to feed of aught but of that which nature without labour bringeth forth. They use the tops of *palmitos* for bread, and kill deer, fish and porks for the rest of their sustenance. They have also many sorts of fruits that grow in the woods, and great variety of birds and fowl. And if to speak of them were not tedious and vulgar, surely we saw in those passages of very rare colours and forms, not elsewhere to be found, for as much as I have either seen or read.

Of these people those that dwell upon the branches of Orinoco called Capuri and Macureo are for the most part carpenters of *Canoas*, for they make the most and fairest houses, and sell them into Guiana for gold, and into Trinidad for *Tobacco*,* in the excessive taking whereof they exceed all nations, and notwithstanding the moistness of the air in which they live, the hardness of their diet, and the great labours they suffer to hunt, fish and fowl for their living, in all my life either in the Indies or in Europe did I never behold a more goodly or better favoured people, or a more manly. They were wont to make war upon all nations, and

deliberate: discreet, thinking before they speak.
manurance: cultivation.
palmitos: palms, whose centre leaves are edible.
vulgar: hackneyed. People had had enough of such travellers' tales.

especially on the Cannibals, so as none durst without a good strength trade by those rivers, but of late they are at peace with their neighbours, all holding the Spaniards for a common enemy. When their commanders die, they use great lamentation, and when they think the flesh of their bodies is putrified and fallen from the bones, then they take up the carcass again, and hang it in the *Cassique's* house that died, and deck his skull with feathers of all colours, and hang all his gold plates about the bones of his arms, thighs, and legs. Those nations which are called Arwacas which dwell on the south of Orinoco (of which place and nation our Indian pilot was), are dispersed in many other places, and do use to beat the bones of their lords into powder, and their wives and friends drink it* all in their several sorts of drinks.

After we departed from the port of these Ciawani, we passed up the river with the flood, and anchored the ebb, and in this sort we went onward. The third day that we entered the river our galley came on ground, and stuck so fast as we thought that even there our discovery had ended, and that we must have left sixty of our men to have inhabited like rooks upon trees with those nations. But the next morning, after we had cast out all her ballast, with tugging and hauling to and fro, we got her afloat and went on. At four days' end we fell into as goodly a river as ever I beheld, which was called the great Amana, which ran more directly without windings or turnings than the other. But soon after the flood of the sea left us, and we enforced either by main strength to row against a violent current, or to return as wise as we went out, we had then no shift but to persuade the companies that it was but two or three day's work, and therefore desired them to take pains, every gentleman and others taking their turns to row, and to spell one the other at the hour's end. Every day we passed by goodly branches of rivers, some falling from the west, others from the east into Amana, but those I leave to the description in the chart of discovery, where every one shall be

spell one the other: relieve for a spell (a time).

named with his rising and descent. When three days more were overgone, our companies began to despair, the weather being extreme hot, the river bordered with very high trees that kept away the air, and the current against us every day stronger than other. But we evermore commanded our pilots to promise an end the next day, and used it so long as we were driven to assure them from four reaches of the river to three, and so to two, and so to the next reach. But so long we laboured as many days were spent, and so driven to draw ourselves to harder allowance, our bread even at the last, and no drink at all; and our men and ourselves so wearied and scorched, and doubtful withal whether we should ever perform it or no, the heat increasing as we drew towards the line; for we were now in five degrees.

The farther we went on (our victual decreasing and the air breeding great faintness) we grew weaker and weaker when we had most need of strength and ability, for hourly the river ran more violently than other against us, and the barge, wherries, and ship's boat of Captain Gifford and Captain Calfield had spent all their provisions, so as we were brought into despair and discomfort, had we not persuaded all the company that it was but only one day's work more to attain the land where we should be relieved of all we wanted, and if we returned that we were sure to starve by the way, and that the world would also laugh us to scorn. On the banks of these rivers were divers sorts of fruits good to eat, flowers and trees of that variety as were sufficient to make ten volumes of herbals. We relieved ourselves many times with the fruits of the country and sometimes with fowl and fish. We saw birds of all colours, some carnation, some crimson, orange-tawny, purple, green, watchet, and of all other sorts both simple and mixed, as it was unto us a great good passing of the time to behold them, besides the relief we found by killing some store of them with our

harder allowance: smaller rations.
discomfort: low spirits.
herbals: botanical books.
watchet: a shade of blue.

fowling pieces, without which, having little or no bread and less drink, but only the thick and troubled water of the river, we had been in a very hard case.

Our old pilot of the Ciawani (whom, as I said before, we took to redeem Ferdinando) told us that if we would enter a branch of a river on the right hand with our barge and wherries, and leave the galley at anchor the while in the great river, he would bring us to a town of the Arwacas where we should find store of bread, hens, fish, and of the country wine, and persuaded us that departing from the galley at noon we might return ere night. I was very glad to hear this speech, and presently took my barge, with eight musketeers, Captain Gifford's wherry, with himself and four musketeers, and Captain Calfield with his wherry and as many, and so we entered the mouth of this river, and because we were persuaded that it was so near, we took no victual with us at all. When we had rowed three hours, we marvelled we saw no sign of any dwelling, and asked the pilot where the town was. He told us a little further. After three hours more, the sun being almost set, we began to suspect that he led us that way to betray us, for he confessed that those Spaniards which fled from Trinidad, and also those that remained with Carapana in Emeria, were joined together in some village upon that river. But when it grew towards night, and we demanding where the place was, he told us but four reaches more. When we had rowed four and four, we saw no sign, and our poor water-men even heart broken and tired were ready to give up the ghost; for we had now come from the galley near forty miles.

At the last we determined to hang the pilot, and if we had well known the way back again by night, he had surely gone, but our own necessities pleaded sufficiently for his safety. For it was as dark as pitch, and the river began so to narrow itself, and the trees to hang over from side to side, as we were driven with arming swords to cut a passage through those branches that covered the water. We were very desirous

fowling pieces: light sporting guns.

to find this town, hoping of a feast, because we made but a short breakfast aboard the galley in the morning, and it was now eight o'clock at night, and our stomachs began to gnaw apace. But whether it was best to return or go on, we began to doubt, suspecting treason in the pilot more and more. But the poor old Indian ever assured us that it was but a little further, and but this one turning, and that turning, and at last about one o'clock after midnight we saw a light, and rowing towards it, we heard the dogs of the village. When we landed we found few people, for the Lord of that place was gone with divers *Canoas* above 400 miles off, upon a journey towards the head of Orinoco to trade for gold, and to buy women of the Cannibals, who afterward unfortunately passed by us as we rode at an anchor in the port of Morequito, in the dark of night, and yet came so near us as his *Canoas* grated against our barges. He left one of his company at the port of Morequito, by whom we understood that he had brought 30 young women, divers plates of gold, and had great store of fine pieces of cotton cloth and cotton beds. In his house we had good store of bread, fish, hens, and Indian drink, and so rested that night, and in the morning after we had traded with such of his people as came down, we returned towards our galley and brought with us some quantity of bread, fish, and hens.

On both sides of this river, we passed the most beautiful country that ever mine eyes beheld. And whereas all that we had seen before was nothing but woods, prickles, bushes and thorns, here we beheld plains of twenty miles in length, the grass short and green, and in divers parts groves of trees by themselves, as if they had been by all the art and labour in the world so made of purpose. And still as we rowed, the deer came down feeding by the water's side, as if they had been used to a keeper's call. Upon this river there were great store of fowl, and of many sorts. We saw in it divers sorts of strange fishes, and of marvellous bigness, but for *Lagartos* it

Lagarto: the caiman or crocodile of South America. Raleigh uses *serpent* as a generic term for all reptiles.

exceeded, for there were thousands of those ugly serpents, and the people call it for the abundance of them the River of *Lagartos* in their language. I had a *Negro*, a very proper young fellow, that leaping out of the galley to swim in the mouth of this river, was in all our sights taken and devoured by one of those *Lagartos*.

In the meanwhile our companies in the galley thought we had been all lost, (for we promised to return before night), and sent the Lion's Whelp's ship's boat with Captain Whiddon to follow us up the river, but the next day after we had rowed up and down some four score miles, we returned and went on our way up the great river, and when we were even at the last cast for want of victuals, Captain Gifford being before the galley and the rest of the boats, seeking out some place to land upon the banks to make fire, espied four *Canoas* coming down the river, and with no small joy caused his men to try the uttermost of their strengths; and after a while two of the 4 gave over and ran themselves ashore, every man betaking himself to the fastness of the woods. The two other lesser got away while he landed to lay hold on these, and so turned into some by-creek, we knew not whither. Those *Canoas* that were taken were laden with bread, and were bound for Margarita in the West Indies, which those Indians (called Arwacas) purposed to carry thither for exchange. But in the lesser, there were three Spaniards, who having heard of the defeat of their governor in Trinidad and that we purposed to enter Guiana, came away in those *Canoas*. One of them was a *Cavallero*,* as the Captain of the Arwacas after told us, another a soldier, and the third a refiner.

In the meantime, nothing on earth could have been more welcome to us next unto gold than the great store of very excellent bread which we found in these *Canoas*, for now our men cried, 'Let us go on, we care not how far!' After that Captain Gifford had brought the two *Canoas* to the galley, I took my barge and went to the bank's side with a dozen

Cavallero: gentleman.

shot, where the *Canoas* first ran themselves ashore, and landed there, sending out Captain Gifford and Captain Thynne on one hand, and Captain Calfield on the other, to follow those that were fled into the woods. And as I was creeping through the bushes I saw an Indian basket hidden, which was the refiner's basket, for I found in it his quick-silver, saltpetre, and divers things for the trial of metals, and also the dust of such ore as he had refined, but in those *Canoas* which escaped there was a good quantity of ore and gold. I then landed more men, and offered 500 pound to what soldier soever could take one of those three Spaniards that we thought were landed. But our labours were in vain in that behalf, for they put themselves into one of the small *Canoas*; and so while the greater *Canoas* were in taking, they escaped. But seeking after the Spaniards, we found the Arwacas hidden in the woods which were pilots for the Spaniards and rowed their *Canoas*, of which I kept the chiefest for a pilot, and carried him with me to Guiana, by whom I understood where and in what countries the Spaniards had laboured for gold, though I made not the same known to all. For when the springs began to break, and the rivers to raise themselves so suddenly as by no means we could abide the digging of any mine, especially for that the richest are defended with rocks of hard stone, which we call the white spar, and that it required both time, men, and instruments fit for such a work, I thought it best not to hover thereabouts, lest if the same had been perceived by the company there would have been by this time many barks and ships set out, and perchance other nations would also have gotten of ours for pilots, so as both ourselves might have been prevented, and all our care taken for good usage of the people been utterly lost, by those that only respect present profit, and such violence or insolence offered, as the nations which are borderers would have changed their desire of our love and defence into hatred and violence.

prevented: forestalled.

And for any longer stay to have brought a more quantity (which I hear hath been often objected) whosoever had seen or proved the fury of that river after it began to arise, and had been a month and odd days as we were from hearing aught from our ships, leaving them meanly manned, above 400 miles off, would perchance have turned somewhat sooner than we did, if all the mountains had been gold or rich stones. And to say the truth all the branches and small rivers which fell into Orinoco were raised with such speed, as if we waded them over the shoes in the morning outward, we were covered to the shoulders homeward the very same day; and to stay to dig out gold with our nails had been *Opus Laboris*, but not *Ingenii*. Such a quantity as would have served our turns we could not have had, but a discovery of the mines to our infinite disadvantage we had made, and that could have been the best profit of further search or stay; for those mines are not easily broken, nor opened in haste, and I could have returned a good quantity of gold ready cast, if I had not shot at another mark than present profit.

This Arwacan pilot, with the rest, feared that we would have eaten them or otherwise have put them to some cruel death, for the Spaniards to the end that none of the people in the passage towards Guiana or in Guiana itself might come to speech with us, persuaded all the nations that we were man eaters and Cannibals. But when the poor men and women had seen us, and that we gave them meat, and to every one some thing or other, which was rare and strange to them, they began to conceive the deceit and purpose of the Spaniards, who indeed (as they confessed) took from them both their wives and daughters daily, and used them for the satisfying of their own lusts, especially such as they took in this manner by strength. But I protest before the majesty of the living God, that I neither know nor believe that any of our company, one or other, by violence or otherwise, ever knew any of their women, and yet we saw many

Opus Laboris etc.: a task demanding physical labour rather than intelligence.

hundreds and had many in our power, and of those very young and excellently favoured which came among us without deceit, stark naked.

Nothing got us more love among them than this usage, for I suffered not any man to take from any of the nations so much as a *Pina* or a *Potato* root,* without giving them contentment, nor any man so much as to offer to touch any of their wives or daughters. Which course, so contrary to the Spaniards (who tyrannize over them in all things) drew them to admire Her Majesty, whose commandment I told them it was, and also wonderfully to honour our nation. But I confess it was a very impatient work to keep the meaner sort from spoil and stealing when we came to their houses, which because in all I could not prevent, I caused my Indian interpreter at every place when we departed to know of the loss or wrong done, and if aught were stolen or taken by violence, either the same was restored and the party punished in their sight, or else it was paid for to their uttermost demand. They also much wondered at us, after they heard that we had slain the Spaniards at Trinidad, for they were before resolved that no nation of Christians durst abide their presence, and they wondered more when I had made them know of the great overthrow that Her Majesty's army and fleet had given them of late years in their own countries.

After we had taken in this supply of bread, with divers baskets of roots which were excellent meat, I gave one of the *Canoas* to the Arwacas which belonged to the Spaniards that were escaped, and when I had dismissed all but the Captain (who by the Spaniards was christened Martin) I sent back in the same *Canoa* the old Ciawan, and Ferdinando my first pilot, and gave them both such things as they desired, with sufficient victual to carry them back, and by them wrote a letter to the ships, which they promised to deliver and performed it, and then I went on with my new hired pilot, Martin the Arwacan. But the next or second day after, we came aground again with our galley, and were like to cast

Pina: pineapple.

her away with all our victual and provision, and so lay on the sand one whole night, and were far more in despair at this time to free her than before, because we had no tide of flood to help us, and therefore feared that all our hopes would have ended in mishaps. But we fastened an anchor upon the land, and with main strength drew her off.

And so the fifteenth day we discovered afar off the mountains of Guiana to our great joy, and towards the evening had a slant of a northerly wind that blew very strong, which brought us in sight of the great river of Orinoco, out of which this river descended wherein we were. We descried afar off three other *Canoas* as far as we could discern them, after whom we hastened with our barge and wherries; but two of them passed out of sight, and the third entered up the great river, on the right hand to the westward, and there stayed out of sight thinking that we meant to take the way eastward towards the province of Carapana, for that way the Spaniards keep, not daring to go upwards to Guiana, the people in those parts being all their enemies; and those in the *Canoas* thought us to have been those Spaniards that were fled from Trinidad and had escaped killing. And when we came so far down as the opening of that branch into which they slipped, being near them with our barge and wherries, we made after them, and ere they could land, came within call, and by our interpreter told them what we were, wherewith they came back willingly aboard us. And of such fish and *Tortuga's* eggs as they had gathered, they gave us, and promised in the morning to bring the Lord of that part with them, and to do us all other services they could.

That night we came to an anchor at the parting of three goodly rivers (the one was the river of Amana by which we came from the north, and ran athwart towards the south, the other two were of Orinoco which crossed from the west and ran to the sea towards the east) and landed upon a fair sand, where we found thousands of *Tortuga's* eggs, which are

Tortugas: fresh water turtles.

very wholesome meat and greatly restoring, so as our men were now well filled and highly contented both with the fare and nearness of the land of Guiana which appeared in sight. In the morning there came down according to promise the Lord of that border called Toparimaca, with some thirty or forty followers, and brought us divers sorts of fruits, and of his wine, bread, fish, and flesh, whom we also feasted as we could; at least he drank good Spanish wine (whereof we had a small quantity in bottles) which above all things they love. I conferred with this Toparimaca of the next way to Guiana, who conducted our galley and boats to his own port, and carried us from thence some mile and a half to his town, where some of our captains caroused of his wine till they were reasonable pleasant; for it is very strong with pepper and the juice of divers herbs and fruits digested and purged. They keep it in great earthen pots of ten or twelve gallons very clean and sweet, and are themselves at their meetings and feasts the greatest carousers and drunkards of the world. When we came to his town we found two *Cassiques* whereof one of them was a stranger that had been up the river in trade, and his boats, people, and wife encamped at the port where we anchored, and the other was of that country a follower of Toparimaca. They lay each of them in a cotton *Hamaca*, which we call Brazil beds, and two women attending them with six cups and a little ladle to fill them out of an earthen pitcher of wine, and so they drank each of them three of those cups at a time, one to the other, and in this sort they drink drunk at their feasts and meetings.

That *Cassique* that was a stranger had his wife staying at the port where we anchored, and in all my life I have seldom seen a better favoured woman. She was of good stature, with black eyes, fat of body, of an excellent countenance, her hair almost as long as herself, tied up again in pretty knots, and it seemed she stood not in that awe of her husband as the

next: nearest.
pleasant: merry.
digested and purged: boiled and clarified.

rest, for she spoke and discoursed and drank among the gentlemen and captains, and was very pleasant, knowing her own comeliness and taking great pride therein. I have seen a lady in England so like her, as but for the difference of colour I would have sworn might have been the same.

The seat of this town of Toparimaca was very pleasant, standing upon a little hill, in an excellent prospect, with goodly gardens a mile compass round about it, and two very fair and large ponds of excellent fish adjoining. This town is called Arowocai. The people are of the nation called Nepoios and are followers of Carapana. In that place I saw very aged people, that we might perceive all their sinews and veins without any flesh, and but even as a case covered only with skin. The Lord of this place gave me an old man for pilot, who was of great experience and travel, and knew the river most perfectly both by day and night; and it shall be requisite for any man that passeth it to have such a pilot, for it is four, five, and six miles over in many places, and twenty miles in other places, with wonderful eddies, and strong currents, many great islands and divers shoals, and many dangerous rocks, and besides upon any increase of wind so great a billow as we were sometimes in great peril of drowning in the galley, for the small boats durst not come from the shore but when it was very fair.

The next day we hasted thence, and having an easterly wind to help us, we spared our arms from rowing. For after we entered Orinoco, the river lieth for the most part east and west, even from the sea unto Quito in Peru. This river is navigable with ships little less than 1000 miles, and from the place where we entered it may be sailed up in small pinnaces to many of the best parts of Nuevo Reyno de Granada and of Popayán. And from no place may the cities of these parts of the Indies be so easily taken and invaded as from hence. All that day we sailed up a branch of that river, having on the left hand a great island, which they call Assapana, which may contain some five and twenty miles

Assapana: Yaya.

in length and six miles in breadth, the great body of the river running on the other side of this island. Beyond that middle branch, there is also another island in the river called Iwana, which is twice as big as the Isle of Wight, and beyond it, and between it and the main of Guiana, runneth a third branch of Orinoco called Arraroopana. All three are goodly branches, and all navigable for great ships. I judge the river in this place to be at least thirty miles broad, reckoning the islands which divide the branches in it, for afterwards I sought also both the other branches.

After we reached to the head of this island called Assapana, a little to the westward on the right hand there opened a river which came from the north, called Europa, and fell into the great river; and beyond it, on the same side, we anchored for that night, by another island six miles long and two miles broad, which they call Ocaywita. From hence in the morning we landed two Guianians, which we found in the town of Toparimaca, that came with us, who went to give notice of our coming to the Lord of that country called Putyma, a follower of Topiawari, Chief Lord of Arromaia, who succeeded Morequito, whom (as you have heard before) Berrio put to death; but his town being far within the land, he came not unto us that day, so as we anchored again that night near the banks of another island, of bigness much like the other, which they call Putapayma, on the mainland, over against which island was a very high mountain called Oecope. We coveted to anchor rather by these islands in the river than by the main, because of the *Tortuga's* eggs which our people found on them in great abundance, and also because the ground served better for us to cast our nets for fish, the main banks being for the most part stony and high, and the rocks of a blue metalline colour, like unto the best steel ore, which I assuredly take it to be. Of the same blue stone are also divers great mountains which border this river in many places.

The next morning towards nine of the clock we weighed

Iwana: Tortola.

anchor, and the breeze increasing, we sailed always west up the river, and after a while opening the land on the right side, the country appeared to be champaign, and the banks showed very perfect red. I therefore sent two of the little barges with Captain Gifford, and with him Captain Thynne, Captain Calfield, my cousin Grenville, my nephew John Gilbert, Captain Eynos, Master Edward Porter, and my cousin Butshead Gorges, with some few soldiers, to march over the banks of that red land and to discover what manner of country it was on the other side; who at their return found it all a plain level, as far as they went or could discern from the highest tree they could get upon. And my old pilot, a man of great travel, brother to the *Cassique* Toparimaca, told me that those were called the plains of the Sayma, and that the same level reached to Cumaná and Caracas in the West Indies, which are 120 leagues to the north, and that there inhabited four principal nations. The first were the Sayma, the next Assawai, the third and greatest the Wikiri, by whom Pedro Hernandez de Serpa before mentioned* was overthrown, as he passed with three hundred horse from Cumaná towards Orinoco in his enterprize of Guiana, the fourth are called Aroras and are as black as *Negros*, but have smooth hair, and these are very valiant or rather desperate people, and have the most strong poison* on their arrows and most dangerous of all nations; of which poison I will speak somewhat, being a digression not unnecessary.

There was nothing whereof I was more curious than to find out the true remedies of these poisoned arrows, for besides the mortality of the wound they make, the party shot endureth the most insufferable torment in the world and abideth a most ugly and lamentable death, sometimes dying stark mad, sometimes their bowels breaking out of their bellies, and are presently discoloured as black as pitch, and so unsavoury as no man can endure to cure or to attend them. And it is more strange to know that in all this time there was never Spaniard either by gift or torment that

champaign: level and open country.

could attain to the true knowledge of the cure, although they have martyred and put to invented torture I know not how many of them. But every one of these Indians know it not, no not one among thousands, but their soothsayers and priests, who do conceal it and only teach it but from the father to the son.

Those medicines which are vulgar and serve for the ordinary poison are made of the juice of a root called *Tupara.* The same also quencheth marvellously the heat of burning fevers, and healeth inward wounds and broken veins that bleed within the body. But I was more beholding to the Guianians than any other, for Antonio de Berrio told me that he could never attain to the knowledge thereof, and yet they taught me the best way of healing as well thereof, as of all other poisons. Some of the Spaniards have been cured in ordinary wounds of the common poisoned arrows with the juice of garlic. But this is a general rule for all men that shall hereafter travel the Indies where poisoned arrows are used, that they must abstain from drink, for if they take any liquor into their body, as they shall be marvellously provoked thereunto by drought, I say, if they drink before the wound be dressed or soon upon it, there is no way with them but present death.

And so I will return again to our journey which for this third day we finished, and cast anchor again near the continent, on the left hand between two mountains, the one called Aroami and the other Aio. I made no stay here but till midnight, for I feared hourly lest any rain should fall, and then it had been impossible to have gone any further up, notwithstanding that there is every day a very strong breeze and easterly wind. I deferred the search of the country on Guiana side, till my return down the river. The next day we sailed by a great island in the middle of the river, called Manoripano, and as we walked a while on the island, while the galley got ahead of us, there came after us from the main a small *Canoa* with seven or eight Guianians, to invite us to

vulgar: commonly known.

anchor at their port, but I deferred it till my return. It was that *Cassique* to whom those Nepoios went which came with us from the town of Toparimaca. And so the fifth day we reached as high up as the province of Arromaia, the country of Morequito whom Berrio executed, and anchored to the west of an island called Murrecotima, ten miles long and five broad. And that night the *Cassique* Aramiari (to whose town we made our long and hungry voyage out of the river of Amana) passed by us.

The next day we arrived at the port of Morequito and anchored there, sending away one of our pilots to seek the King of Arromaia, uncle to Morequito, slain by Berrio as aforesaid. The next day following, before noon, he came to us on foot from his house, which was 14 English miles (himself being 110 years old) and returned on foot the same day, and with him many of the borderers, with many women and children, that came to wonder at our nation and to bring us down victual, which they did in great plenty; as venison, pork, hens, chickens, fowl, fish, with divers sorts of excellent fruits and roots, and great abundance of *Pinas*, the princess of fruits that grow under the sun, especially those of Guiana. They brought us also store of bread, and of their wine, and a sort of *Paraquitos*, no bigger than wrens, and of all other sorts both small and great. One of them gave me a beast called by the Spaniards *Armadilla*, which they call *Cassacam*, which seemeth to be all barred over with small plates somewhat like to a *Renocero*, with a white horn growing in his hinder parts, as big as a great hunting horn, which they use to wind instead of a trumpet. Monardus* writeth that a little of the powder of that horn, put into the ear, cureth deafness.

After this old King had rested a while in a little tent that I caused to be set up, I began by my interpreter to discourse with him of the death of Morequito his predecessor, and afterward of the Spaniards; and ere I went any further I made him know the cause of my coming thither, whose servant I was, and that the Queen's pleasure was I should undertake the voyage for their defence, and to deliver them from the tyranny of the Spaniards, dilating at large (as I had done before to those of Trinidad) Her Majesty's greatness, her justice, her charity to all oppressed nations, with as many of the rest of her beauties and virtues as either I could express or they conceive. All which being with great admiration attentively heard, and marvellously admired, I began to sound the old man as touching Guiana and the state thereof, what sort of commonwealth it was, how governed, of what strength and policy, how far it extended, and what nations were friends or enemies adjoining, and finally of the distance and way to enter the same. He told me that himself and his people with all those down the river towards the sea, as far as Emeria, the province of Carapana, were of Guiana, but that they called themselves Orenoqueponi, because they bordered the great river of Orinoco, and that all the nations between the river and those mountains in sight called Wacarima were of the same caste and appellation; and that on the other side of those mountains of Wacarima there was a large plain (which after I discovered in my return) called the valley of Amariocapana. In all that valley the people were also of the ancient Guianians.

I asked what nations those were which inhabited on the further side of those mountains, beyond the valley of Amariocapana. He answered with a great sigh (as a man which had inward feeling of the loss of his country and liberty, especially for that his eldest son was slain in a battle on that side of the mountains, whom he most entirely loved) that he remembered in his father's lifetime when he was very old, and himself a young man, that there came down into that large valley of Guiana a nation from so far off as the sun slept (for such were his own words) with so great a multitude as they could not be numbered nor resisted, and that they wore large coats and hats of crimson colour, which colour he expressed by showing a piece of red wood, wherewith my tent was supported; and that they were called Oreiones and Epuremei, those that had slain and rooted out so many of the ancient people as there were leaves in the wood upon all the trees, and had now made themselves lords of all, even to that mountain foot called Curaa, saving only of two nations, the one called Iwarawakiri and the other Cassipagotos; and that in the last battle fought between the Epuremei and the Iwarawakiri his eldest son was chosen to carry to the aid of the Iwarawakiri a great troop of the Orenoqueponi, and was there slain with all his people and friends, and that he had now remaining but one son. And further told me that those Epuremei had built a great town called Macureguarai,* at the said mountain foot, at the beginning of the great plains of Guiana, which have no end. And that their houses have many rooms, one over the other, and that therein the great king of the Oreiones and Epuremei kept three thousand men to defend the borders against them, and withal daily to invade and slay them. But that of late years since the Christians offered to invade his territories and those frontiers, they were all at peace and traded one with another, saving only the Iwarawakiri and those other nations upon the head of the river of Caroni, called Cassipagotos, which we afterwards discovered, each one holding the Spaniard for a common enemy.

After he had answered thus far, he desired leave to depart, saying that he had far to go, that he was old and weak and was every day called for by death, which was also his own phrase. I desired him to rest with us that night, but I could not entreat him, but he told me that at my return from the country above, he would again come to us, and in the meantime provide for us the best he could of all that his country yielded. The same night he returned to Orocotona his own town, so as he went that day twenty-eight miles, the weather being very hot, the country being situate between four and five degrees of the equinoctial. This Topiawari is held for the proudest and wisest of all the Orenoqueponi, and so he behaved himself towards me in all his answers at my return, as I marvelled to find a man of that gravity and judgement and of so good discourse, that had no help of learning nor breed.

The next morning we also left the port and sailed westward up the river to view the famous river called Caroni, as well because it was marvellous of itself, as also for that I understood it led to the strongest nations of all the frontiers that were enemies to the Epuremei, which are subjects to Inca, Emperor of Guiana and Manoa; and that night we anchored at another island called Caiama, of some five or six miles in length, and the next day arrived at the mouth of Caroni. When we were short of it as low or further down as the port of Morequito we heard the great roar and fall of the river; but when we came to enter with our barge and wherries, thinking to have gone up some forty miles to the nations of the Cassipagotos, we were not able with a barge of eight oars to row one stone's cast in an hour, and yet the river is as broad as the Thames at Woolwich, and we tried both sides, and the middle, and every part of the river; so as we encamped upon the banks adjoining, and sent off our Orenoqueponi (which came with us from Morequito) to give knowledge to the nations upon the river of our being there and that we desired to see the Lords of Canuria, which dwelt within the province upon that river, making them know that we were enemies to the Spaniards (for it was on this river's side that Morequito slew the friar and those nine Spaniards which came from Manoa, the city of Inca, and took from them 40000 pesoes of gold).

So as the next day there came down a Lord or *Cassique* called Wanuretona with many people with him, and brought all store of provisions to entertain us, as the rest had done. And as I had before made my coming known to Topiawari, so did I acquaint this *Cassique* therewith, and how I was sent by Her Majesty for the purpose aforesaid, and gathered also what I could of him touching the estate of Guiana; and I found that those also of Caroni were not only enemies to the Spaniards but most of all to the Epuremei,

breed: upbringing. *peso*: a standard Spanish coin.

which abound in gold. And by this Wanuretona I had knowledge that on the head of this river were three mighty nations, which were seated on a great lake, from whence this river descended, and were called Cassipagotos, Eparagotos, and Arawagotos, and that all those either against the Spaniards or the Epuremei would join with us, and that if we entered the land over the mountains of Curaa, we should satisfy ourselves with gold and all other good things. He told us further of a nation called Iwarawakiri before spoken of, that held daily war with the Epuremei that inhabited Macureguarai, the first civil town of Guiana, of the subjects of Inca the Emperor.

Upon this river one Captain George,* that I took with Berrio, told me there was a great silver mine, and that it was near the banks of the said river. But by this time as well Orinoco, Caroni, as all the rest of the rivers were risen four or five foot in height so as it was not possible by the strength of any men or with any boat whatsoever to row into the river against the stream. I therefore sent Captain Thynne, Captain Grenville, my nephew John Gilbert, my cousin Butshead Gorges, Captain Clarke, and some thirty shot more to coast the river by land, and to go to a town some twenty miles over the valley called Amnatapoi, and if they found guides there, to go further towards the mountain foot to another great town, called Capurepana, belonging to a *Cassique* called Haharacoa (that was a nephew to old Topiawari King of Arromaia our chiefest friend) because this town and province of Capurepana adjoined to Macureguarai, which was the frontier town of the empire.

And the meanwhile myself with Captain Gifford, Captain Calfield, Edward Hancocke, and some half a dozen shot marched overland to view the strange overfalls of the river Caroni, which roared so far off, and also to see the plains adjoining and the rest of the province of Canuri. I sent also Captain Whiddon, W. Connocke, and some eight shot with them, to see if they could find any mineral stone along the river's side. When we ran to the tops of the first hills of the plains adjoining to the river, we beheld that wonderful breach of waters, which ran down Caroni; and might from that mountain see the river how it ran in three parts, above twenty miles off, and there appeared some ten or twelve overfalls in sight, every one as high over the other as a church tower, which fell with that fury that the rebound of waters made it seem as if it had been all covered over with a great shower of rain. And in some places we took it at the first for a smoke that had risen over some great town. For mine own part I was well persuaded from thence to have returned, being a very ill footman, but the rest were all so desirous to go near the said strange thunder of waters, as they drew me on by little and little, till we came into the next valley, where we might better discern the same.

I never saw a more beautiful country, nor more lively prospects, hills so raised here and there over the valleys, the river winding into divers branches, the plains adjoining without bush or stubble, all fair green grass, the ground of hard sand easy to march on either for horse or foot, the deer crossing in every path, the birds towards the evening singing on every tree with a thousand several tunes, cranes and herons of white, crimson, and carnation perching on the river's side, the air fresh with a gentle easterly wind, and every stone that we stooped to take up promised either gold or silver by his complexion. Your Lordships shall see of many sorts, and I hope some of them cannot be bettered under the sun, and yet we had no means but with our daggers and fingers to tear them out here and there, the rocks being most hard of that mineral spar aforesaid, and is like a flint, and is altogether as hard or harder, and besides the veins lie a fathom or two deep in the rocks. But we wanted all things requisite save only our desires and good will to have performed more if it had pleased God.

To be short, when both our companies returned, each of them brought also several sorts of stones that appeared very

wanted: lacked.

fair, but were such as they found loose on the ground and were for the most part but coloured, and had not any gold fixed in them, yet such as had no judgement or experience kept all that glistered, and would not be persuaded but it was rich because of the lustre, and brought of those and of marcasite withal from Trinidad, and have delivered of those stones to be tried in many places, and have thereby bred an opinion that all the rest is of the same. Yet some of these stones I showed afterward to a Spaniard of the Caracas who told me that it was *El Madre del Oro*, and that the mine was further in the ground. But it shall be found a weak policy in me either to betray myself or my country with imaginations, neither am I so far in love with that lodging, watching, care, peril, diseases, ill savours, bad fare, and many other mischiefs that accompany these voyages, as to woo myself again into any of them, were I not assured that the sun covereth not so much riches in any part of the earth. Captain Whiddon and our surgeon, Nicholas Millechap, brought me a kind of stones like sapphires; what they may prove I know not. I showed them to some of the Orenoqueponi and they promised to bring me to a mountain that had of them very large pieces growing diamond-wise. Whether it be crystal of the mountain, Bristol Diamond,* or sapphire I do not yet know, but I hope the best. Sure I am that the place is as likely as those from whence all the rich stones are brought, and in the same height or very near.

On the left hand of this river Caroni are seated those nations which are called Iwarawakiri before remembered, which are enemies to the Epuremei. And on the head of it adjoining to the great lake Cassipa* are situate those other nations which also resist Inca and the Epuremei, called Cassipagotos, Eparagotos, and Arawagotos. I further understood that this lake of Cassipa is so large as it is above one day's journey for one of their *Canoas* to cross, which may be some 40 miles, and that therein fall divers rivers, and that

marcasite: iron or copper pyrites, wrongly supposed from their sheen to contain minute particles of gold.

the great store of grains of gold are found in the summer time when the lake falleth by the banks in those branches. There is also another goodly river beyond Caroni which is called Arui, which also runneth through the lake Cassipa, and falleth into Orinoco further west, making all that land between Caroni and Arui an island, which is likewise a most beautiful country.

Next unto Arui there are two rivers Atoica and Caora, and on that branch which is called Caora are a nation of people whose heads appear not above their shoulders, which though it may be thought a mere fable, yet for mine own part I am resolved it is true, because every child in the provinces of Arromaia and Canuri affirm the same. They are called Ewaipanoma.* They are reported to have their eyes in their shoulders and their mouths in the middle of their breasts, and that a long train of hair groweth backward between their shoulders. The son of Topiawari, which I brought with me into England, told me that they are the most mighty men of all the land, and use bows, arrows, and clubs thrice as big as any of Guiana or of the Orenoqueponi, and that one of the Iwarawakiri took a prisoner of them the year before our arrival there and brought him into the borders of Arromaia, his father's country. And further when I seemed to doubt of it, he told me that it was no wonder among them, but that they were as great a nation and as common as any other in all the provinces, and had of late years slain many hundreds of his father's people, and of other nations their neighbours, but it was not my chance to hear of them till I was come away, and if I had but spoken one word of it while I was there, I might have brought one of them with me to put the matter out of doubt. Such a nation was written of by Mandeville, whose reports were held for fables many years, and yet since the East Indies were discovered, we find his relations true of such things as heretofore were held incredible. Whether it be true or no the matter is not great, neither can there be any profit in the imagination. For mine own part I saw them not, but I am resolved that so many people did not all combine or forethink to make the report.

When I came to Cumaná in the West Indies afterwards, by chance I spake with a Spaniard dwelling not far from thence, a man of great travel, and after he knew that I had been in Guiana and so far directly west as Caroni, the first question he asked me was whether I had seen any of the Ewaipanoma, which are those without heads; who being esteemed a most honest man of his word, and in all things else, told me that he had seen many of them. I may not name him because it may be for his disadvantage,* but he is well known to Monsieur Mucheron's son of London, and to Peter Mucheron, merchant, of the Flemish ship that was there in trade, who also heard what he avowed to be true of those people.

The fourth river to the west of Caroni is Casnero which falleth into Orinoco on this side of Amapaia, and that river is greater than Danubius or any of Europe. It riseth on the south of Guiana from the mountains which divide Guiana from Amazon, and I think it to be navigable many hundred miles. But we had no time, means, nor season of the year, to search those rivers for the causes aforesaid, the winter being come upon us, although the winter and summer as touching cold and heat differ not, neither do the trees ever sensibly lose their leaves, but have always fruit either ripe or green, and most of them both blossoms, leaves, ripe fruit and green at one time. But their winter only consisteth of terrible rains and overflowings of the rivers, with many great storms and gusts, thunder and lightnings, of which we had our fill ere we returned.

[*There follows a detailed account of the Orinoco and its tributaries, considered as a means of invading Peru and New Granada.*]

I thought it time lost to linger any longer in that place, especially for that the fury of Orinoco began daily to threaten us with dangers in our return. For no half day passed but the river began to rage and overflow very fear-

sensibly: perceptibly.

fully, and the rains came down in terrible showers and gusts in great abundance. And withal, our men began to cry out for want of shift, for no man had place to bestow any other apparel than that which he wore on his back, and that was thoroughly washed on his body for the most part ten times in one day. And we had now been well near a month, every day passing to the westward, further and further from our ships. We therefore turned towards the east, and spent the rest of the time in discovering the river towards the sea, which we had not yet viewed and which was most material. The next day following we left the mouth of Caroni, and arrived again at the port of Morequito where we were before (for passing down the stream we went without labour, and against the wind, little less than 100 miles a day).

As soon as I came to anchor I sent away one for old Topiawari, with whom I much desired to have further conference, and also to deal with him for someone of his country to bring with us into England, as well to learn the language as to confer withal by the way (the time being now spent of any longer stay there). Within three hours after my messenger came to him, he arrived also, and with him such a rabble of all sorts of people, and every one laden with somewhat, as if it had been a great market or fair in England; and our hungry companies clustered thick and threefold among their baskets, every one laying hand on what he liked. After he had rested awhile in my tent, I shut out all but ourselves and my interpreter, and told him that I knew that both the Epuremei and the Spaniards were enemies to him, his country and nations; that the one had conquered Guiana already, and that the other sought to regain the same from them both. And therefore I desired him to instruct me what he could, both of the passage into the golden parts of Guiana, and to the civil towns and apparelled people of Inca.

[*Topiawari offered to lead his people against Guiana the following year, if Raleigh would leave fifty of his men with him over the*

shift: change of clothes.

winter. Calfield, Grenville and Gilbert—who seem to have been the fire-eaters of the party—were eager to stay, but Raleigh said this was impossible since he '*had not above fifty good men in all there, the rest were labourers and rowers*'*, and after what had happened at Trinidad the Spaniards would be merciless. Topiawari then said that for his own sake he must appear to have had as little to do with the English as possible but when the war began Raleigh could count on the help of the borderers.*]

Divers of his followers afterwards desired me to make haste again, that they might sack the Epuremei, and I asked them 'Of what?' They answered, 'Of their women for us and their gold for you'. For the hope of many of those women they more desire the war than either for gold or for the recovery of their ancient territories. For what between the subjects of Inca and the Spaniards, those frontiers are grown thin of people, and also great numbers are fled to other nations further off for fear of the Spaniards. After I received this answer of the old man we fell into consideration whether it had been of better advice to have entered Macureguarai and to have begun a war upon Inca at this time, yea or no, if the time of the year and all things else had sorted. For mine own part (as we were not able to march it for the rivers, neither had any such strength as was requisite, and durst not abide the coming of the winter or to tarry any longer from our ships) I thought it very evil counsel to have attempted it at that time, although the desire of gold will answer many objections. But it would have been in mine opinion an utter overthrow to the enterprize if the same should be hereafter by Her Majesty attempted. For then (whereas now they have heard we were enemies to the Spaniards and were sent by Her Majesty to relieve them) they would as good cheap have joined with the Spaniards at our return, as to have yielded unto us, when they had proved that we came both for one errand, and that both sought but to sack and spoil them; but as yet

make haste again: come back quickly.
sorted: agreed.
as good cheap: as profitably.

our desire of gold or our purpose of invasion is not known unto those of the empire. And it is likely that if Her Majesty undertake the enterprize, they will rather submit themselves to her obedience than to the Spaniards, of whose cruelty both themselves and the borderers have already tasted. And therefore till I had known Her Majesty's pleasure, I would rather have lost the sack of one or two towns (although they might have been very profitable) than to have defaced or endangered the future hope of so many millions, and the great good, and rich trade that England may be possessed of thereby. I am assured now that they will all die even to the last man against the Spaniards, in hope of our succour or return. Whereas otherwise if I had either laid hands on the borderers, or ransomed the Lords as Berrio did, or invaded the subjects of Inca, I know all had been lost for hereafter.

After that I had resolved Topiawari, Lord of Arromaia, that I could not at this time leave with him the companies he desired, and that I was contented to forbear the enterprize against the Epuremei till the next year, he freely gave me his only son to take with me into England, and hoped that though he himself had but a short time to live, yet that by our means his son should be established after his death. And I left with him one Francis Sparrow,* a servant of Captain Gifford, (who was desirous to tarry, and could describe a country with his pen), and a boy of mine called Hugh Goodwin,* to learn the language.

I after asked the manner how the Epuremei wrought those plates of gold, and how they could melt it out of the stone. He told me that the most of the gold which they made in plates and images was not severed from the stone, but that on the lake of Manoa, and in a multitude of other rivers, they gathered it in grains of perfect gold and in pieces as big as small stones, and that they put to it a part of copper, otherwise they could not work it, and that they used a great earthen pot with holes round about it, and when they had

resolved: satisfied.

mingled the gold and copper together, they fastened canes to the holes, and so with the breath of men they increased the fire till the metal ran, and then they cast it into moulds of stone and clay, and so make those plates and images. I have sent your Honours of two sorts such as I could by chance recover, more to show the manner of them than for the value. For I did not in any sort make my desire of gold known, because I had neither time nor power* to have a greater quantity. I gave among them many more pieces of gold than I received, of the new money* of twenty shillings with Her Majesty's picture to wear, with promise that they would become her servants thenceforth.

I have also sent your Honours of the ore, whereof I know some is as rich as the earth yieldeth any, of which I know there is sufficient, if nothing else were to be hoped for. But besides that we were not able to tarry and search the hills, so we had neither pioneers, bars, sledges, nor wedges of iron to break the ground, without which there is no working in mines. But we saw all the hills with stones of the colour of gold and silver, and we tried them to be no marcasite, and therefore such as the Spaniards call *El Madre del Oro*, which is an undoubted assurance of the general abundance. And myself saw the outside of many mines of the white spar, which I know to be the same that all covet in this world, and of those, more than I will speak of.

Having learned what I could in Canuri and Arromaia, and received a faithful promise of the principalest of those provinces to become servants to Her Majesty and to resist the Spaniards, if they made any attempt in our absence, and that they would draw in the nations about the lake of Cassipa, and those Iwarawakiri, I then parted from old Topiawari, and received his son for a pledge between us, and left with him two of ours as aforesaid. To Francis Sparrow I gave instructions to travel to Macureguarai, with such merchandizes as I left with him, thereby to learn

pioneers: soldiers trained for mining operations (such as were required in siege work). *sledges*: sledge-hammers.

the place, and if it were possible to go on to the great city of Manoa. Which being done, we weighed anchor and coasted the river on Guiana side, because we came up on the north side, by the lawns of the Sayma and Wakiri.

[*Raleigh gives a brief account of the journey downstream in terrible weather. Keymis and a small party went overland to see a gold mine. If this was the famous mine which was the objective of Raleigh's last desperate venture to Guiana, he had himself never seen it.*]

To speak of what passed homeward were tedious, either to describe or name any of the rivers, islands, or villages of the Tivitivas which dwell on trees. We will leave all those to the general map. And to be short, when we were arrived at the seaside, then grew our greatest doubt and the bitterest of all our journey forepassed, for I protest before God that we were in a most desperate estate. For the same night which we anchored in the mouth of the river of Capuri, where it falleth into the sea, there arose a mighty storm, and the river's mouth was at least a league broad, so as we ran before night close under the land with our small boats, and brought the galley as near as we could; but she had as much ado to live as could be, and there wanted little of her sinking and all those in her. For mine own part, I confess, I was very doubtful which way to take, either to go over in the pestered galley, there being but six foot water over the sands for two leagues together, and that also in the channel, and she drew five; or to adventure in so great a billow, and in so doubtful weather, to cross the seas in my barge. The longer we tarried the worse it was, and therefore I took Captain Gifford, Captain Calfield, and my cousin Grenville into my barge, and after it cleared up, about midnight, we put ourselves to God's keeping, and thrust out into the sea, leaving the galley at anchor, who durst not adventure but by daylight. And so being all very sober and melancholy, one faintly cheering another to show courage, it pleased God that the next day about nine of the clock we descried the island of Trinidad, and steering for the nearest part of it, we kept the shore till we came to Curiapan, where we found our ships at anchor, than which there was never to us a more joyful sight.

Now that it hath pleased God to send us safe to our ships, it is time to leave Guiana to the sun, whom they worship, and steer away towards the north. I will therefore in a few words finish the discovery thereof. Of the several nations which we found upon this discovery I will once again make repetition, and how they are affected. At our first entrance into Amana, which is one of the outlets of Orinoco, we left on the right hand of us, in the bottom of the bay, lying directly against Trinidad, a nation of inhuman Cannibals, which inhabit the rivers of Guanipa and Berbeese. In the same bay there is also a third river which is called Areo, which riseth on Paria side towards Cumaná, and that river is inhabited with the Wakiri, whose chief town upon the said river is Sayma. In this bay there are no more rivers but these three before rehearsed, and the four branches of Amana, all which in the winter thrust so great abundance of water into the sea as the same is taken up fresh two or three leagues from the land. In the passages towards Guiana (that is, in all those lands which the eight branches of Orinoco fashion into islands), there are but one sort of people, called Tivitivas, but of two castes as they term them, the one called Ciawani, the other Waraweeti, and those war one with the other.

On the hithermost part of Orinoco, as at Toparimaca and Winicapora, those are of a nation called Nepoios, and are of the followers of Carapana, Lord of Emeria. Between Winicapora and the port of Morequito which standeth in Arromaia, and all those in the valley of Amariocapana, are called Orenoqueponi, and did obey Morequito, and are now followers of Topiawari. Upon the river of Caroni are the Canuri, which are governed by a woman (who is inheritrix of that province) who came [from] far off to see our nation, and asked me divers questions of Her Majesty, being much delighted with the discourse of Her Majesty's greatness, and wondering at such reports as we truly made of Her

Highness's many virtues. And upon the head of Caroni, and on the lake of Cassipa, are the three strong nations of the Cassipagotos. Right south into the land are the Capurepani and Emparepani, and beyond those adjoining to Macureguarai (the first city of Inca) are the Iwarawakiri. All these are professed enemies to the Spaniards and to the rich Epuremei also. To the west of Caroni are divers nations of Cannibals, and of those Ewaipanoma without heads. Directly west are the Amapaias and Anebas, which are also marvellous rich in gold. The rest towards Peru we will omit. On the north of Orinoco, between it and the West Indies are the Wakiri, Saymi, and the rest before spoken of, all mortal enemies to the Spaniards. On the south side of the main mouth of Orinoco are the Arwacas; and beyond them the Cannibals; and to the south of them the Amazons.

To make mention of the several beasts, birds, fishes, fruits, flowers, gums, sweet woods, and of their several religions and customs, would for the first require as many volumes as those of Gesnerus,* and for the rest another bundle of Decades.* The religion of the Epuremei is the same which the Incas, Emperors of Peru used, which may be read in Cieca and other Spanish stories, how they believe the immortality of the soul, worship the sun, and bury with them alive their best beloved wives and treasure, as they likewise do in Pegu in the East Indies and other places. The Orenoqueponi bury not their wives with them, but their jewels, hoping to enjoy them again. The Arwacas dry the bones of their Lords, and their wives and friends drink them in powder. In the graves of the Peruvians the Spaniards found their greatest abundance of treasure. The like also is to be found among these people in every province. They have all many wives, and the Lords fivefold to the common sort. Their wives never eat with their husbands, nor among the men, but serve their husbands at meals and afterwards feed by themselves. Those that are past their younger years make all their bread and drink, and work their cotton beds, and do all else of service and labour, for the men do nothing but hunt, fish, play, and drink, when they are out of the wars.

I will enter no further into discourse of their manners, laws and customs. And because I have not myself seen the cities of Inca I cannot avow on my credit what I have heard, although it be very likely, that the Emperor Inca hath built and erected as magnificent palaces in Guiana as his ancestors did in Peru, which were for their riches and rareness most marvellous and exceeding all in Europe, and I think of the world, China excepted; which also the Spaniards (which I had) assured me to be of truth, as also the nations of the borderers, who being but *Salvaios* to those of the inland do cause much treasure to be buried with them, for I was informed of one of the *Cassiqui* of the valley of Amariocapana which had buried with him a little before our arrival a chair of gold most curiously wrought, which was made either in Macureguarai adjoining or in Manoa. But if we should have grieved them in their religion at the first, before they had been taught better, and had digged up their graves, we had lost them all. And therefore I held my first resolution, that Her Majesty should either accept or refuse the enterprize, ere anything should be done that might in any sort hinder the same. And if Peru had so many heaps of gold, whereof those Incas were princes, and that they delighted so much therein, no doubt but this which now liveth and reigneth in Manoa hath the same humour, and I am assured hath more abundance of gold within his territory than all Peru and the West Indies.

For the rest, which myself have seen, I will promise these things that follow and know to be true. Those that are desirous to discover and to see many nations, may be satisfied within this river, which bringeth forth so many arms and branches leading to several countries and provinces, above 2000 miles east and west, and 800 miles south and north. And of these, the most either rich in gold or in other merchandizes. The common soldier shall here fight for gold,

Salvaios: savages.

and pay himself instead of pence with plates of half a foot broad, whereas he breaketh his bones in other wars for provant and penury. Those commanders and chieftains that shoot at honour and abundance, shall find there more rich and beautiful cities, more temples adorned with golden images, more sepulchres filled with treasure, than either Cortez found in Mexico or Pizzaro in Peru: and the shining glory of this conquest will eclipse all those so far extended beams of the Spanish nation. There is no country which yieldeth more pleasure to the inhabitants, either for these common delights of hunting, hawking, fishing, fowling, and the rest than Guiana doth. It hath so many plains, clear rivers, abundance of pheasants, partridges, quails, rails, cranes, herons, and all other fowl; deer of all sorts, porks, hares, lions, tigers, leopards, and divers other sorts of beasts, either for chase or food. It hath a kind of beast called *Cama*, or *Anta*, as big as an English beef and in great plenty.

To speak of the several sorts of every kind, I fear would be troublesome to the reader, and therefore I will omit them, and conclude that both for health, good air, pleasure, and riches, I am resolved it cannot be equalled by any region either in the east or west. Moreover the country is so healthful, as [out of] 100 persons and more (which lay without shift most sluttishly, and were every day almost melted with heat in rowing and marching, and suddenly wet again with great showers, and did eat of all sorts of corrupt fruits, and made meals of fresh fish without seasoning, of *Tortugas*, of *Lagartos*, and of all sorts good and bad, without either order or measure, and besides lodged in the open air every night) we lost not any one, nor had one ill disposed to my knowledge, nor found any *Callentura* or other of those pestilent diseases which dwell in all hot regions, and so near the equinoctial line.

Where there is store of gold, it is in effect needless to remember other commodities for trade. But it hath towards

provant: allowance of food, army rations.
Cama: tapir. *Callentura*: tropical fever.

the south part of the river great quantities of Brazil wood, and of divers berries that dye a most perfect crimson and carnation. And for painting, all France, Italy, or the East Indies yield none such. For the more the skin is washed, the fairer the colour appeareth, and with which even those brown and tawny women spot themselves and colour their cheeks. All places yield abundance of cotton, of silk, of *Balsamum*, and of those kinds most excellent, and never known in Europe; of all sorts of gums, of Indian pepper; and what else the countries may afford within the land we know not, neither had we time to abide the trial and search. The soil besides is so excellent and so full of rivers, as it will carry sugar, ginger, and all those other commodities which the West Indies hath.

The navigation is short, for it may be sailed with an ordinary wind in six weeks, and in the like time back again, and by the way neither lee shore, enemies' coast, rocks, nor sands, all which in the voyages to the West Indies and all other places we are subject unto; as the channel of Bahama, coming from the West Indies, cannot be passed in the winter, and when it is at the best, it is a perilous and fearful place. The rest of the Indies for calms and diseases very troublesome, and the Bermudas a hellish sea for thunder, lightning, and storms.

This very year there were seventeen sail of Spanish ships lost in the channel of Bahama, and the great Philip* like to have sunk at the Bermudas was put back to San Juan de Puerto Rico. And so it falleth out in that navigation every year for the most part, which in this voyage are not to be feared. For the time of the year to leave England is best in July, and the summer in Guiana is in October, November, December, January, February, and March, and then the ships may depart thence in April, and so return again into

painting: cosmetic paint.

Balsamum: vegetable oils of various kinds, used in medicine for soothing inflammation.

lee shore: a shore towards which the wind blows, dangerous for shipping.

England in June, so as they shall never be subject to winter weather, either coming, going, or staying there, which for my part, I take to be one of the greatest comforts and encouragements that can be thought on, having (as I have done) tasted in this voyage by the West Indies so many calms, so much heat, such outrageous gusts, foul weather, and contrary winds.

To conclude, Guiana is a country that hath yet her maidenhead, never sacked, turned, nor wrought, the face of the earth hath not been torn, nor the virtue and salt of the soil spent by manurance, the graves have not been opened for gold, the mines not broken with sledges, nor their images pulled down out of their temples. It hath never been entered by any army of strength, and never conquered or possessed by any Christian prince. It is besides so defensible, that if two forts be builded in one of the provinces which I have seen, the flood setteth in so near the bank where the channel also lieth that no ship can pass up but within a pike's length of the artillery, first of the one and afterwards of the other. Which two forts will be a sufficient guard both to the empire of Inca and to an hundred other several kingdoms, lying within the said river, even to the city of Quito in Peru.

There is therefore great difference between the easiness of the conquest of Guiana and the defence of it being conquered, and the West or East Indies. Guiana hath but one entrance by the sea (if it have that) for any vessels of burden, so as whosoever shall first possess it, it shall be found inaccessible for any enemy except he come in wherries, barges, or *Canoas*, or else in flat bottomed boats, and if he do offer to enter it in that manner, the woods are so thick 200 miles together upon the rivers of such entrance, as a mouse cannot sit in a boat unhit from the bank. By land it is more impossible to approach, for it hath the strongest situation of any region under the sun, and is so environed with impassable mountains on every side as it is impossible to

turned: tilled with plough or spade. *wrought*: quarried or mined.

victual any company in the passage, which hath been well proved by the Spanish nation, who since the conquest of Peru have never left five years free from attempting this empire or discovering some way into it, and yet of 23 several gentlemen, knights, and noblemen, there was never any that knew which way to lead an army by land or to conduct ships by sea anything near the said country. Orellana, of which the River of Amazons taketh name, was the first, and Don Antonio de Berrio (whom we displanted) the last; and I doubt much, whether he himself or any of his, yet know the best way into the said empire. It can therefore hardly be regained, if any strength be formerly set down, but in one or two places, and but two or three crumsters or galleys built and furnished upon the river within. The West Indies hath many ports, watering places, and landings, and nearer than 300 miles to Guiana no man can harbour a ship, except he know one only place, which is not learned in haste and which I will undertake there is not any one of my companies that knoweth, whosoever hearkened most after it.

Besides by keeping one good fort, or building one town of strength, the whole empire is guarded, and whatsoever companies shall be afterwards planted within the land, although in twenty several provinces, those shall be able all to reunite themselves upon any occasion either by the way of one river or be able to march by land without either wood, bog, or mountain. Whereas in the West Indies there are few towns or provinces that can succour or relieve one the other, either by land or sea. By land the countries are either desert, mountainous, or strong enemies. By sea, if any man invade to the eastward, those to the west cannot in many months turn against the breeze and easterwind. Besides the Spaniards are therein so dispersed as they are nowhere strong but in Nueva Hispania only. The sharp mountains, the thorns and poisoned prickles, the sandy and deep ways in the valleys, the smothering heat and air and want of water in other places, are their only and best defence, which

crumsters: wherries of Dutch design.

(because those nations which invade them are not victualled or provided to stay, neither have any place to friend adjoining) do serve them instead of good arms and great multitudes.

The West Indies were first offered Her Majesty's grandfather by Columbus,* a stranger in whom there might be doubt of deceit, and besides it was then thought incredible that there were such and so many lands and regions never written of before. This empire is made known to Her Majesty by her own vassal, and by him that oweth to her more duty than an ordinary subject, so that it shall ill sort with the many graces and benefits which I have received to abuse Her Highness either with fables or imaginations. The country is already discovered, many nations won to Her Majesty's love and obedience, and those Spaniards which have latest and longest laboured about the conquest, beaten out, discouraged and disgraced, which among these nations were thought invincible. Her Majesty may in this enterprize employ all those soldiers and gentlemen that are younger brethren,* and all captains and chieftains that want employment, and the charge will be only the first setting out in victualling and arming them. For after the first or second year I doubt not but to see in London a Contractation House* of more receipt for Guiana than there is now in Seville for the West Indies.

And I am resolved that if there were but a small army afoot in Guiana, marching towards Manoa the chief city of Inca, he would yield Her Majesty by composition so many hundred thousand pounds yearly as should both defend all enemies abroad and defray all expences at home, and that he would besides pay a garrison of 3000 or 4000 soldiers very royally to defend him against other nations. For he cannot but know how his predecessors, yea how his own great uncles Huascar and Atabalipa, sons to Huayna Capac, Emperor of Peru, were (while they contended for the empire) beaten out by the Spaniards, and that both of late years and ever since the said conquest, the Spaniards have sought the passages and entry of his country; and of their cruelties used to the borderers he cannot be ignorant. In which respects no doubt but he will be brought to tribute with great gladness. If not, he hath neither shot nor iron weapon in all his empire and therefore may easily be conquered.

And I further remember that Berrio confessed to me and others (which I protest before the Majesty of God to be true) that there was found among prophecies in Peru (at such time as the empire was reduced to the Spanish obedience) in their chiefest temples, amongst divers others which foreshowed the loss of the said empire, that from Inglatierra those Incas should be again in time to come restored and delivered from the servitude of the said conquerors. And I hope, as we with these few hands have displanted the first garrison and driven them out of the said country, so Her Majesty will give order for the rest, and either defend it and hold it as tributary, or conquer and keep it as Empress of the same. For whatsoever prince shall possess it shall be greatest, and if the King of Spain enjoy it, he will become unresistible. Her Majesty hereby shall confirm and strengthen the opinions of all nations as touching her great and princely actions. And where the south border of Guiana reacheth to the dominion and empire of the Amazons, those women shall hereby hear the name of a virgin which is not only able to defend her own territories and her neighbours, but also to invade and conquer so great empires and so far removed.

To speak more at this time, I fear would be but troublesome. I trust in God, this being true will suffice, and that he which is King of all kings, and Lord of lords, will put it into her heart which is Lady of ladies to possess it. If not, I will judge those men worthy to be kings thereof that by her grace and leave will undertake it of themselves.

THE HISTORY OF THE WORLD.

In Fiue Bookes.

1. *Ntreating of the Beginning and first Ages of the same from the Creation vnto* Abraham.
2. *Of the Times from the Birth of* Abraham, *to the destruction of the Temple of* Salomon.
3. *From the destruction of* Ierusalem, *to the time of* Philip *of* Macedon.
4. *From the Reigne of* Philip *of* Macedon, *to the establishing of that Kingdome, in the Race of* Antigonus.
5. *From the setled rule of* Alexanders *successors in the East, vntill the* Romans *(preuailing ouer all) made Conquest of* Asia *and* Macedon.

By Sir Walter Ralegh, *Knight*.

PREFACE TO THE HISTORY OF THE WORLD: INTRODUCTION

RALEIGH was a prisoner in the Tower from about the middle of 1603 until early in 1616, when he was released to set out upon his last Guiana voyage. His imprisonment varied in severity. It must always have been a hardship to be confined from year's end to year's end within damp walls beside London's unsavoury river, but for at least some of the time he had his wife and children with him, and he was allowed to talk with other prisoners, among whom the Earl of Northumberland was a man with serious intellectual interests. Eventually he was able to gather a library around him and to equip a small laboratory in which he carried out chemical experiments and assayed metals.

His major occupation, when the first shock was over and he had settled down to his strange death-in-life, was compiling a history of the world. It was a kind of adventure in time, now that he could no longer adventure in space. It may have been only his many active occupations that had prevented him from embarking upon it sooner. It had at any rate flitted across his mind in 1592 in the shape of an image in *Cynthia*. Now he was thrown in upon himself and in a mood to take stock not only of his own life but of life in general. Philip Edwards describes *The History of the World* as 'an interpretation of man, explained in terms of his history'. What, Raleigh seems to be enquiring, looking ruefully at the ruins of his own fortune, has any man, even the greatest, made of his life? And the answer, to quote Professor Edwards again, is 'precious little'. But by being shown as part of the eternal scheme of things, both the situation perceived and the clear eyes of the percipient gain a kind of sad dignity.

Raleigh was encouraged in his project by the heir-apparent, Prince Henry. The charm, which had failed so completely with James, easily won the young prince and his mother, Queen Anne of Denmark. But in 1612, at the age of eighteen, Prince Henry died of typhoid fever. Thus it fell to his younger brother Charles to ascend the throne when his time came and to meet the challenge of the Civil Wars. History under Henry would have been different though how different it is impossible to say. He was a spirited and intelligent young man. Raleigh was delighted to contribute to his education a number of manuscript works, notably a couple of treatises against a proposal to match him and his sister Elizabeth with a son and daughter of the House of Savoy. They were composed in 1611 at the Prince's own request, and emphasize the danger of England's making an alliance with a Catholic and pro-Spanish family. Another work, which survives only in fragments, was to have been a naval history.

The first book of *The History of the World* was ready in April 1611, when it was entered in the Stationers' Register. Publication was delayed while Raleigh expanded it to meet the wishes of an unnamed critic, whom we may suppose to have been the Prince. By the time it actually appeared, in March 1614, the Prince had been dead two years, and Raleigh pays a mournful tribute to him in his final paragraph, and says that he has no heart to take the work further. He deals first with the ancient world, beginning with Hebrew history as the oldest, most reliable and most important, the Bible being the inspired Word of God. After that, he writes of the empires of the Babylonians, the Persians, the Greeks and the Romans, breaking off at the Roman conquest of Macedon. He had intended to concentrate, as soon as records permitted it, upon the history of England, and we can only regret that he took the work no further. He must, on the death of his royal protector, have considered very seriously the wisdom of embarking upon anything so politically dangerous as modern history. His brief survey of the English monarchy in the *Preface* did enough damage as it was.

Some months after publication the book was officially recalled upon the King's orders. In 1617 it was in circulation again, in a second edition with Raleigh's name on a newly devised title-page. He was no longer a prisoner, who might be thought presumptuous had he appeared before the public as an author. The engraved frontispiece which prefaces the first edition carries no author's name, though it was freely spoken of as his. It has long been supposed that a title-page was removed from this edition, after which the book was released, the King's main objection having been met. Recent scholarship now challenges this assumption. There is very little solid evidence that any such page was in the book in the first place. It would have been difficult to arrange for its removal from all copies and it would not have gone far towards placating King James.

James prided himself upon his learning and was in a position to appreciate Raleigh's achievement. He could not easily quarrel with his main thesis, that in history we may trace the working of God's providence. To James Stuart, however, it was pleasing to reflect that the good ruler has God's authority for his actions. Raleigh, on the other hand, devoted himself to showing that in the eyes of God monarchs are no better than other men and retribution is exacted for all their crimes. He was careful in his *Preface* to represent James as a shining example of a good king, but the whole tenour of the book belittles human greatness and the pretensions of kings. Though James doubtless tried to school himself to a pious humility, he cannot have relished Raleigh of all people turning schoolmaster and teaching this lesson. It was openly said that the King disliked the work because it was 'too saucy in censuring princes'. In particular he was thought to have objected to the treatment of Henry VIII, and it must be admitted that in dealing with Henry, who as Queen Elizabeth's father was not such ancient history, the author does not mince his words. Nor are his references to Spain at all ingratiating, and King James was trying to establish good relations with Spain.

Raleigh was interested in what men have tried to do, how they have succeeded and why they have failed. He not infrequently draws parallels between the ancient and the modern world, and introduces comments based upon his own experience, in the French Wars of Religion, in Ireland, or in the New World. At one point he enquires how contemporary English soldiers would compare with Greeks and Romans, and decides in favour of his countrymen. History, he says, makes the past live for us. But much more important for him than reviving the past and expanding our intellectual horizon is the possibility of tracing in history a record of the justice of God. This makes his book entirely unlike the work of a modern historian, and particularly satisfying to the seventeenth-century reader, who was at one with him in wishing to trace God's guiding hand in world events. The magnificent engraved frontispiece of the first edition shows History holding on high the globe of the world. She treads underfoot the figures of Death and Oblivion, supported on one hand by Experience, with measuring rod and plumb line, and on the other by the light of the naked Truth. Good Fame and Bad Fame blow their trumpets, and over all broods the ever-open Eye of God.

Raleigh's history begins with the beginning of all things, the Creation. It is essential to his thesis to establish the fact that the world is of God's making and governed by his laws. A considerable section of the *Preface* counters pagan and materialistic theories of creation and nature. It is too specialized for inclusion here but it is interesting to know that Raleigh included it. The section in which he surveys English history shows very clearly his view of it as a cycle of personal crime and personal retribution. Anyone familiar with Shakespeare's history plays will recognize the version of events which Raleigh gives, and which is that common to the chronicle histories of the day. He concentrates upon the lives of great kings and leaders because they are the people whose stories have been preserved. They provide moreover a particularly telling text for his melancholy sermon upon the littleness of man. At the back of his thinking, as of all the orthodox Christian thought of his time, is the concept of man as fallen through sin from his first perfection, and of the world as a place in which materialistic values, desires and ambitions are always distracting us from what matters most, our obedience to God and the promise of eternal life.

It was in some ways easy for a prisoner to set a low value upon a world in which he no longer had any stake. But as soon as he was given the opportunity, Raleigh plunged again into all the greed and treachery and triviality. This behaviour, though he himself was guilty of it, would in no way have surprised the disillusioned author of *The History of the World.* It was what he would expect, of himself as of other worldlings. As he said in a farewell letter to his son, 'All is vanity and weariness, yet such a weariness and vanity that we shall ever complain of it and love it for all that.'

In writing the *Preface*, which sums up the mood in which the whole work is conceived, Raleigh naturally turns to those of the ancients who, in the name of human dignity, taught a detachment from worldly desires and disasters, that is to say to authors with a moral and stoical bent, such as Seneca, Cicero and Plutarch. Among Christian writers he found an even stronger renunciation of worldly values. He was drawn to the Old Testament, notably to Job and Ecclesiastes. He seems in fact happier with the Old Testament than the New. It reflects his theme of the power and justice of God and the fallibility of man.

The *History* itself, being mainly narrative, lacks the emotional quality which makes the *Preface* a kind of muted poetry. It lacks also the life and vigour of Raleigh's narratives of contemporary events, such as *The Last Fight of the Revenge* and *The Discovery of Guiana*, but the style is admirably compact, pointed and sinewy. Some of the most interesting parts, over and above the digressions into recent events and personal experiences, are the character studies of great men.

It must be admitted that it makes little appeal to the general reader today and, apart from the personal digressions, has little value for the historian. The subject matter is largely outmoded. We know a good deal more about the ancient world than Raleigh did and look at the historian's task in a rather different light. The elaborate chronological tables, for instance, whereby he synchronized Biblical history, which he regarded as absolutely true, with secular records, seem so much labour wasted. In the seventeenth century, however, the work was highly valued, frequently reprinted, and several times summarized. The *Preface* acquired the appropriate title of *Sir Walter Raleigh's Premonition to Princes.*

Cromwell recommended the work to his son. 'It is a body of history', he said, 'and will add much more to your understanding than fragments.' John Locke, the philosopher, was another who admired it. It was attractive because it was a comprehensive world history, because it was written in clear and forceful language, and because it said what Cromwell and so many other Englishmen most fervently believed, that man is a fallen creature, inhabiting a sad and fallen world, but that it is not a purposeless chaos, for all lies ultimately in the disposition of a just God. The optimistic temper of the Commonwealth seized upon the second and more optimistic part of Raleigh's thesis. He had given up hoping that men would act rationally and well. The Puritans were momentarily sure that, unlike everybody else, *they* would.

It may seem curious after this to turn to Raleigh's reputation as an atheist, which dogged him through life, or at least until the publication of the *History*, with its strong, severe, and rather impersonal religious bent. The word 'atheist' was in common use in the sixteenth century as an indiscriminate term of abuse. It could be hurled at anybody who appeared to the speaker to be unprincipled, irreverent, and liable to question accepted beliefs, and whether deserved or not, its impact was shattering to reputations. It fitted the public picture of Raleigh as a dangerous and incalculable person.

The Queen's favourite was the natural target of envious criticism. There must however have been some quality in the man himself, over and above his rather unscrupulous fortune-hunting, which allowed this particular mud to stick. Raleigh had intellectual interests. He read sceptical philosophy and sometimes retailed it. He was not a profound thinker nor a professional philosopher, but he enjoyed ideas and the exchange of ideas. He probably enjoyed shocking staid and hidebound people. Some of his studies were scientific. Because of his voyages, he was interested in mathematics and astronomy as aids to navigation. He had instruction from one of the best mathematicians of the day, a man called Thomas Hariot. Some of the suspicion which clung round advanced science, as possibly materialistic and irreligious, transferred itself to him. He was far too sure of himself to care about this or to take any steps to avoid the imputation.

Raleigh was a Protestant, and the quarrel he pursued with Spain was heated by religious prejudice. He had fought with the Huguenots in France and against Catholic rebels in Ireland. At home he was an enemy to the missionary priests who were trying to bring Protestant England back to her old loyalties. He held the government's view that they spread political disaffection. It was they who first put upon him the brand of 'atheist'. In 1592 a pamphlet appeared in which the Jesuit, Father Robert Parsons, attacked Queen Elizabeth's heretical court. In it was an allusion to 'Sir Walter Raleigh's school of atheism, and of the conjuror that is Master thereof [Hariot] and of the diligence used to get young gentlemen to this school'. The phraseology is that of witty metaphor. Father Parsons did not mean that Raleigh kept a school in any literal sense. When Marlowe was charged with atheism, Raleigh and Hariot were mentioned as scoffers at religion. By 1594 gossip had risen to such a pitch that a Church commission met in Dorset to enquire into charges of atheism laid against Sir Walter and his free-thinking friends. A neighbouring parson, the Reverend

Ralph Ironside, had been deeply shocked and disturbed by their dinner-table conversation on the nature of the soul.

The charges were not substantiated, but the scandal did Raleigh no good. He had fallen from favour and his reputation, of which he had been so careless, was now open to attack. His enemies felt free to label him atheist. He was represented in this light to douce King James. At the treason trial in 1603 great play was made with it. The publication of *The History of the World* did much to silence such attacks and to re-establish Raleigh in public esteem. 'Your faith hath heretofore been questioned', said the judge who sentenced him in 1618, 'but I am satisfied you are a good Christian, for your book, which is an admirable work, doth testify as much.' The earlier view of him as one who flouted established sanctities explains why his name is so persistently associated with the poem called *The Lie*. He may not have written it, but it is just the kind of poem people expected him to write.

Some scholars believe that Shakespeare's *Love's Labour's Lost* was a veiled attack upon Raleigh, his alleged atheism, his mathematical interests, and his scandalous marriage. The casual phrase 'school of night', used rather awkwardly in the course of a laboured joke about fair and dark beauty (IV. iii. 272), is equated with Father Parsons's expression 'school of atheism', which indubitably did refer to Raleigh, and a picturesque legend has recently grown up about Sir Walter Raleigh and the School of Night. The whole idea should be treated with great caution.

The reader is recommended to consult the textual notes, p. 236 for an explanation of editorial practice with regard to quotations. Biblical references have been supplied where possible. Raleigh's precise sources are not always easy to identify.

Sir Walter Raleigh's Premonition to Princes

The Preface to *The History of the World*

HOW unfit and how unworthy a choice I have made of myself to undertake a work of this mixture, mine own reason, though exceeding weak, hath sufficiently resolved me. For had it been begotten then with my first dawn of day, when the light of common knowledge began to open itself to my younger years, and before any wound received, either from fortune or time; I might yet well have doubted that the darkness of age and death would have covered over both it and me, long before the performance. For beginning with the Creation, I have proceeded with the history of the world, and lastly purposed (some few sallies excepted) to confine my discourse within this our renowned island of Great Britain.

I confess that it had better sorted with my disability, the better part of whose times are run out in other travails, to have set together (as I could) the unjointed and scattered frame of our English affairs, than of the universal: in whom had there been no other defect (who am all defect) than the time of the day, it were enough: the day of a tempestuous life, drawn on to the very evening ere I began. But those inmost and soul-piercing wounds*, which are ever aching while uncured; with the desire to satisfy those few friends which I have tried by the fire of adversity, the former enforcing, the latter persuading, have caused me to make my thoughts legible, and myself the subject of every opinion wise or weak.

run out: suggested by an hour-glass.

To the world I present them, to which I am nothing indebted. Neither have others that were (fortune changing) sped much better in any age. For prosperity and adversity have evermore tied and untied vulgar affections. And as we see it in experience, that dogs do always bark at those they know not, and that it is in their nature to accompany one another in those clamours, so is it with the inconsiderate multitude. Who wanting that virtue which we call honesty in all men, and that especial gift of God which we call charity in Christian men, condemn without hearing, and wound without offence given; led thereunto by uncertain report only, which His Majesty truly acknowledgeth* for the author of all lies. 'Blame no man', saith Siracides,* 'before thou have enquired the matter. Understand first and then reform righteously'.† 'Rumour is without witness, without judge, malicious and deceivable'.‡ This vanity of vulgar opinion it was that gave Saint Augustine argument to affirm that he feared the praise of good men and detested that of the evil. And herein no man hath given a better rule than this of Seneca:* 'Let us satisfy our own consciences and not trouble ourselves with fame. Be it never so ill, it is to be despised so we deserve well.'§

For myself, if I have in anything served my country and prized it before my private, the general acceptation can yield me no other profit at this time than doth a fair sunshine day to a seaman after shipwreck; and the contrary no other harm than an outrageous tempest after the port attained. I know that I lost the love of many for my fidelity towards Her* whom I must still honour in the dust; though further than the defence of her excellent person, I never persecuted any man. Of those that did it, and by what device they did it, He that is the supreme Judge of all the

my private: my personal advantage.

† Ecclesiasticus, ch. ix, v. 7.

‡ Rumor, res sine teste, sine iudice, maligna, fallax.

§ Conscientiae satisfaciamus: nihil in famam laboremus: sequatur vel mala, dum bene merearis.

world hath taken the account. So as for this kind of suffering, I must say with Seneca, '*It is a pleasure to have a bad name in a good cause*'.†

As for other men, if there be any that have made themselves fathers of that fame which hath been begotten for them, I can neither envy at such their purchased glory, nor much lament mine own mishap in that kind; but content myself to say with Virgil *Sic vos non vobis** in many particulars.

To labour other satisfaction were an effect of frenzy not of hope; seeing it is not truth, but opinion, that can travel the world without a passport. For were it otherwise, and were there not as many internal forms of the mind as there are external figures of men, there were then some possibility to persuade by the mouth of one advocate, even equity alone.

But such is the multiplying and extensive virtue of dead earth and of that breath-giving life which God hath cast upon slime and dust, as that among those that were, of whom we read and hear, and among those that are, whom we see and converse with, every one hath received a several picture of face, and every one a diverse picture of mind; every one a form apart, every one a fancy and cogitation differing; there being nothing wherein Nature so much triumpheth as in dissimilitude. From whence it cometh that there is found so great diversity of opinions, so strong a contrariety of inclinations, so many natural and unnatural, wise, foolish, manly and childish affections and passions in mortal men. For it is not the visible fashion and shape of plants and of reasonable creatures that makes the difference of working in the one and of condition in the other, but the form internal.

And though it hath pleased God to reserve the art of reading men's thoughts to himself; yet as the fruit tells the name of the tree, so do the outward works of men (so far as their cogitations are acted) give us whereof to guess at the rest.

† Mala opinio, bene parta, delectat.

Nay, it were not hard to express the one by the other very near the life; did not craft in many, fear in the most, and the world's love in all, teach every capacity according to the compass it hath to qualify and mask over their inward deformities for a time. Though it be also true, 'No man can long continue masked in a counterfeit behaviour. The things that are forced for pretences, having no ground of truth, cannot long dissemble their own natures.'† Neither can any man (saith Plutarch*) so change himself but that his heart may be sometime seen at his tongue's end.

In this great discord and dissimilitude of reasonable creatures, if we direct ourselves to the multitude, 'The common people are evil judges of honest things'‡ and 'whose wisdom' (saith Ecclesiastes) 'is to be despised'. If to the better sort, every understanding hath a peculiar judgement, by which it both censureth other men and valueth itself. And therefore unto me it will not seem strange though I find these my worthless papers torn with rats; seeing the slothful censurers of all ages have not spared to tax the reverend Fathers of the Church with ambition; the severest men to themselves with hypocrisy; the greatest lovers of justice with popularity; and those of the truest valour and fortitude with vainglory. But of these natures which lie in wait to find fault and to turn good into evil, seeing Solomon complained long since; and that the very age of the world renders it every day after other more malicious, I must leave the professors to their easy ways of reprehension, than which there is nothing of more facility.

To me it belongs in the first part of this preface, following the common and approved custom of those who have left the memories of time past to after ages, to give as near as I can the same right to history which they have done. Yet

peculiar: private to itself. *popularity*: courting popular favour.

† Nemo potest diu personam ferre fictam: cito in naturam suam recidunt, quibus veritas non subest.

‡ Omnis honestae rei malus iudex est vulgus.

seeing therein I should but borrow other men's words, I will not trouble the reader with the repetition. True it is, that among many other benefits for which it hath been honoured, in this one it triumpheth over all human knowledge, that it hath given us life in our understanding, since the world itself had life and beginning, even to this day. Yea, it hath triumphed over time, which besides it, nothing but eternity hath triumphed over. For it hath carried our knowledge over the vast and devouring space of so many thousands of years, and given so fair and piercing eyes to our mind, that we plainly behold living now, as if we had lived then, that great world, 'the wise work' (saith Hermes*) 'of a great God',† as it was then, when but new to itself. By it I say it is that we live in the very time when it was created. We behold how it was governed. How it was covered with waters, and again repeopled. How kings and kingdoms have flourished and fallen, and for what virtue and piety God made prosperous and for what vice and deformity he made wretched both the one and the other. And it is not the least debt which we owe unto history, that it hath made us acquainted with our dead ancestors; and out of the depth and darkness of the earth, delivered us their memory and fame. In a word, we may gather out of history a policy no less wise than eternal, by the comparison and application of other men's forepassed miseries with our own like errors and ill-deservings.

But it is neither of examples the most lively instructions, nor the words of the wisest men, nor the terror of future torments that hath yet so wrought in our blind and stupified minds as to make us remember that the infinite eye and wisdom of God doth pierce through all our pretences; as to make us remember that the justice of God doth require none other accuser than our own consciences; which neither the false beauty of our apparent actions, nor all the formality which (to pacify the opinions of men) we put on,

formality: rigid decorum.

† Magni Dei sapiens opus.

can in any, or the least kind, cover from His knowledge. And so much did that heathen wisdom confess, no way as yet qualified by the knowledge of a true God. If any, saith Euripides,* 'having in his life committed wickedness, think he can hide it from the everlasting gods, he thinks not well'.

To repeat God's judgements in particular upon those of all degrees which have played with His mercies, would require a volume apart; for the sea of examples hath no bottom. The marks set on private men are with their bodies cast into the earth, and their fortunes written only in the memories of those that lived with them; so as they who succeed, and have not seen the fall of others, do not fear their own faults. God's judgements upon the greater and greatest have been left to posterity; first by those happy hands which the Holy Ghost hath guided;* and secondly, by their virtue who have gathered the acts and ends of men mighty and remarkable in the world.

Now to point far off, and to speak of the conversion of angels into devils* for ambition; or of the greatest and most glorious of kings, who have gnawn the grass* of the earth with beasts, for pride and ingratitude towards God; or of that wise working of Pharoah* when he slew the infants of Israel, ere they had recovered their cradles; or of the policy of Jezebel,* in covering the murder of Naboth by a trial of the Elders, according to the law, with many thousands of the like—what were it other than to make a hopeless proof that far-off examples would not be left to the same far-off respects as heretofore? For who hath not observed what labour, practice, peril, bloodshed and cruelty the kings and princes of the world have undergone, exercised, taken on them and committed, to make themselves and their issues masters of the world? And yet hath Babylon, Persia, Egypt, Syria, Macedon, Carthage, Rome and the rest no fruit, flower, grass, nor leaf springing upon the face of the earth, of those seeds. No! Their very roots and ruins do hardly

recovered: arrived at, i.e. while still in their mothers' arms.
practice: plotting.

remain. 'All that the hand of man can make is either overturned by the hand of man, or at length by standing and continuing consumed.'† The reasons of whose ruins are diversely given by those that ground their opinions on second causes.*

All kingdoms and states have fallen (say the politicians) by outward and foreign force, or by inward negligence and dissension, or by a third cause arising from both. Others observe that the greatest have sunk down under their own weight, of which Livy* hath a touch. '*It grew till it staggered under its own great size.*'‡ Others that the divine providence (which Cratippus* objected to Pompey) hath set down the date and period of every estate, before their first foundation and erection. But hereof I will give myself a day over to resolve.

For seeing the first books of the following story have undertaken the discourse of the first kings and kingdoms, and that it is impossible for the short life of a preface to travel after and overtake far-off antiquity and to judge of it, I will for the present examine what profit hath been gathered by our own kings and their neighbour princes; who having beheld both in divine and human letters the success of infidelity, injustice, and cruelty, have (notwithstanding) planted after the same pattern.

True it is that the judgements of all men are not agreeable; nor (which is more strange) the affection of any one man stirred up alike with examples of like nature. But everyone is touched most with that which most nearly seemeth to touch his own private, or otherwise best suiteth with his apprehension. But the judgements of God are forever unchangeable, neither is He wearied by the long process of time, and won to give His blessing in one age to that which He hath cursed in another. Wherefore those that are

a day over: a little longer time. *agreeable*: in accord.

† Omnia quae manu hominum facta sunt, vel manu hominum evertuntur, vel stando et durando deficiunt.

‡ Eo crevit, ut magnitudine laboret sua.

wise, or whose wisdom if it be not great yet is true and well grounded, will be able to discern the bitter fruits of irreligious policy as well among those examples that are found in ages removed far from the present as in those of latter times. And that it may no less appear by evident proof, than by asseveration, that ill doing hath always been attended with ill success, I will here by way of preface run over some examples which the work ensuing hath not reached.

Among our kings of the Norman race, we have no sooner passed over the violence of the Norman Conquest than we encounter with a singular and most remarkable example of God's justice upon the children of Henry the First. For that King, when both by force, craft, and cruelty he had dispossessed, over-reached, and lastly made blind and destroyed his elder brother, Robert Duke of Normandy, to make his own sons lords of this land, God cast them all, male and female, nephews and nieces (Maud excepted) into the bottom of the sea,* with above a hundred and fifty others that attended them, whereof a great many were noble and of the King dearly beloved.

To pass over the rest, till we come to Edward the Second.* It is certain that after the murder of that king, the issue of blood then made, though it had some times of stay and stopping, did again break out; and that so often and in such abundance as all our princes of the masculine race (very few excepted) died of the same disease. And although the young years of Edward the Third made his knowledge of that horrible fact no more than suspicious; yet in that he afterwards caused his own uncle, the Earl of Kent,* to die, for no other offence than the desire of his brother's redemption, whom the Earl as then supposed to be living; (the King making that to be treason in his uncle which was indeed treason in himself, had his uncle's intelligence been true); this I say made it manifest that he was not ignorant of what had passed, nor greatly desirous to have had it otherwise, though he caused Mortimer to die for the same.

the same disease: i.e. by violence. *suspicious*: to be suspected.

This cruelty the secret and unsearchable judgement of God revenged on the grandchild of Edward the Third. And so it fell out, even to the last of that line, that in the second or third descent they were all buried under the ruins of those buildings of which the mortar had been tempered with innocent blood. For Richard the Second,* who saw both his Treasurers, his Chancellor, and his Steward, with divers others of his counsellors, some of them slaughtered by the people, others in his absence executed by his enemies; yet he always took himself for overwise to be taught by examples. The Earls of Huntingdon and Kent, Montagu and Spencer, who thought themselves as great politicians in those days as others have done in these, hoping to please the King and to secure themselves by the murder of Gloucester,* died soon after with many other their adherents by the like violent hands; and far more shamefully than did that Duke. And as for the King himself (who in regard of many deeds unworthy of his greatness cannot be excused, as the disavowing himself by breach of faith, charters, pardons, and patents), he was in the prime of his youth deposed and murdered* by his cousin-german and vassal, Henry of Lancaster, afterwards Henry the Fourth.

This King, whose title was weak and his obtaining the crown traitorous, who broke faith with the Lords at his landing, protesting to intend only the recovery of his proper inheritance, broke faith with Richard himself, and broke faith with all the kingdom in Parliament, to whom he swore that the deposed King should live. After that he had enjoyed this realm some few years—and in that time had been set upon on all sides by his subjects, and never free from conspiracies and rebellions—he saw (if souls immortal see and discern any things after the body's death) his grandchild Henry the Sixth and his son the Prince suddenly and without mercy murdered; the possession of the crown (for which he had caused so much blood to be poured out) transferred from his race, and by the issues of his enemies worn and enjoyed; enemies whom by his own practice he supposed that he had left no less powerless than the succession of the kingdom questionless; by entailing the same upon his own issues by Parliament. And out of doubt, human reason could have judged no otherwise but that these cautious provisions of the father, seconded by the valour and signal victories of his son, Henry the Fifth, had buried the hopes of every competitor under the despair of all reconquest and recovery. I say, that human reason might so have judged, were not this passage of Casaubon* also true, 'A day, an hour, a moment, is enough to overturn the things that seemed to have been founded and rooted in adamant.'†

Now for Henry the Sixth, upon whom the great storm of his grandfather's grievous faults fell, as it formerly had done upon Richard, the grandchild of Edward. Although he was generally esteemed for a gentle and innocent Prince, yet as he refused the daughter of Armagnac, of the house of Navarre, the greatest of the Princes of France, to whom he was affianced (by which match he might have defended his inheritance in France) and married the daughter of Anjou, (by which he lost all that he had* in France), so as in condescending to the unworthy death of his uncle of Gloucester, the main and strong pillar of the House of Lancaster, he drew on himself and this kingdom the greatest joint loss and dishonour that ever it sustained since the Norman Conquest. Of whom it may truly be said, which a counsellor of his own spoke of Henry the Third of France, 'That he was a very gentle Prince, but his reign happened in a very unfortunate season.'‡

[*The next paragraph treats of the guilt of Suffolk, Buckingham and the Queen as parties to Gloucester's murder, and how they were paid home for it.*]

And now came it to Edward the Fourth's turn (though after many difficulties) to triumph. For all the plants of

† Dies, hora, momentum, evertendis dominationibus sufficit, quae adamantinis credebantur radicibus esse fundatae.

‡ Qu'il estait un fort gentil Prince; mais son reigne est advenu en une fort mauvais temps.

Lancaster were rooted up, one only Earl of Richmond* excepted, whom also he had once bought of the Duke of Brittany but could not hold him. And yet was not this of Edward such a plantation as could any way promise itself stability. For this Edward the King (to omit more than many of his other cruelties) beheld and allowed the slaughter which Gloucester, Dorset, Hastings and others made of Edward the Prince* in his own presence; of which tragical actors there was not one that escaped the judgement of God in the same kind. And he which (besides the execution of his brother of Clarence* for none other offence than he himself had formed in his own imagination) instructed Gloucester to kill Henry the Sixth, his predecessor, taught him also by the same art to kill his own sons and successors, Edward and Richard. For those kings which have sold the blood of others at a low rate have but made the market for their own enemies to buy of theirs at the same price.

To Edward the Fourth succeeded Richard the Third, the greatest master in mischief of all that forewent him. Who although for the necessity of his tragedy he had more parts to play and more to perform in his own person than all the rest, yet he so well fitted every affection that played with him, as if each of them had but acted his own interest. For he wrought so cunningly upon the affections of Hastings and Buckingham, enemies to the Queen and to all her kindred, as he easily allured them to condescend that Rivers and Grey, the King's maternal uncle and half-brother, should (for the first) be severed from him; secondly he wrought their consent to have them imprisoned, and lastly (for the avoiding of future inconvenience) to have their heads severed from their bodies. And having now brought those his chief instruments to exercise that common precept which the Devil hath writ on every post, namely to depress those whom they had grieved and to destroy those whom they had depressed, he urged that argument so far and so forcibly as nothing but the death of the young King himself and of his brother could fashion the conclusion. For he caused it to be hammered into Buckingham's head, that whensoever the King or his brother should have able years to exercise their power, they would take a most severe revenge of that cureless wrong offered to their uncle and brother, Rivers and Grey.

But this was not his manner of reasoning with Hastings, whose fidelity to his master's sons was without suspect. And yet the Devil, who never dissuades by impossibility, taught him to try him. And so he did. But when he found by Catesby, who sounded him, that he was not fordable, he first resolved to kill him sitting in council; wherein having failed with his sword, he set the hangman upon him, with a weapon of more weight. And because nothing else could move his appetite, he caused his head to be stricken off before he ate his dinner. A greater judgement of God than this upon Hastings I have never observed in any story. For the selfsame day that the Earl Rivers, Grey, and others were (without trial of law or offence given) by Hastings' advice executed at Pomfret, I say Hastings himself in the same day and (as I take it) in the same hour, in the same lawless manner had his head stricken off in the Tower of London.

But Buckingham lived a while longer, and with an eloquent oration persuaded the Londoners to elect Richard for their King. And having received the Earldom of Hereford for reward, besides the high hope of marrying his daughter to the King's only son, after many grievous vexations of mind and unfortunate attempts, being in the end betrayed and delivered up by his trustiest servant, he had his head severed from his body at Salisbury, without the trouble of any of his peers.* And what success had Richard himself after all these mischiefs and murders, policies and counter-policies to Christian religion, and after such time as with a most merciless hand he had pressed out the breath of his nephews and natural Lords, other than the prosperity of so short a life as it took end ere himself could well look over

fordable: suggested by 'sounded', tried the depth.

and discern it? The great outcry of innocent blood obtaining at God's hands the effusion of his, who became a spectacle of shame and dishonour both to his friends and enemies.

This cruel King, Henry the Seventh cut off,* and was therein (no doubt) the immediate instrument of God's justice. A politic prince he was if ever there were any, and who by the engine of his wisdom beat down and overturned as many strong oppositions both before and after he wore the crown as ever king of England did. I say by his wisdom, because as he ever left the reins of his affections in the hands of his profit, so he always weighed his undertakings by his abilities, leaving nothing more to hazard than so much as cannot be denied it in all human actions. He had well observed the proceedings of Louis the Eleventh, whom he followed in all that was royal or royal-like, but he was far more just, and began not their processes whom he hated or feared by the execution, as Louis did.

He could never endure any mediation in rewarding his servants, and therein exceeding wise, for whatsoever himself gave, he himself received back the thanks and the love, knowing it well that the affections of men (purchased by nothing so readily as by benefits) were trains that better became great Kings than great subjects. On the contrary, in whatsoever he grieved his subjects, he wisely put it off on those that he found fit ministers for such actions. Howsoever, the taking off of Stanley's head,* who set the crown on his, and the death of the young Earl of Warwick,* son to George Duke of Clarence, shows, as the success also did, that he held somewhat of the errors of his ancestors, for his possession in the first line ended in his grandchildren, as that of Edward the Third and Henry the Fourth had done.

Now for King Henry the Eighth. If all the pictures and patterns of a merciless prince were lost in the world, they might all again be painted to the life out of the story of this king. For how many servants did he advance in haste (but

engine: skill, ingenuity.
their processes: legal actions against them.

for what virtue no man could suspect) and with the change of his fancy ruined again, no man knowing for what offence? To how many others of more desert gave he abundant flowers from whence to gather honey, and in the end of harvest burnt them in the hive? How may wives did he cut off and cast off as his fancy and affection changed? How many princes of the blood (whereof some of them for age could hardly crawl towards the block) with a world of others of all degrees (of whom our common chronicles have kept the account) did he execute? Yea, in his very deathbed, and when he was at the point to have given his account to God for the abundance of blood already spilt, he imprisoned the Duke of Norfolk, the father, and executed the Earl of Surrey, the son; the one, whose deservings he knew not how to value, having never omitted anything that concerned his own honour and the King's service, the other, never having committed anything worthy of his least displeasure; the one exceeding valiant and advised, the other no less valiant than learned,* and of excellent hope. But besides the sorrows which he heaped upon the fatherless and widows at home, and besides the vain enterprises abroad, wherein it is thought that he consumed more treasure than all our victorious kings did in their several conquests, what causeless and cruel wars did he make upon his own nephew, King James the Fifth?* What laws and wills did he devise to establish this kingdom in his own issues? Using his sharpest weapons to cut off and cut down those branches which sprang from the same root that himself did.

And in the end (notwithstanding these his so many irreligious provisions) it pleased God to take away all his own without increase; though for themselves in their several kinds all princes of eminent virtue.* For these words of Samuel to Agag, King of the Amelekites, have been verified upon many others. 'As thy sword hath made other women childless, so shall thy mother be childless among other women.'† And that blood, which the same King Henry

† Samuel, ch. xv, v. 33.

affirmed that the cold air of Scotland had frozen up in the North, God hath diffused by the sunshine of His grace; from whence His Majesty now living and long to live is descended. Of whom I may say it truly, that if all the malice of the world were infused into one eye, yet could it not discern in his life, even to this day, any one of those foul spots by which the consciences of all the forenamed princes (in effect) have been defiled; nor any drop of that innocent blood on the sword of his justice, with which the most that forewent him have stained both their hands and fame.

[*Raleigh praises James for waiting till the crown came peaceably and rightfully to him. He praises the benefit to England of the union of the crowns. How fatal had James taken advantage of 1588 to invade! He praises his liberality and learning. How gentle his disposition and unlike the wicked kings aforementioned! Then follows at some length further proof from French and Spanish history that God is not mocked.*]

Oh by what plots, by what forswearings, betrayings, oppressions, imprisonments, tortures, poisonings, and under what reasons of state and politic subtlety have these forenamed kings, both strangers and of our own nation, pulled the vengeance of God upon themselves, upon theirs, and upon their prudent ministers! And in the end have brought those things to pass for their enemies, and seen an effect so directly contrary to all their own counsels and cruelties, as the one could never have hoped for themselves, and the other never have succeeded, if no such opposition had ever been made. God hath said it and performed it ever, 'I will destroy the wisdom of the wise.'†

But what of all this? And to what end do we lay before the eyes of the living the fall and fortunes of the dead? Seeing the world is the same that it hath been, and the children of the present time will still obey their parents. It is in the present time that all the wits of the world are exercised. To hold the times we have, we hold all things lawful; and either we hope to hold them forever, or at least we hope that there

† Perdam sapientiam sapientum. 1 Corinthians, ch. i, v. 19.

is nothing after them to be hoped for. For as we are content to forget our own experience, and to counterfeit the ignorance of our own knowledge in all things that concern ourselves; or persuade ourselves that God hath given us letters patents to pursue all our irreligious affections, with a *non obstante*; so we neither look behind us what hath been nor before us what shall be. It is true that the quantity which we have is of the body. We are by it joined to the earth. We are compounded of earth and we inhabit it. The heavens are high, far off and unsearchable. We have sense and feeling of corporal things; and of eternal grace but by revelation. No marvel then that our thoughts are also earthly; and it is less to be wondered at that the words of worthless men cannot cleanse them, seeing their doctrine and instruction, whose understanding the Holy Ghost vouchsafed to inhabit, have not performed it. For as the prophet Isaiah cried out long agone, 'Lord, who hath believed our reports?'†

And out of doubt, as Isaiah complained then for himself and others, so are they less believed every day after other. For although religion and the truth thereof be in every man's mouth, yea in the discourse of every woman, who for the greatest number are but *Idols of vanity*, what is it other than an universal dissimulation? We profess that we know God; but by works we deny him. For beatitude doth not consist in the knowledge of divine things, but in a divine life;‡ for the Devils know them better than men. And certainly there is nothing more to be admired and more to be lamented than the private contention, the passionate dispute, the personal hatred, and the perpetual war, massacres and murders for religion among Christians; the discourse whereof hath so occupied the world as it hath well near driven the practice thereof out of the world. Who would not

letters patents: documents conferring some kind of official privilege, which included a clause beginning *non obstante* (notwithstanding), an indication that nothing was to over-ride the powers conferred.

† Isaiah, ch. lii, v. 1.

‡ Beatitudo non est divinorum cognitio, sed vita divina.

soon resolve, that took knowledge but of the religious disputations among men, and not of their lives which dispute, that there were no other thing in their desires than the purchase of heaven; and that the world itself were but used as it ought and as an inn or place wherein to repose ourselves in passing on towards our celestial habitation? When on the contrary, besides the discourse and outward profession, the soul hath nothing but hypocrisy. We are all (in effect) become comedians in religion; and while we act in gesture and voice divine virtues, in all the course of our lives we renounce our persons and the parts we play. For charity, justice, and truth have but their being *in terms*, like the philosophers' *materia prima.**

Neither is it that wisdom which Solomon defineth to be the 'Schoolmistress of the knowledge of God' that hath valuation in the world. It is enough that we give it our good word. But the same which is altogether exercised in the service of the world, as the gathering of riches chiefly; by which we purchase and obtain honour, with the many respects which attend it.

These indeed be the marks which (when we have bent our consciences to the highest) we all shoot at. For the obtaining whereof it is true that the care is our own; the care our own in this life, the peril our own in the future. And yet when we have gathered the greatest abundance, we ourselves enjoy no more thereof than so much as belongs to one man. For the rest, he that had the greatest wisdom and the greatest ability that ever man had, hath told us that this is the use. 'When goods increase' (saith Solomon) 'they also increase that eat them; and what good cometh to the owners but the beholding thereof with their eyes?'† As for those that devour the rest, and follow us in fair weather; they again forsake us in the first tempest of misfortune and steer away before the sea and wind, leaving us to the malice of our destinies.

Of these, among a thousand examples, I will take but one out of Master Dannet,* and use his own words. 'Whilst the

† Ecclesiastes, ch. v, v.11, traditionally believed to be by Solomon.

Emperor Charles the Fifth,* after the resignation of his estates, stayed at Flushing for wind to carry him his last journey into Spain, he conferred on a time with Seldius, his brother Ferdinand's ambassador, till the deep of the night. And when Seldius should depart, the Emperor calling for some of his servants, and nobody answering him (for those that attended upon him were some gone to their lodgings and all the rest asleep) the Emperor took up the candle himself and went before Seldius to light him down the stairs and so did, notwithstanding all the resistance that Seldius could make. And when he was come to the stairs foot, he said thus unto him. "Seldius, remember this of Charles the Emperor, when he shall be dead and gone, that him whom thou hast known in thy time environed with so many mighty armies and guards of soldiers, thou hast also seen alone, abandoned, and forsaken, yea even of his own domestical servants . . . I acknowledge this change of fortune to proceed from the mighty hand of God, which I will by no means go about to withstand."'

[*Raleigh considers reasons why we might value our own position in the world and the fame and fortune we are able to leave to our posterity and decides that they can mean nothing to us when we are dead. Nonetheless they have their proper place in life.*]

Shall we therefore value honour and riches at nothing? And neglect them as unnecessary and vain? Certainly no. For that infinite wisdom of God, which hath distinguished his angels by degrees; which hath given greater and less light and beauty to heavenly bodies; which hath made differences between beasts and birds—created the eagle and the fly, the cedar and the shrub; and among stones given the fairest tincture to the ruby and the quickest light to the diamond; hath also ordained kings, dukes, or leaders of the people, magistrates, judges, and other degrees among men. And as honour is left to posterity for a mark and ensign of the virtue and understanding of their ancestors; so, seeing Siracides preferreth death before beggary,† and that titles,

Quickest: liveliest. † Ecclesiasticus, ch. xi, v. 28.

without proportionable estates, fall under the miserable succour of other men's pity, I account it foolishness to condemn such a care. Provided that worldly goods be well gotten and that we raise not our own buildings out of other men's ruins. For as Plato doth first prefer the perfection of bodily health, secondly the form and beauty, and thirdly '*Wealth honestly won*',† so Jerome cries, 'Woe unto them that erect their houses by unrighteousness and their chambers without equity!' And Isaiah the same, 'Woe to those that spoil and were not spoiled!'‡ And it was out of the true wisdom of Solomon that he commandeth us 'not to drink the wine of violence; not to lie in wait for blood; and not to swallow them up alive whose riches we covet. For such are the ways'* (saith he) 'of everyone that is greedy of gain.'§

And if we could afford ourselves but so much leisure as to consider that he which hath most in the world hath, in respect of the world, nothing in it; and that he which hath the longest time lent him to live in it hath yet no proportion at all therein, setting it either by that which is past when we were not, or by that time which is to come in which we shall abide for ever. I say, if both, to wit our proportion in the world and our time in the world, differ not much from that which is nothing, it is not out of any excellency of understanding that we so much prize the one, which hath (in effect) no being; and so much neglect the other, which hath no ending; coveting those mortal things of the world, as if our souls were therein immortal, and neglecting those things which are immortal, as if ourselves after the world were but mortal.

But let every man value his own wisdom as he pleaseth. Let the rich man think all fools that cannot equal his abundance; the revenger esteem all negligent that have not trodden down their opposites; the politician all gross that

In respect of: in comparison with all the rest.

† Divitias nulla fraude quaesitas.

‡ Isaiah, ch. xxxiii, v. 1.

§ Proverbs, ch. i, v. 12, 18, 19.

cannot merchandize their faith. Yet when we once come in sight of the port of death, to which all winds drive us; and when by letting fall that fatal anchor which can never be weighed again, the navigation of this life takes end; then it is, I say, that our own cogitations (those sad and severe cogitations, formerly beaten from us by our health and felicity) return again, and pay us to the uttermost for all the pleasing passages of our lives past. It is then that we cry out to God for mercy; then, when ourselves can no longer exercise cruelty towards others. And it is only then that we are stricken through the soul with this terrible sentence, that 'God will not be mocked.'† For if, according to Saint Peter, 'The righteous scarcely be saved, and that God spared not his angels',‡ where shall those appear who having served their appetites all their lives, presume to think that the severe commandments of the All-powerful God were given but in sport; and that the short breath which we draw when death presseth us, if we can but fashion it to the sound of 'Mercy!' (without any kind of satisfaction or amends) is sufficient? 'Oh how many', saith a reverend Father, 'descend to eternal torments and sorrows with this hope!'§

[*Raleigh expatiates upon the folly of deathbed repentances and the instability of all earthly hopes.*]

For myself, this is my consolation, and all that I can offer to others, that the sorrows of this life are but of two sorts; whereof the one hath respect to God, the other to the world. In the first we complain to God against ourselves for our offences against Him, and confess, 'And Thou, O Lord, art just in all that hath befallen us.'|| In the second we complain to ourselves against God; as if He had done us wrong, either in not giving us worldly goods and honours answering our appetites; or for taking them again from us, having had them; forgetting that humble and just acknowledgement of

merchandize their faith: sell their loyalty to the highest bidder.

† Galatians, ch. vi, v. 7. ‡ I, Peter ch. iv, v. 18.

§ O quam multi cum hac spe ad eternos labores et bella descendunt.

|| Et tu justus es in omnibus quae venerunt super nos.

Job, 'The Lord hath given, and the Lord hath taken.'† To the first of which Saint Paul hath promised blessedness, to the second death. And out of doubt he is either a fool or ungrateful to God, or both, that doth not acknowledge, how mean soever his estate be, that the same is yet far greater than that which God oweth him; or doth not acknowledge, how sharp soever his afflictions be, that the same are yet far less than those which are due unto him. And if an heathen wise man call the adversities of the world but 'the tributes of living',‡ a wise Christian man ought to know them and bear them, but as the tributes of offending. He ought to bear them manlike and resolvedly, not as those whining soldiers do '*who follow their General murmuring*'.§

For seeing God, who is the author of all our tragedies, hath written one for us and appointed us all the parts we are to play; and hath not in their distribution been partial to the most mighty princes of the world; that gave unto Darius* the part of the greatest emperor and the part of the most miserable beggar, a beggar begging water of an enemy to quench the great drought of death; that appointed Bajazeth* to play the Grand Signior of the Turks in the morning, and in the same day the footstool of Tamerlane (both which parts Valerian* had also played, being taken by Sapores); that made Belisarius* play the most victorious captain and lastly the part of a blind beggar; of which examples many thousands may be produced—why should other men, who are but as* the least worms, complain of wrongs?

Certainly there is no other account to be made of this ridiculous world than to resolve that the change of fortune on the great theatre is but as the change of garments on the less. For when, on the one and the other, every man wears but his own skin, the players are all alike. Now if any man out of weakness prize the passages of this world otherwise, for (saith Petrarch*), '*It is an exceptional gift to be able to*

† Job, ch. i, v. 21.
‡ Tributa vivendi. Seneca, *De remediis fortuitorum*, xvi, 10.
§ qui gementes sequuntur imperatorem.

withdraw the mind from the world of sense',† it is by reason of that unhappy fantasy of ours, which forgeth in the brains of man all the miseries (the corporal excepted) whereunto he is subject. Therein it is that misfortune and adversity work all that they work. For seeing Death, in the end of the play, takes from all whatsoever fortune or force takes from anyone; it were a foolish madness in the shipwreck of worldly things, where all sinks but the sorrow, to save it. That were, as Seneca saith, 'to fall under fortune, of all other the most miserable destiny'.‡

But it is now time to sound a retreat, and to desire to be excused of this long pursuit; and withal, that the good intent which hath moved me to draw the picture of time past (which we call history) in so large a table, may also be accepted in place of a better reason.

[*Raleigh goes on to explain why he began with Creation, since Creation implies Providence, his main subject. He then embarks upon a long and interesting discussion, scientific and theological, of the nature of God and the world.*

Thereafter he explains something of the plan of the work and admits that he has had the help of friends.]

I know that it will be said by many that I might have been more pleasing to the reader if I had written the story of mine own times, having been permitted to draw water as near the well-head as another. To this I answer, that whosoever in writing a modern history shall follow truth too near the heels, it may happily strike out his teeth. There is no mistress or guide that hath led her followers and servants into greater miseries. He that goes after her too far off loseth her sight and loseth himself; and he that walks after her at a middle distance, I know not whether I should call that kind of course temper or baseness. It is true that I never travailed after men's opinions when I might have made the best use of them; and I have now too few days remaining to

happily: by chance. *temper*: moderation.

† Magni ingenii est revocare mentem a sensibus.

‡ Fortunae succumbere, quod tristius est omni fato.

imitate those that either out of extreme ambition or extreme cowardice or both, do yet (when Death hath them on his shoulders) flatter the world between the bed and the grave. It is enough for me (being in that state I am) to write of the eldest times; wherein also why may it not be said that in speaking of the past I point at the present and tax the vices of those that are yet living, in their persons that are long since dead? And have it laid to my charge? But this I cannot help, though innocent. And certainly if there be any, that finding themselves spotted like the tigers of old time, shall find fault with me for painting them over anew, they shall therein accuse themselves justly and me falsely.

For I protest before the Majesty of God that I malice no man under the sun. Impossible I know it is to please all; seeing few or none are so pleased with themselves or so assured of themselves, by reason of their subjection to their private passions, but that they seem diverse persons in one and the same day. Seneca hath said it, and so do I, '*One is to me instead of all*',† and to the same effect Epicurus, '*I mean this for you and not for the crowd*';‡ or (as it hath since lamentably fallen out) I may borrow the resolution of an ancient philosopher, '*One is enough, none is enough*'.§ For it was for the service of that inestimable Prince Henry, the successive hope and one of the greatest of the Christian world, that I undertook this work. It pleased him to peruse some part thereof and to pardon what was amiss. It is now left to the world without a master, from which all that is presented hath received both blows and thanks. '*For we approve and reprehend the same things. And this is the end of every judgement, when the controversy is committed to many*'.||

But these discourses are idle. I know that as the charitable will judge charitably; so against those '*who delight in malice*'¶

† Unus mihi pro populo erat.
‡ Hoc ego non multis sed tibi.
§ Satis est unus, satis est nullus.
|| Eadem probamus, eadem reprehendemus: hic exitus est omnis iudicii. in quo lis secundum plures datur.
¶ qui gloriantur in malitia.

my present adversity hath disarmed me. I am on the ground already, and therefore have not far to fall. And for rising again, as in the natural privation* there is no recession to habit, so is it seldom seen in the privation politic. I do therefore forbear to style my readers 'gentle', 'courteous' and 'friendly', thereby to beg their good opinions, or to promise a second and third volume (which I also intend) if the first receive grace and good acceptance. For that which is already done may be thought enough—and too much. And it is certain, let us claw the reader with never so many courteous phrases, yet shall we evermore be thought fools, that write foolishly. For conclusion; all the hope I have lies in this, that I have already found more ungentle and uncourteous readers of my love towards them, and well-deserving of them, than ever I shall do again. For had it been otherwise, I should hardly have had this leisure to have made myself a fool in print.

THE CONCLUSION OF THE WORK

By this which we have already set down is seen the beginning and end of the three first monarchies of the world; whereof the founders and erectors thought that they could never have ended. That of Rome, which made the fourth, was also at this time almost at the highest. We have left it flourishing in the middle of the field; having rooted up or cut down all that kept it from the eyes and admiration of the world. But after some continuance, it shall begin to lose the beauty it had. The storms of ambition shall beat her great boughs and branches one against another. Her leaves shall fall off, her limbs wither, and a rabble of barbarous nations enter the field and cut her down.

Now these great kings and conquering nations have been

claw: flatter.

the subject of those ancient histories which have been preserved and yet remain among us; and withal of so many tragical poets as in the persons of powerful princes and other mighty men have complained against infidelity, time, destiny, and most of all against the variable success of worldly things and instability of fortune. To these undertakings the greatest lords of the world have been stirred up rather by the desire of fame, which plougheth up the air and soweth in the wind, than by the affection of bearing rule, which draweth after it so much vexation and so many cares. And that this is true, the good advice of Cineas* to Pyrrhus proves. And certainly, as fame hath often been dangerous to the living, so is it to the dead of no use at all, because separate from knowledge. Which were it otherwise, and the extreme ill bargain of buying this lasting discourse understood by them which are dissolved, they themselves would then rather have wished to have stolen out of the world without noise, than to be put in mind that they have purchased the report of their actions in the world by rapine, oppression, and cruelty, by giving in spoil the innocent and labouring soul to the idle and insolent, and by having emptied the cities of the world of their ancient inhabitants and filled them again with so many and so variable sorts of sorrows.

Since the fall of the Roman Empire (omitting that of the Germans, which had neither greatness nor continuance) there hath been no state fearful in the East but that of the Turk. Nor in the West any prince that hath spread his wings far over his nest but the Spaniard, who since the time that Ferdinand expelled the Moors* out of Granada have made many attempts to make themselves masters of all Europe. And it is true, that by the treasures of both Indies and by the many kingdoms which they possess in Europe, they are at this day the most powerful. But as the Turk is now counterpoised by the Persian, so instead of so many millions as have been spent by the English, French, and Netherlands in a defensive war, and in diversions against them, it is easy to demonstrate that with the charge of two hundred thousand pound* continued but for two years or three at the most, they may not only be persuaded to live in peace, but all their swelling and overflowing streams may be brought back into their natural channels and old banks. These two nations, I say, are at this day the most eminent and to be regarded; the one seeking to root out the Christian religion altogether, the other the truth and sincere profession thereof, the one to join all Europe to Asia, the other the rest of all Europe to Spain.

For the rest, if we seek a reason of the succession and continuance of this boundless ambition in mortal men, we may add to that which hath been already said, that the kings and princes of the world have always laid before them the actions, but not the ends, of those great ones which preceded them. They are always transported with the glory of the one, but they never mind the misery of the other till they find the experience in themselves. They neglect the advice of God while they enjoy life or hope it; but they follow the counsel of Death upon his first approach.

It is he that puts into man all the wisdom of the world, without speaking a word; which God with all the words of His law, promises, or threats doth not infuse. Death which hateth and destroyeth man, is believed; God, which hath made him and loves him, is always deferred. 'I have considered', saith Solomon, 'all the works that are under the sun, and behold, all is vanity and vexation of spirit.'† But who believes it, till Death tells it us?* . . .

It is therefore Death alone that can suddenly make man to know himself. He tells the proud and insolent that they are but abjects, and humbles them at the instant; makes them cry, complain, and repent, yea, even to hate their forepassed happiness. He takes the account of the rich, and proves him a beggar—a naked beggar, which hath interest in nothing but in the gravel that fills his mouth. He holds a glass before

interest: a share in.

† Ecclesiastes, ch. i, v. 14.

the eyes of the most beautiful, and makes them see therein their deformity and rottenness; and they acknowledge it.

O eloquent, just and mighty Death! Whom none could advise, thou hast persuaded; what none hath dared, thou hast done; and whom all the world hath flattered, thou only hast cast out of the world and despised. Thou hast drawn together all the far-stretched greatness, all the pride, cruelty, and ambition of man, and covered it all over with these two narrow words—*Hic Jacet.*

Lastly, whereas this book, by the title it hath, calls itself *The First Part of the General History of the World*, implying a second and third volume; which I also intended and have hewn out; besides many other discouragements persuading my silence, it hath pleased God to take that glorious Prince out of the world to whom they were directed; whose unspeakable and never enough lamented loss hath taught me to say with Job, '*My harp also is turned to mourning, and my organ into the voice of them that weep.*'†

Hic Jacet: 'Here lies . . . .'

† Versa est in luctum cithara mea, et organum meum in vocem flentium. Job, ch. xx, v. 31.

NOTES

POEMS

1. **Sweet were the sauce** (p. 29). From Gascoigne's *Steel Glass*, 1576.

George Gascoigne was a soldier-poet of the 1570's, whose motto *Tam Marti quam Mercurio* pleased Raleigh so much that he adopted it as his own. *The Steel Glass* is a verse satire in which Gascoigne claims to hold up a mirror to the times and to show people their true likenesses. The cheaper kind of mirror in the sixteenth century was made of highly polished steel. Gascoigne draws a distinction between old-fashioned steel, trusty and true, and

> The crystal glass, which glimseth brave and bright
> And shows the thing much better than it is.

Raleigh, who is in his early twenties, assumes a rather blustering tone in defence of Gascoigne, whose unflattering likenesses are not going to make him popular; but one feels that the aggression is as much part of Raleigh's nature as of this particular occasion. Gascoigne seems to have had a stormy career and to have made enemies, but the details of his troubles are obscure.

The heavy pauses, marked in the original by a comma within every line, are typical of verse in the seventies, as is the equally heavy alliteration.

2. **Methought I saw** (p. 30). From Spenser's *Faerie Queene*, 1590.

Raleigh's good offices on Spenser's behalf are set out in the General Introduction, pp. 11, 12. Among many complimentary sonnets to patrons which Spenser prefixed to *The Faerie Queene* there is one to Raleigh, hailing him as 'the summer's nightingale Thy sovereign goddess's most dear delight'. He also printed a long letter addressed to Raleigh in which he clarifies his purpose in the poem. Since it was designed to be in twelve books, and in 1590 only the first three were published, it does not fully explain itself.

Spenser was nothing if not loyal to his friends, and his feelings about them tend to be reflected in his poem, which like Raleigh's

Cynthia but in a much more public and publishable way, glorifies England's Queen. The squire Timias, who falls hopelessly in love with the maiden-huntress Belphoebe, is in something like Raleigh's situation. His love can be no more than faithful service, since his rank is as yet lowly, and Belphoebe is a foster-child of Diana, dedicated to virginity and proudly self-sufficient. She is however deeply hurt when her squire turns momentarily aside from her to succour a distressed lady, and she rejects him as false to her.

> Is this the faith? she said, and said no more,
> But turned her face, and fled away for evermore.

In Book IV Canto 8, Spenser contrives a happy reunion, after devoting many stanzas to the despair of Timias. There also seems to be an allusion to Raleigh's marriage in Book VI, where the power of slander and evil tongues is embodied in a monster called the Blatant Beast, which wounds guiltless knights and ladies. An account of Spenser's own relationship with Raleigh appears, under a light disguise, in *Colin Clout's Come Home Again.*

In his sonnet Raleigh compliments Spenser by declaring that he has surpassed Petrarch, the most admired love-poet of the Renaissance, and has made even Homer uneasy. Petrarch's sonnets to Laura were the model for the sonnets of Italian, French and English poets.

2. *vestal flame.* In ancient Rome the symbolic flame in the Temple of Vesta, goddess of hearthfire and home, was kept perpetually alight by her priestesses, the Vestal Virgins. Raleigh describes Petrarch's love for Laura as a vestal flame because it was chaste and undying. He uses a similar image in *Cynthia*, I.

8. *those graces*: fair love and fairer virtue.

3. **If all the world and love were young** (p. 31). From *England's Helicon*, 1603.

This poem is written in answer to, and consequently is to some extent modelled upon, some well-known verses by Marlowe. The parallels and contrasts would be difficult to enjoy without Marlowe's poem for comparison. It is therefore printed, from the same source. The shepherd's charming and fantastic gifts are Marlowe's invention, not Raleigh's. Raleigh takes the more cynical, or at any rate more realistic point of view, and thereby transposes Marlowe's major into a minor key.

4. **Praised be Diana** (p. 32). From *The Phoenix Nest*, 1593.

In this sonnet Raleigh is making the most of his identification of Queen Elizabeth with the moon-goddess, here given her familiar name of Diana. In his long poem he calls her Cynthia, which is an alternative name for the goddess, from her birthplace, Mount Cynthus. The moon is feminine, in contrast to the masculine sun, the usual emblem of royalty. She is sole queen of the heavens when she appears. She is a maiden goddess and Raleigh praises her purity. He stresses her 'harmless light', as opposed to the fierce and hurtful power of the sun, and he contrives to associate her with fertility in that the moon was thought to be the cause of dew. Raleigh is speaking as a poet and not as a scientist, but he is using some scientific theories of the time to construct this curious poem. The one which serves him best is the belief he borrows from the orthodox Ptolemaic astronomy of his day, that whereas everything below the sphere of the moon is corrupt and subject to decay, everything above is pure and immortal. Hence 'mortality below her orb is placed'. Since the sphere of the moon is the closest to the earth, any heavenly 'influences' must pass through it before they reach the earth. It is possible that 'In aye she mistress-like makes all things pure' refers less to time than to the eternal regions she inhabits. The fact that the moon continually changes and continually renews herself makes her in another way an immortality emblem. The division of time by lunar months constitutes her 'guide' of 'time's chariot'.

The power of the moon to influence the tides is another image very much to Raleigh's purpose. It is not exploited fully here, but it is plainly the reason why his long poem was called *The Book of the Ocean to Cynthia*. In *Colin Clout's Come Home Again* Spenser refers to Raleigh as 'The Shepherd of the Ocean'. He had to be a shepherd because it was essentially a pastoral poem. The Queen, an inveterate nicknamer, called him quite simply 'Water', playing on his baptismal name, and perhaps on his passion for the sea and ships. The use of Circe, in the last line, as a type of sensual and deceitful love follows a common enough custom, but Raleigh intent upon his moon imagery may have remembered that the enchantress who turned Ulysses's wayweary men into swine was the daughter of the Sun.

5. **Like to a hermit poor** (p. 33). From *The Phoenix Nest*, 1593.

Set to music, this poem became very popular. It is a free translation of a sonnet by Phillipe Desportes. It affords a good example of what the Elizabethans meant by a poetical conceit. There is not just a momentary comparison of a disappointed lover to a hermit renouncing the world, but an elaboration of the idea throughout a complete sonnet, making point after point of contact after the initial parallel has been stated. It is interesting to note that to Raleigh the whole of Spenser's *Faerie Queene* was a conceit.

6. **Like truthless dreams** (p. 34). From *The Phoenix Nest*, 1593.

This poem is strikingly like the extant stanzas of *Cynthia.*

7. **Feed still thyself** (p. 34). From *The Phoenix Nest*, 1593.

This poem and the five that follow it, numbers 7–12, are given to Raleigh upon the assumption that there is a 'Raleigh group' among the poems in *The Phoenix Nest.* That the editor of the anthology tended to group together poems by one author is testified by those which show an author's initials. A few poems elsewhere ascribed to Raleigh, e.g. 5 and 6, help to establish the group. In style and temper the poems resemble his known work. The subject, though it is generally the common one of a hopeless love for a superlative lady, is strikingly appropriate to Raleigh and the Queen. See especially 9–11.

8. **My first born love** (p. 35). From *The Phoenix Nest*, 1593.

The poet is here perhaps experimenting with a classical metre. The last stanza seems hardly a statement Raleigh would dare to make to the Queen. It is the conventional curse of the lover who is scorned.

9. **Those eyes which set my fancy** (p. 36). From *The Phoenix Nest*, 1593.

This poem affords a good example of the rhetorical ordering of material. Cp. 3 and 11.

10. **A secret murder** (p. 37). From *The Phoenix Nest*, 1593.

Raleigh must have congratulated himself here upon the ingenuity of his conceit. The point of the last line is that the wounds of a dead man were popularly supposed to bleed afresh in the presence of the murderer, an idea which is deftly associated with the metaphorical wounds of the faithful lover bleeding in the presence of his mistress.

11. **Sought by the world** (p. 37). From *The Phoenix Nest*, 1593.

10. *Envy herself shall swim*: the spirit of rivalry will give way to pity and admiration.

12. **What else is hell** (p. 38). From *The Phoenix Nest*, 1593.

8. *To strive against earth, water, fire and air*. Since these are the four basic elements of which, according to the science of the day, the whole world was compounded, Raleigh is pursuing his love in defiance of the very nature of things.

13. **My body in the walls captived** (p. 39). From the autograph manuscript at Hatfield House.

This sonnet clearly refers to Raleigh's spell in the Tower in 1592. It is the opposite of the poetical conceit in which the writer is literally imprisoned but rejoices in the freedom of his mind. e.g. Lovelace's 'Stone walls do not a prison make'. Raleigh laments that his mind, fettered by an unhappy love, is an even worse prison.

14. **Sufficeth it to you, my joys interred** (p. 39). From the autograph manuscript at Hatfield House.

It is difficult to follow the thought of this poem, in which ideas pour out pell-mell, and sentences start which do not always finish. This is not really like Raleigh, who tends to write in a particularly orderly way, obscure only because he is so very concise. (See for instance *Conceit begotten by the Eyes*, 17, and *The Lie*, 19.) The disorder of *Cynthia* may be intentional, to indicate his desperation. The poem is copied in a neat hand, with no division into stanzas. It is clearly not a first draft.

One source of confusion lies in the fact that it refers to times past, with shared memories which need not be explained to the person for whom it is written, and perhaps to shared images and emblems from the earlier *Cynthia*. It has survived only by chance and illustrates very clearly the private and personal nature of much of Raleigh's verse. It was intended for an audience of one. Elizabeth had a taste for elaborately enigmatic writing. Her own letters are both flowery and tortuous. The metaphorical way in which Raleigh writes, however, seems to be natural to him. It can be paralleled in those passages in the Preface to *The Discovery of Guiana*, in which he alludes to his marriage and disgrace, and in the Preface to *The History of the World*. Unlike the proliferating and intertwining metaphors, many of them of archetypal simplicity (dead joys, fallen flowers, sunless days, changing seasons, wounds and flames of love), his similes are precise, clear, and very individual. Set similes were one of the rhetorical conventions of the Renaissance, and Raleigh's use of the lamb lately weaned, the body violently slain, the idly-turning water wheel is not perhaps any more unexpected than some of Shakespeare's similes in *Venus and Adonis*.

The poem ebbs and flows perpetually, as the author describes past joy and present despair, the impossibility of a love such as his decaying, and the inescapable fact that on one side, at any rate, it has decayed.

The parallel with what had actually happened is at times so close that the reader may not realize that what he is getting is at two removes. The personal situation, between a man and a woman, an ambitious, pushing, middle-aged man and a resentful, ageing, self-willed woman, is first transformed into wider terms, which are not untrue—of happiness, once enjoyed, now lost; hopes once lively, now dashed; long efforts come to nothing, and rich rewards still available to others but no longer to the writer. What Raleigh faced in 1592 was—momentarily at least—the ruin of a great and promising career. 'Of great erections such the sudden fall'. His emotion, extreme as it is in *Cynthia*, could hardly be in excess of cause. This genuine passion of loss, he then restates in the conventional terms of faithful lover and cruel lady. It had become a convention precisely because it was so effective a way of commenting upon what happens in life. Its essence is unattained and unattainable desire, and that covers a great deal more than what happened to Sir Walter Raleigh in 1592.

The division here into stanzas (which the rhyme controls) and into short numbered passages, has been introduced for the reader's convenience. Whereas poems which Raleigh intended to be complete in themselves build up to a bold climax, these fragments are noticeably inconclusive, and reflect the fluid nature of the poem. Parts i and ii are consecutive in the manuscript. Between ii and iii seventeen stanzas are omitted, between iii and iv twelve stanzas, between iv and v thirty-four, and between v and vi five.

the Ocean to Cynthia: the beloved is Cynthia, Diana, Belphoebe, the maiden moon-goddess, with the moon's power to sway the tides of ocean.

5. *If to the living*. There is no implication here that the Queen is dead. Raleigh is addressing his 'joys interred'.

17. *those high-flowing streams*: of the Queen's favour.

28. *Philomen*. However sadly the nightingale sang, it implied a love-relationship, which now no longer exists.

29. *No feeding flocks*. It is not clear what the pastoral allusions mean in the existing fragment. The earlier *Cynthia* may well have been pastoral in form, and it is significant that the present poem reverts to pastoral imagery at the conclusion. The pastoral was a way of veiling feelings and situations which could not be literally stated. In its world of shepherds, nymphs and goddesses the poet could give his imagination rein.

41. *my fancy's adamant*: drawing it, as adamant draws iron.

45–6. *my Muse Gathered those flowers*: his earlier poems, well received by the Queen.

61. *To seek new worlds*. This could refer to the many occasions when Raleigh planned voyages and was not allowed to sail. In particular it seems to apply to the voyage of 1592, upon which he actually set out. It was something rather more specific than the Queen's memory that brought him back.

101. *by such a parting light*. It is odd that Raleigh should mention writing a history of the world. The general intention of the image is to express the plight of a person undertaking an impossibly long and difficult task in an impossibly short and unpropitious time. The task is to retell the whole story of his love.

146. *The tokens hung on breast*. We have no record of the tokens Raleigh gave Elizabeth, but they would be such jewelled pendants as she herself gave to favoured servants, such as the 'anchor guided by a lady' that she gave to Sir Humphrey Gilbert, setting out on his last voyage, and the pendant containing her picture with which she honoured Drake after he had sailed round the world.

154. *Belphoebe*. This is the name of the nymph who in Spenser's *Faerie Queene* is loved by the squire Timias, an allegorical picture of Raleigh and Elizabeth. Whether Spenser took the name from

Raleigh, or Raleigh from Spenser, it is hard to say. Phoebe was a name for Diana, as sister of Phoebus, the sun.

15. **My day's delights** (p. 48). From the autograph manuscript at Hatfield House.

Many years later, Raleigh remade these plaintive verses into an address to Jame's Queen, Anne of Denmark. After the last stanza, there is the beginning of one to follow, 'For tender stalks . . .', which breaks off abruptly.

20. *unburied bones.* There were plenty of these in Ireland, where Sir Henry Sidney wrote to the Queen 'such horrible and lamentable spectacles there are to behold as . . . the view of the bones and skulls of your dead subjects, who partly by murder, partly by famine, have died in the fields.'

16. **As you came from the holy land** (p. 49). From a commonplace book in the Bodleian Library, MS Rawlinson Poetry 85.

This graceful poem is modelled on the popular ballads concerned with a pilgrimage to the shrine of Our Lady of Walsingham. Ophelia sings a snatch of one.

> How should I your true love know
>   From another one?
> By his cockle hat and staff
>   And his sandal shoon.

It repeats some of the imagery and some of the sentiments of *Cynthia.*

9. *She is neither white nor brown.* This presumably distinguishes golden hair (Elizabeth's was red-gold) from flaxen and brown.

17. **Conceit begotten by the eyes** (p. 51). From Davison's *Poetical Rhapsody*, 1602.

Raleigh here treats in a very incisive and haunting way a favourite theme, the distinction between a shallow, sensual love and 'a passion of the mind'.

18. **Nature that washt her hands in milk** (p. 52). From MS Harleian 6917, in the British Museum.

Here we are dealing with a poem Raleigh could not have meant for the Queen. The descriptions are too sensuous, and the theme of time destroying love and beauty would have been far from congenial. It is not really a love poem at all, but a lament for the inevitable passing of life and joy. That is why, in 1618, he could pick up the last stanza and remake it as his farewell to the world.

19. **Go soul, the body's guest** (p. 53). From Davison's *Poetical Rhapsody*, 1611.

There are several claimants for this poem, Raleigh coming high among them. Its bold and wholesale condemnation of an unworthy world, which may well reproduce a mood of his, seems to have evoked a slightly shocked response. There are some doggerel answers, one at least directed to him as the supposed author.

> Go, echo of the mind,
> A careless troth protest,
> Make answer that rude Rawly
> No stomach can digest.

(MS Chetham 8012, in Chetham's Hospital, Manchester.)

It was current long before the treason trial of 1603, and is perhaps connected with Raleigh's unpopularity as the rival of Essex. 'To give the lie' was a final insult, which could be wiped out only in blood.

8. *rotten wood.* It is a property of wood in a particular state of decay to become phosphorescent.

16. *affection.* Some texts read 'a faction', which gives a perfect rhyme and an obvious sense. There are, however, places where Raleigh uses 'affection' in an uncomplimentary way. In *The Discovery of Guiana* it means a political alliance, and at one point he says 'it is to be doubted how those that in time of victory *seem to affect* their neighbour nations, will remain after the first view of misfortune and ill success'.

25. *them that brave it most.* Raleigh should know about this, for his extravagance in dress was notorious. 'To brave it' is to show off, particularly in dress and personal adornment. The courtiers make themselves splendid in order to catch the prince's eye and win his favour, hence they 'beg for more by spending'.

50. *prevention.* The meaning is not clear. Some late texts read 'pretention', which makes obvious sense.

74. *done blabbing*. To blab is to blurt out secrets, to give the show away.

20. **What is our life** (p. 56). From Orlando Gibbons's *First Set of Madrigals and Mottets*, 1612.

The popularity of this short piece may be because the idea was not at the time a hackneyed one. Theatres were new and very fashionable.

2. *music of division*: long notes divided into many shorter ones, in order to elaborate and diversify a melody.

3. *tiring houses*: dressing rooms.

4. *Comedy*. Many texts read 'Tragedy'.

8. *drawn curtains*. This is a curious comment in view of the fact that contemporary stages had no front curtains.

21. **Give me my scallop-shell of quiet** (p. 56). From *Daiphantus, or The Passions of Love*, 1604.

Raleigh's poem, if it is his, seems to have been added as a make-weight to this little book. The text is better than that which appeared as his in *Sir Walter Raleigh's Sceptick*, 1651. It is an extraordinary piece of work, and if he did in fact write it at the point of death (that would be some time in 1603, when the death sentence was deliberately kept hanging over him till the last possible moment) it may well be explained as the result of psychological shock. An Elizabethan poet did not normally abandon himself to whatever images and rhythms slid into his mind. The powerful drive of the poem overcomes what might seem odd and grotesque about it, though some anthologists prefer to print only the first six lines.

Philip Edwards doubts whether the piece is Raleigh's at all, finding the dominant religious imagery uncharacteristic. Yet a man facing death might well choose to meditate upon Christ's atonement and his hopes of salvation. The lines which conclude *Even such is Time* reflect a similar concern, with a greater detachment. The prospect of death in 1618 cannot have affected Raleigh quite as the sentence of 1603 did, for it did not come out of a clear sky, but was the culmination of many unhappy years and ominous events.

1. *Give me my scallop-shell etc.* A pilgrim was traditionally equipped for wayfaring with a coarse gown, a staff, a wallet (scrip) for food and a drinking-bottle. The scallop shell, the sign that the wearer

had reached the renowned shrine of St James of Compostella on the Spanish coast, later became a common emblem of the dedicated pilgrim.

7. *Blood must be my body's balmer*: man gains eternal life through the blood of Christ shed for us on the cross. 'Balm' seems to have several associations here, which is typical of how this poem works: (i) 'embalming' as a means of preserving a body and thus in a sense conferring everlasting life (ii) a ritual anointing, the due preparation for leaving this world (iii) a medicinal 'balm' used to soothe the aching of weary limbs.

35. *heaven's bribeless hall.* What follows is a general arraignment of faulty human justice, with a particular stress upon mercenary lawyers. This does not seem a very apt comment upon Raleigh's own case, as victim of a politically rigged trial and of the treachery of friends. However badly the prosecution treated him, nobody has ever thought it was in response to 'bribed palms'. It is possible however that an angry sense of political blackmail may have expressed itself in this impersonal and conventional way. The absence of any reference to false friends, Raleigh's constant complaint, is perhaps the more surprising. How, when he had once let himself go, as he does in this poem, did he keep it out?

44. *our sins and sinful fury.* Some texts read 'with sinful fury' which shows that as it stands the phrase presents some difficulty, though the emendation hardly improves it. 'Fury' is a word often used as equivalent to 'madness' and implies perhaps the violent, passionate and unthinking way in which we live our lives. Cp. Sir Thomas Browne who says in *Religio Medici* (Part II, section vii), that having repented and been absolved at the last, 'therefore [I] am not terrified with the sins or madness of my youth'.

22. **Cowards fear to die** (p. 58). From *Sir Walter Raleigh's Sceptick*, 1651.

23. **Even such is time** (p. 59). From a manuscript in the Bibliothèque Nationale, Paris, Cinque Cents de Colbert 467.

These lines were much admired and endlessly copied, in sympathy for Raleigh, outrage at his death, and in the romantic belief that he composed the poem the night before he was beheaded. They do not become any less interesting when we see their original setting, as the last stanza of 'Nature that washt her hands in milk'.

The documents in the Bibliothèque Nationale have some official authority. They were sent to the French government by the English government as part of an official enquiry into Raleigh's last-minute attempt to escape to France. The text is good and may well be a direct transcript from the original, assuming that any papers Raleigh left were sifted by security agents. The story runs that he wrote them upon a fly-leaf of his Bible. After hearing his sentence in Westminster Hall he was removed to the Abbey Gatehouse, which was in use as a convenient prison. He was beheaded in Parliament Square.

THE LAST FIGHT OF THE REVENGE

p. 72. *the year 1588.* Raleigh gives a succinct account of the fate of the Great Armada, including the famous fireships, 'squibs' as he contemptuously calls them, with which the Spaniards were driven in confusion from their anchorage off Calais.

p. 73. *Sir Francis Drake.* In 1585 King Philip invited English merchants to bring corn into Spain, promising them safe-conduct, but he broke his word and seized their ships to supply his Great Armada, then in preparation. The Queen retorted by sending Drake to raid the West Indies. He took Santiago in the Cape Verde Islands, San Domingo in Hispaniola, Cartagena, capital of the Spanish mainland, and St Augustine in Florida. Sickness among his crews prevented him from attempting Havana and Panama. After that there could be no doubt that England and Spain were at war.

p. 74. *Sir John Norris.* This expedition of 1589, in which Sir John Norris commanded the land-forces and Sir Francis Drake the fleet, was intended as a retort to the Great Armada and suffered the usual fate of a divided command under Elizabeth. It was only a qualified success. Drake attacked the remnants of the Spanish fleet in harbour at Corunna, but this meant that any further attacks had lost the advantage of surprise. There was much sickness among the men. The two forces failed to synchronize in the attack on Lisbon and the lack of guns equal to siege operations, the 'provision to batter' to which Raleigh alludes, made this particular proceeding pointless. The Portuguese, who had been under Spanish rule since 1580, when Philip II claimed and seized the throne, and whom Raleigh represents as groaning under the yoke, were supposed to rise in favour of the pretender, Don Antonio, but this was just another of the things that failed to happen according to plan.

p. 74. *the Brazil fleet.* With the union of the crowns of Spain and Portugal, Brazil was added to Spain's overseas empire.

p. 74. *the Bark Ralegh*: a small vessel built by Sir Walter when he hoped to go with Sir Humphrey Gilbert in 1583 in search of the North West Passage. The Queen kept Raleigh at home and his ship turned back on the second day out, pleading a serious epidemic aboard.

p. 75. *a bark of Sir George Carey's.* Sir George was Marshal of the Household and Captain of the Isle of Wight.

p. 75. *shrouded their approach*: i.e. they came in from the west, which lends a little colour to Monson's statement that Grenville took them for the West Indian fleet.

p. 76. *Bertendona.* Martin de Bertendona had fought with the Great Armada, and had had to burn his ship when Drake raided Corunna in 1589, so he had old scores to pay. It was not uncommon for the Spaniards to burn their ships rather than surrender. Raleigh had the last word, when he led the English fleet into Cadiz harbour in 1596, and forced the San Philip to beach and burn herself. 'The St. Philip', he writes, in his account of the action, 'the great and famous Admiral of Spain was the mark I shot at . . . being resolved to be revenged for the Revenge or to second her with my own life'.

p. 78. *Sir Francis Godolphin*: a Cornishman, Governor of the isles of Scilly, knighted in 1580.

p. 78. *Master William Killigrew*: another Cornishman, Groom of the Privy Chamber, which was the Queen's household establishment, and steward of the Stannary Court, knighted in 1603. His friendship with Raleigh was lasting, since his son visited him in the Tower in 1613, and was himself arrested for speaking to another friend on the way out.

p. 80. *Don Alonso Bazan*: brother of the great Spanish Admiral, Santa Cruz, who had died in the Armada year.

p. 83. *Master Watts.* Alderman Watts was a city merchant and a great adventurer by sea. Between April and September 1591 he had five ships out, bound amongst other things to the assistance of Raleigh's Virginia colony. They failed to find the colonists, but they took five prizes, laden with bullion, plate, cochineal, ginger, sugar and hides. Watts, in his statement of accounts (MS Lansdowne 67), valued them at £31,380, a very large sum in the currency of the time. Out of that he had to pay a third for the seamen's shares, something to the Queen's Customs and something to the Lord Admiral, as well as defraying the initial expenses of fitting out and provisioning the ships.

p. 84. *Maurice Fitz John.* The Earls of Desmond were one of the great Anglo-Irish families, settled since Norman times. The Desmond Rebellion (1579–82) was sparked off by a Catholic enthusiast, James Fitzmaurice, and carried on by the Earl, partly to work off a grudge against the rival house of Ormonde, who held the Lord Lieutenancy of Munster. The Earl's brothers, John and James, joined Fitzmaurice with great promptitude, and Sir John led the rebel armies for a time between the death of Fitzmaurice and the accession of the Earl. They all, as Raleigh relates, came to miserable ends. He knew what he was talking about since he went to Munster in 1580 as a captain of foot soldiers. When the rebellion was quelled, the ravaged land was divided into 'seignories' and given to English landlords who undertook to settle English families and keep out the native Irish; an ill-judged policy, which sowed the seeds of fresh rebellion. Ireland was an open sore in the side of Elizabeth's England, liable both by geographical position and by religion to offer a strategic foothold to her enemies. The survivors of the Great Armada, however, did not find much mercy at the hands of the Irish. No English 'undertaker' was to have more than one seignory, but Raleigh had three and a half, in Cork and Waterford.

p. 84. *rich pay.* The first edition reads 'praie', which Hakluyt emends to 'pay'. It is not inconceivable that Raleigh's pen slipped and he did originally write 'prey'. There were a number of different ways in which seamen were paid, one being an agreed share of the profits.

p. 85. *runagate Jesuits.* Devoted Jesuit priests undertook the desperate mission of keeping the Catholic religion alive in England and Ireland. Because the Pope had absolved English Catholics from their allegiance to the Queen, they were, whether they would or no, a politically unreliable party in the state. It was for this, rather than for their religious beliefs and practices, that they suffered hardship.

p. 86. *Bartholomew de las Casas*: a Spanish priest who denounced the exploitation of the South American Indians in his *Brevissima Relacion de la Destruycion de las Indias*. See p. 93.

THE DISCOVERY OF GUIANA

p. 102. *Charles Howard*: Baron Howard of Effingham, in 1585 appointed Lord High Admiral. The kinship which Raleigh claims was not very close. His mother's sister had married into the family from which Howard's mother came.

p. 102. *Sir Robert Cecil*. He was the son of Elizabeth's Chancellor, Lord Burleigh. A man of considerable acumen, he slowly rose to great power but not to popularity. In 1596 he had been five years a Privy Councillor, a position which Raleigh never in his life obtained. At first the two were close friends, but towards the end of the Queen's reign a coldness grew between them and Raleigh ultimately came to think of Cecil as a secret and bitter enemy. Because of this friendship we have many of Raleigh's letters, and some of his verses, kept with the rest of the Cecil papers at Hatfield House, seat of the present Lord Salisbury. Cecil became Secretary of State in 1596, first Lord Salisbury in 1605, and Lord Treasurer in 1608. It is characteristic of him that we do not know what he adventured. He probably shared in Raleigh's ship. His privateering was always kept private. Howard comes out into the open as the owner of the Lion's Whelp.

p. 102. *malice and revenge*. This allusion, and much that follows, is to Raleigh's fall from favour upon the discovery of his secret marriage in 1592.

p. 104. *Pizzaro*. See introduction, p. 91.

p. 104. *my servant Jacob Whiddon*. We hear of Whiddon many times in command of Raleigh's privateers. He led a prospecting voyage to Guiana in 1594.

p. 104. *Captain Parker*: described by Hakluyt as Master William Parker of Plymouth, gentleman.

p. 104. *400 miles*. Schomburgk says not more than 250 miles, allowing for the winding of the river.

p. 105. *if they could not.* The copy-text reads *that if* but *that* is here omitted as syntactically superfluous.

p. 105. *taken by Captain Preston.* Captain Amyas Preston, with four ships, set off in Raleigh's company, but they parted en route. It may have been deliberate on Preston's part, bad weather conditions providing an easy excuse. When Preston finally arrived in the West Indies he took Coro and Santiago, on the coast of Venezuela, meeting little opposition.

Except here, Raleigh is significantly silent about his attempt on Cumaná, which he tried to sack on his way back from Guiana. Spanish accounts represent the attempt as a disastrous failure. Captain Calfield, Captain Thynne and John Grenville were killed. Raleigh put Berrio ashore in exchange for his own wounded. The transaction can have pleased neither. Berrio was delivered over to his enemy, Governor Vides, and Raleigh had to forgo the rich ransom he had been expecting. Spanish reports claim between seventy and eighty English dead, a figure undoubtedly exaggerated, but suggesting that losses were heavy. Lady Raleigh wrote to Cecil, announcing her husband's safe return, 'Sir, It is true, I thank the living God, Sir Walter is safely landed at Plymouth with as great honour as ever man can, but with little riches. . . . Many of his men slain. Himself well now.' If he had been ill, perhaps he was troubled in mind more than in body. Keymis reported in the following year that 'the Indians our friends did fear lest you with your company were all slain, and your ships sunk at Cumaná (for so the Spaniards noised it amongst them)'. The successful surprise attack on San Josef, the town Berrio had founded in Trinidad, is described in the course of Raleigh's narrative.

p. 105. *not so easily invaded.* The towns that Raleigh mentions here and hereafter are mostly in Venezuela and New Granada. He seems to be making a distinction between coast towns, not very rich and easily raided, and the many inland settlements in which the Spaniards were secure. They were not to be left long in peace if he had his way. One reason why Spanish settlements were concentrated inland was the unhealthiness of coastal districts.

p. 105. *Nuevo Reyno and Popayán.* The full-stop after Popayán in the copy-text is here replaced by a comma.

p. 106. *treatise of the West Indies.* A lost work.

p. 108. *situate in 8 degrees.* Actually 10 degrees north. Raleigh is consistently out in his reckoning.

p. 108. *your Lordship.* Raleigh presumably sent separate and perhaps slightly different accounts to Cecil and Howard, whose names he combines in his dedication, but not always in the text.

p. 108. *oysters . . . upon trees.* The trees were mangroves, growing below tide level, and thus quite able to support oysters.

p. 108. *Andrew Thevet*: a great writer of travels, went to Brazil in 1555, and published *Les Singularités de la France Antarctique* in 1558, and *La Cosmographie Universelle* in 1571. His scholarly conscience revolted at the idea of calling the New World the Indies, which it was not, and he preferred to call the great southern continent the Antarctic. His delightful books are liberally illustrated with pictures of strange flora and fauna, but there is not any representation of mangroves.

p. 108. *Pliny in . . . his* Natural History. Book XII, section 20, describes mangroves growing below tide-level in the Persian Gulf.

p. 108. *stone pitch.* Natural asphalt occurs near Tierra de Brea, still a major source of the world's supplies.

p. 109. *Mais, Cassavi.* Two major food products of these regions are maize and manioc. The Indians make cassava bread from manioc, a root which when processed we call tapioca.

p. 110. *those English . . . in Virginia.* Raleigh's second attempt to colonize Virginia, in 1587, ended in the loss of the whole party, perhaps at the hands of Indians. A company sent to relieve them in 1589 could learn nothing of their fate. Alderman Watts's ships looked for them in 1591 (see p. 217).

p. 112. *I set upon the Corp du Guard.* These must be the 'company of Spaniards who kept a guard' at Port of Spain, and may well have included those who were 'entertained kindly and feasted after our manner'. Spanish accounts say that the Governor sent a party in charge of his nephew, Don Rodrigo, to ask the English what they were doing on the island. When his men failed to return, he sent a second contingent. The English showed a flag of truce, protested that they meant no harm, laid on food and drink, and then slaughtered their guests while they were eating. Thereafter they fell without warning upon San Josef. The only part of this story which Raleigh omits is the cold-blooded treachery. He is careful however to supply some justification, enlarging on the treachery of the Spaniards towards Whiddon's men in '94 and the maltreatment of the native caçiques, which suggests that there was something to justify. Even if Rodrigo and the Spanish soldiers were not actually butchered with the food still in their mouths, the slaughter as Raleigh relates it followed hard upon friendly overtures and pledges. He was naturally anxious to protect his rear. Berrio was expecting reinforcements from New Granada and from Spain.

p. 112. *Berrio and his companion.* Raleigh gives a good account further on of Don Antonio de Berrio, Governor of Trinidad. His companion was Alvaro Jorge, who survived to lead yet another expedition to Manoa. By that time old and sick, he died of the rigours of the journey, after which his men ran riot, alienated the Indians, and made no more progress towards their objective. The next year, 1597, Berrio died. Professor Harlow has written his epitaph. 'So ended the career of one who had devoted seventeen years of continuous hardship and disappointment to the pursuit of a delusion'.

p. 112. *Captain Keymis.* Lawrence Keymis, before he was thirty, had left a fellowship at Balliol to become Raleigh's right-hand man. He was in charge of the second Guiana expedition, in 1596, contributing an account to Hakluyt's *Voyages.* He divided his enthusiasm between his leader and his leader's cherished project. 'Myself, and the remain of my few years, I have bequeathed wholly to Raleana [his name for the Orinoco], and all my thoughts live only in that action.' In 1603 his known closeness to Raleigh led to his arrest as a possible witness against him, and Raleigh indignantly protested that his loyal henchman had been threatened with the rack in order to extract some damaging confession. Maybe he was better as a lieutenant than as a leader, for left in sole charge of the expedition up-river in 1617 he failed miserably, and took his own life on the voyage home; a man perhaps of too sanguine a temperament, as bad for Raleigh as Raleigh was for him.

p. 112. *my Indian interpreter.* It was a fine stroke on Raleigh's part to have Captain Whiddon bring home an Indian from his pioneering voyage to learn English. It had already been tried by the early settlers in Virginia.

p. 113. *my ships.* Raleigh had no more than three ships of any size, his own flagship, whose name curiously enough we do not know, the Lion's Whelp, and 'a small bark of Captain Cross's', also nameless. Those reports which say he had four ships are including the gallego, which seems to have been rather flimsy. Some responsible officer must have been left in charge of the ships, in which Berrio and Alvaro Jorge were kept under guard, but again no name has survived.

p. 114. *victuals being most fish.* In a manuscript work, which is sometimes attributed to Raleigh, called *Observations concerning the Royal Navy and Sea Service*, there is a selection of cold menus for seamen, appropriate to stormy weather and circumstances in which cooking is difficult. They include beer, biscuit, butter, cheese, pickled herrings, smoked herrings, dry sprats, oil, vinegar, mustard and onions. Fortunately for the health of the party, which was excellent, they were able to supplement their basic rations from the resources of the country.

p. 114. *the Emperor now reigning.* Raleigh speaks with such assurance of the Emperor of Guiana that it requires some effort to remember that he was as much a myth as his capital city of Manoa and that there *was* no empire. Rumours of an advanced civilization in Guiana related in fact to the Chibcha civilization in Colombia, out of which the Spaniards had already carved the New Kingdom of Granada.

p. 114. *Pedro de Cieza*: author of the *Cronica de Peru* (1553).

p. 114. *Francisco Lopez*: author of the *Cronica de Indias*, and *Historia de la Conquista de Nueva-Espania* (1552–3).

p. 115. *a lake of salt water*: quite imaginary.

p. 117. *Orellana.* Francisco de Orellana was the first to explore the Amazon, which was named after him the Orellana. The name that has lasted, however, is the one that he gave it after he had encountered women-warriors there. Raleigh calls it the River of Amazons, (which I have retained) or just Amazons, which I have emended to the more familiar Amazon.

p. 117. *Diego Ordaz*: went more than 1000 miles up the Orinoco in 1531.

p. 117. *Johannes Martines*: has been identified as Juan Martin de Albujar, who was captured and lived ten years with the Indians.

On his return he told a fascinating story about the golden city of Manoa.

p. 120. *Robert Dudley*: son of Lord Leicester and a great navigator. He was raiding in Trinidad and exploring the Orinoco a month or two before Raleigh arrived there. He wrote a rather charming account of his doings at Hakluyt's request.

p. 120. *large chart or map*. There is a map in the British Museum, MS Addit. 17940A, which marks some of the rivers explored by Keymis in '96. It was probably drawn by Thomas Hariot, when Raleigh was at Cadiz, 'out of some such of Sir Walter's notes and writings which he hath left behind him'. Facsimiles are to be found in the books by G. E. Hadow and V. T. Harlow.

p. 120. *from Virginia*. Presumably in 1586, when the first colonists, who went out in 1585, abandoned the attempt to settle and came home. Raleigh had sent two ships to prospect in '84.

p. 121. *those warlike women*. Raleigh had doubtless met with references to the Amazons in Greek and Latin historians, and was familiar with their alleged custom of mutilating the right breast so that it should not impede them when they drew back their bowstrings. On this occasion he did not trouble to check his reading. He simply takes over what Thevet has to say in *Singularités de la France Antarctique*, retaining even the name of the gorgon Medusa, who figures unexpectedly as an Amazon. He gives a much expanded account in *The History of the World* (Book IV, ch. ii, par. 15) from which it appears that his previous observations had been sceptically received. Orellana certainly encountered women-warriors, 'very white and tall, with very long hair twisted over their heads'. Seven or eight were killed in a tough battle, but the great majority of the combatants were men. The legends were probably based upon the actual existence in the ancient world of women-warriors, of powerful priestess castes, and of matriarchally ordered societies. The existence of purely female communities has not been substantiated.

p. 122. *green stones*. Schomburgk said it was still possible when he knew Guiana in the middle of the last century to acquire charms carved from green jade or jadeite. Monardus (see p. 226) who was interested in their supposed medicinal virtues, describes them as 'green with a milkish colour . . . made in divers forms and fashions, for so the Indians had them in old time, some like to fishes, other like to heads of birds, other like to bills of popinjays [parrots], other like round bead-stones, but all pierced through, for that the Indians did use to wear them hanging'.

p. 122. [*Berrio*] *being utterly unlearned.* It is clear from the reports Berrio sent to Spain that this was not so. He must have been trying to evade Raleigh's questions by an affectation of ignorance.

p. 123. *Maria Tamball.* Peter Martyr, in the *First Decade*, (see p. 227) describes a region of islands, possibly the estuary of the Amazon, called by the natives Mariatamball.

p. 124 *dispatched his Campmaster for Spain.* Domingo de Vera Ybarguen went to Spain in 1594 and returned in '96, having been only too successful in attracting colonists. A company of fifteen hundred, including women and children in gala dress, toiled up the Orinoco to the new town of San Thomé, which Berrio had built to guard the entrance to the Caroni river and where there was less than nothing for them.

p. 125. *well spent.* Later editions read *all spent.*

p. 126. *what they could possibly.* The text reads *possible*, which may reproduce a trick of spelling characteristic of Raleigh, who sometimes intends a final 'e' to be syllabic. In the Preface to the *History of the World*, Stanley's appears as Stanles.

p. 128. *about 50 more* [i.e. personnel of the voyage]. The voyage seems to have been almost a family affair, which may explain why Amyas Preston deserted. Many of the names are recognisable as those of Raleigh's kin or faithful followers. John Grenville was the son of Sir Richard of the Revenge. John Gilbert was the son of Raleigh's half-brother, Sir Humphrey. Butshed Gorges was a son of Winnifred Budockshide, or Butshed, Raleigh's first cousin on the mother's side, who had married a Somersetshire Gorges. Captain Whiddon was a trusted servant. Edward Hancocke was a secretary. Henry Thynne was Captain of the Bark Raleigh in 1591 with Howard at the Azores. Raleigh's elder brother had married a Thynne. Connock and Enos are Cornish names. Captain Calfield seems to have carried considerable weight. He led the attack on Cumaná. With the commanders so united a group, it cannot have been too hard to keep control of the men, even in the trying conditions of the voyage; they in their turn were probably picked crews.

The same cannot be said of the voyage of 1617, when Raleigh was a man in disgrace who had been long out of touch with the world.

p. 128. *thus it chanced.* The text reads *this*, which is sometimes Raleigh's spelling of *thus*, just as he writes *mich* for *much.*

p. 131. *Tobacco.* Explorers found tobacco in use among the natives of both Americas. Raleigh was by no means the first to introduce it into England, but he certainly cut a dash as a smoker in days when it was a very modern and rather daring thing to smoke. It did not endear him to King James, who wrote a pamphlet against the habit, which he considered dangerous and disgusting. It was, however, frequently recommended as healthful and medicinal.

p. 132. *their wives and friends drink it.* They still do.

p. 136. *a Cavallero.* He was Don Phelipe de Santiago, who escaped to Margarita. It was he who captured John Sparrow. See p. 227.

p. 139. *a Pina or a Potato root.* These tropical products were just becoming known in England. Raleigh has been credited with introducing the potato from Virginia, but he was never himself in Virginia nor were there any potatoes there other than sweet potatoes.

p. 144. *de Serpa before mentioned.* In 1569 Diego Fernando de Serpa was set upon as Raleigh describes. A survivor from the expedition died a prisoner on board one of Amyas Preston's ships, after the sack of Santiago de Leon in 1595. Raleigh alludes to it in his account of Spanish attempts on Guiana.

p. 144. *strong poison.* This is the famous arrow-poison of the South American Indians, called curare.

p. 146. *Monardus.* Dr Nicholas de Monardes of Seville wrote two very popular treatises on the drugs and medicinal herbs of the New World. In 1574 he combined them in one volume, which was translated into English by John Frampton and published in 1577 as *Joyful News out of the New Found World.* Tobacco and its properties are described in great detail, also maize, cassavi, etc.

p. 148. *Macureguarai.* Since Raleigh never reached this town, which he calls 'the first civil town in Guiana', he can hardly be said to have been in Guiana, as he conceived it, at all.

p. 150. *Captain George.* Alvaro Jorge, Berrio's lieutenant. See p. 222.

p. 152. *Bristol Diamond*: a kind of rock crystal found near Bristol and used as a gem stone.

p. 152. *the great lake Cassipa*. The flooding of the River Paragua was mistaken for a lake.

p. 153. *Ewaipanoma*. This improbable legend gained credence from having been known in the Middle Ages through Sir John Mandeville's travel-books. Since these were a mine of fantastic stories, they are a doubtful recommendation, but in a world only partly explored Raleigh was perhaps wiser than his stay-at-home critics allowed when he kept an open mind.

p. 154. *disadvantage*. The man, called Lucas Fajardo, had already been noted by the disapproving eye of authority as one who fraternized with the English.

p. 157. *Sparrow and Goodwin*: aged 25 and 16 according to a Spanish report, which goes on to say that Goodwin was torn in pieces by four tigers. In the New World jaguars were 'tigers'. The story, with its excess of tigers above the needful, was a figment of the Indian imagination devised to put the Spaniards off the boy's track. Raleigh found him again in 1617, having almost forgotten his English. Sparrow was captured and sent to Spain. When he finally reached England again he wrote a not very interesting description of Trinidad and Guiana, printed in *Purchas His Pilgrims* (XVI), 1625.

p. 158. *time nor power*. The copy text reads *not*. Later editions emend.

p. 158. *the new money*. There was a new minting in 1592, which included some handsome gold pieces with the Queen's head on them.

p. 161. *Gesnerus*. Konrad Gesner, a Swiss naturalist of the early sixteenth century, compiled a *Catalogus plantarum* and a magnificent *Historia animalium* (1551–8).

p. 161. *bundle of Decades*. Peter Martyr d'Anghera was an Italian who migrated to Spain in 1487, promising his friends that he would send them all the news. He found himself in a unique position to tell the Old World what was happening in the New. His *Decades* take the form of news-letters, and begin with an account of the voyages of Columbus. In 1555 the first four *Decades* were translated from the original Latin by Richard Eden, as *The Decades of the*

New World. In 1587 Hakluyt reprinted the complete collection (eight in all) as *De Orbe Novo*, with a dedication to Raleigh.

p. 164. *the great Philip*: the galleon that Raleigh would destroy at Cadiz, 'to be revenged for the Revenge'.

p. 167. *first offered . . . by Columbus*. In 1488 a brother of Columbus submitted his plan for a voyage of discovery to Henry VII who rejected it.

p. 167. *younger brethren*: consequently without patrimony.

p. 167. *Contractation House*. The Casa de Contratacion, established at Seville in 1503, supervised the whole of the overseas trade with the Indies in all its branches, thus enabling the kings of Spain to keep a close control over it.

PREFACE TO 'THE HISTORY OF THE WORLD'

p. 178. *inmost and soul-piercing wounds*: his being a convicted traitor, and the failure of some he thought his friends to stand by him.

p. 179. *His Majesty truly acknowledgeth*: in his *Daemonology* (1597), a book against witches.

p. 179. *Siracides*: author of the apocryphal Book of Ecclesiasticus, The Wisdom of Jesus the Son of Sirach.

p. 179. *Seneca*: a very famous Latin moralist and stylist of the first century A.D.

p. 179. *my fidelity towards Her*. Towards the end of the Queen's life, when others, notably Raleigh's friend Sir Robert Cecil who was by then Secretary of State, were corresponding secretly with King James as the likeliest to succeed, Raleigh still placed all his hopes in his old patroness, and does not seem to have known what was going on. It is noticeable that his gallantry to Elizabeth survived her death and he continued to praise her even when she was no longer there to reward him. A rumour was current in the seventeenth century that upon her death he was all for setting up a republic. It increased the esteem in which he was held by Cromwell, Milton and other anti-monarchists. Cecil's negotiations with James may look ugly from a purely personal point of view, in that he might appear to have abandoned his royal mistress and his old friends in order to smooth his way with the next comer.

They were actually of great political value. They smoothed the way not only for Cecil, but for the two nations of the Scots and the English, about to be for the first time united. The transfer of power to James after the Queen's long reign was effected without undue danger and disturbance. We do not know enough about the treason trial of 1603 to know whether this inevitably involved the sacrifice of Raleigh. It is plain that Raleigh himself never forgave Cecil (who died in May 1612) or his friend Lord Cobham, upon whose evidence he was convicted.

p. 180. *Sic vos non vobis*: Virgil is alleged to have shamed a plagiarist by a couplet in which he said that as the sheep produce wool and the bees honey, but haven't the use of it, so he has produced verses and another has profited by them. The Latin words, which have become a very familiar tag, mean 'You do the work while others profit'.

p. 181. *Plutarch*: a Greek historian and philosopher, with a strong moral bias.

p. 182. *Hermes*: Hermes Trismegistos (Thrice Great Hermes), the supposed author or inspirer of a number of semi-mystical books, highly valued by the Alexandrian Greeks, from whom they passed to the Middle Ages and to the Renaissance.

p. 183. *Euripides.* It is unlikely that Raleigh was familiar with the works of the Greek tragic dramatists other than in excerpts.

p. 183. *hands which the Holy Ghost hath guided*: authors of biblical books assumed to be divinely inspired.

p. 183. *angels into devils*: the fall of Lucifer. Isaiah, ch. xiv, vv. 12–15.

p. 183. *gnawn the grass*: the madness of King Nebuchadnezzar. Daniel, ch. iv.

p. 183. *that wise working of Pharoah*; Matthew, ch. xi, v. 16.

p. 183. *policy of Jezebel*: I Kings, ch. xxi and xxv. 2 Kings, ch. x.

p. 184. *second causes.* The ultimate cause is that God willed it. If one looks for natural explanations, one is investigating second causes.

p. 184. *Livy*: a Roman historian, 59 B.C.–A.D. 17.

p. 184. *Cratippus*: a peripatetic philosopher, contemporary with Cicero, whose son he taught. Plutarch, in his *Life of Pompey*, describes Cratippus comforting Pompey after his defeat at Pharsalia. When Pompey 'raised questions about Providence' (i.e. enquired how such things could happen in a well-ordered world), Cratippus forebore to point out that viewed detachedly his defeat might be thought providential. 'How, O Pompey, and by what evidence, can we be persuaded that thou wouldst have made a better use of fortune than Caesar, hadst thou got the mastery?' is the retort he refrained from making. (Plutarch's *Lives*, Loeb edition, volume v.)

p. 185. *the bottom of the sea*. This refers to the famous loss of the White Ship, in which Henry's son and a great number of young nobles were drowned, returning from Normandy in 1120. Henry made his daughter Maud his heir.

p. 185. *Edward the Second*. In 1327 Edward was deposed by his barons for misgovernment and shortly after was murdered in Berkeley Castle.

p. 185. *the Earl of Kent*. Edmund of Woodstock, Earl of Kent (1301–30), because he opposed Queen Isabella and her favourite Mortimer, was by them tricked into believing Edward the Second was still alive. When he tried to raise the country on Edward's behalf he was accused of treason and beheaded, an outrage which led to the fall of Mortimer.

p. 186. *Richard the Second*. Richard's reign saw much bloodshed, the consequence of Wat Tyler's rebellion and the struggle of the barons to maintain their power.

p. 186. *murder of Gloucester*. The Duke of Gloucester, who had wielded despotic power during the youth of Richard, died in prison at Calais, where he was thought to have been murdered with Richard's connivance.

p. 186. *deposed and murdered*. In 1399 Henry of Lancaster, who had been banished, returned to claim his father's estates, deposed Richard and had himself crowned Henry IV. Richard died in prison, it is thought by deliberate starvation.

p. 187. *Casaubon*. Isaac Casaubon, 1559–1613, a French classical scholar of immense industry. He came to London in 1610, to be free to practise his Protestant religion.

p. 187. *lost all that he had.* Anjou and Maine were ceded to Charles VII on the King's marriage. This was followed by the loss of Normandy.

p. 188. *Earl of Richmond.* Henry Tudor, who became Henry VII, fled to Brittany after the battle of Tewkesbury.

p. 188. *slaughter . . . of Edward the Prince.* The young prince, son of Henry VI, was stabbed on the field of Tewkesbury, while the new King Edward IV, so it was said, looked on and approved. Henry was murdered in the Tower. The Duke of Gloucester, here charged with the murders, was a younger brother of Edward. He was to ascend the throne as Richard III, and to instigate the murder of Edward's sons, the little King Edward V and his brother, famous as the Princes in the Tower. Modern historians tend to see Richard in a less lurid light.

p. 188. *his brother of Clarence*: a younger brother, put up as a rival.

p. 189. *without the trouble of any of his peers*: without a trial by jury.

p. 190. *Henry the Seventh cut off*: at the battle of Bosworth, 1485.

p. 190. *Stanley's head.* Stanley had deserted to Henry at a critical moment in the battle.

p. 190. *the young Earl of Warwick.* He was kept in prison all his life and ended on the scaffold at the age of twenty-one. The King, plagued by pretenders, took this drastic way with a dynastic threat.

p. 191. *no less valiant than learned.* He was a gifted poet, whose translation of Book IV of the *Æneid* is the first example of English blank verse.

p. 191. *James the Fifth*: of Scotland, grandfather of James VI who became James I of England.

p. 191. *all princes of eminent virtue.* King Edward VI, Queen Mary, and Queen Elizabeth, all of whom were childless.

p. 194. *materia prima*: the original material from which, in the opinion of some philosophers, the universe was made. Elsewhere (Book I, ch. i, par. 4) Raleigh calls it 'this potential and imaginary *materia prima*'.

p. 194. *Master Dannet.* Thomas Dannett published in 1600 a translation of the *Memoirs of Louis XI*, by Philippe de Comines, and *A Continuation of the History of France*. Raleigh is quoting from the second. He omits a short portion of the original, which adds nothing of value.

p. 195. *Charles the Fifth*: King of Spain and Holy Roman Emperor, voluntarily abdicated in 1555 and retired to a monastery, worn out by the burden of his immense empire. His son was Philip II of Spain, Elizabeth's great rival.

p. 196. *ways*: corrected by hand from 'wages', implying a manuscript which read 'wayes'.

p. 198. *Darius*. Darius III, King of Persia 336–330 B.C., unable to defend his country against Alexander the Great, was destroyed by his own followers, who wounded and abandoned him. 'Polystratus a Macedonian, being by pursuit of the vanquished pressed with thirst, as he was refreshing himself with some water that he had discovered, espying a cart with a team of wounded beasts breathing for life and not able to move, searched the same and therein found Darius bathing in his own blood. And by a Persian captive which followed this Polystratus, he understood that it was Darius, and was informed of this barbarous tragedy. Darius also seemed greatly comforted (if dying men ignorant of the living God can be comforted) that he cast not out his last sorrows unheard. . . . As he was thus speaking, impatient death pressing out his few remaining spirits, he desired water, which Polystratus presented him, after which he lived but to tell him that of all the best things that the world had which were lately in his power, he had nothing remaining but his last breath wherewith to desire the gods to reward his compassion' (*The History of the World*, Book IV, ch. ii, par. 14). Many ancient historians enlarged upon the sad end of Darius, but a nineteenth-century scholar, George Grote, observes unsympathetically that 'If we follow his conduct throughout the struggle, we shall find little that renders a defeated prince either respectable or interesting'.

p. 198. *Bajazeth*: Sultan of Turkey in the fourteenth century. He was defeated and taken prisoner by the Persian Timur. The story that he was kept in a cage and that Timur used him as his footstool is introduced as an incident in Marlowe's *Tamburlaine*. There is conflicting evidence as to the treatment actually meted out by the one conqueror to the other.

p. 198. *Valerian*: Emperor of Rome, defeated and taken prisoner by Sapor, King of Persia, in A.D. 260. History ran riot in describing the humiliations which were alleged to have been heaped upon him.

p. 198. *Belisarius*: a brilliant Byzantine general, inadequately rewarded by the Emperor Justinian, whom he served. Legend exaggerated the facts, making-believe he was blinded and died a beggar.

p. 198. *as*: corrected by hand from 'of'.

p. 198. *Petrarch*: famous in his lifetime (1304–74) as a scholar and even more famous thereafter for his poetry. He wrote a series of dialogues called the *Secretum* (1343) in which he imagined himself taken to task by Saint Augustine for his overmuch love of this world.

p. 201. *in the natural privation*. The comparison is presumably between the physical body and the body politic. Loss of a bodily faculty is rarely made good and the same is true of place and power. *privation* = degradation from office.

p. 202. *Cineas to Pyrrhus*: Cineas was the counsellor of the fourth-century conqueror, Pyrrhus, King of Epirus. Raleigh tells at length in another place (*The History of the World*, Book IV, ch. VI, par. 7) the story he alludes to here. Cineas having led Pyrrhus on little by little to avow an ambition to conquer the world, asked 'what they should do, when they were lords of all. Whereunto Pyrrhus (finding his drift) answered pleasantly that they would live merrily; a thing (as Cineas then told him) that they presently might do, without any trouble, if he could be content with his own.' Pleasantly=jokingly. Presently=at the present moment. i.e. without initiating an endless chain of conquests.

p. 202. *Ferdinand expelled the Moors*. The expulsion of the Moors from Spain was completed by Ferdinand II of Aragon, upon the capitulation of Granada in 1492.

p. 203. *the charge of two hundred thousand pound*: presumably for establishing a colony in Guiana.

p. 203. *till Death tells it us*: at this point one or two particular instances of no great interest break the majesty of the passage. 'It was Death, which opening the conscience of Charles the Fifth, made him enjoin his son Philip to restore Navarre; and King Francis the First of France, to command that justice should be done upon the murderers of the Protestants in Merindol and Cabrieres, which till then he neglected.'

TEXTUAL NOTES

THE LAST FIGHT OF THE REVENGE

I have taken my text from a copy of the first edition (1591) in the British Museum (292.e.26). The name by which the pamphlet is now generally known, *The Last Fight of the Revenge at Sea*, is not used on the title-page, but as running headline within the book. The version printed by Richard Hakluyt, in his *Second Volume of the Principal Navigations, Voyages, Traffics and Discoveries of the English Nation*, in 1599, differs very little, except that Hakluyt reduces to more reasonable proportions the figures at which Raleigh assesses Spanish casualties.

The original text is carefully even fussily punctuated, and cannot in this respect be easily modernised since the construction of the sentences is not modern. I have changed colons to full stops, added commas to phrases in apposition, and expunged much of the irritating excess of commas which occur with demonstrative clauses, and in other places where they would not be used today. I have also introduced some new paragraphs, where the Elizabethans were content to accept rather daunting blocks of print. Spelling is brought into line with modern practice, including the spelling of place-names and personal names, where there is an accepted modern style. In the sixteenth century Grenville's name was so often spelt Greenfield that the Spaniards knew him as Ricardo da Campo Verde.

THE DISCOVERY OF GUIANA

The length of *The Discovery* is such that if it were printed in its entirety it would take up a disproportionate amount of space in a collection such as this. It is therefore cut by about one sixth. Four main items selected for omission are (i) Raleigh's preface 'To the Reader' in which he defends himself against charges of bringing back worthless ore, or passing off gold from North Africa as South American. (ii) His summary of earlier Spanish attempts on Guiana. (iii) His detailed account of Berrio's third journey. (iv) The journey of his own party down-river. Anyone who wants to locate the famous mine which was the goal of the last voyage must study this part with great care, but it does not hold the same appeal for the general reader as the voyage up-stream with all its fresh impressions. Raleigh tends to repetition and his very full record of the names of native tribes, with their chieftains, districts, towns, rivers and tributary streams, though important to his purpose, can grow tedious.

There are two excellent annotated editions of *The Discovery*, that of Sir Robert Schomburgk (1848) and that of V. T. Harlow (1928). Schomburgk, himself an explorer familiar with the terrain, has followed Raleigh's journey step by step. The value of Harlow's contribution lies in his long and scholarly introduction, and in the appended transcripts of Spanish records, which were made at the time of the Venezuela Boundary Dispute, and are now in the British Museum.

The Discovery of Guiana was an immediate best-seller, and there seem to have been four different English editions in 1596. (See N. M. Penzer's introductory note to Harlow's edition.) It was translated into Latin, German, and Dutch. I print from a copy in the British Museum (C.32.g.25), normalizing spelling and punctuation, and introducing some additional paragraph divisions. Proper names, of which there are many, constitute a special problem, especially names which Raleigh must have taken down phonetically from the Indians. Many of the tribes he met are still to be found. Except in a few instances (e.g. Orinoco and Caroni, which he writes *Orenoque* and *Caroli*) I have not attempted to supply the modern equivalents of Indian names, though I have tried to make Raleigh's spellings consistent. He will write Waqueri, Wakeri and Wakiri. I have used what are now accepted forms of Spanish names, e.g. Trinidad for his *Trinidado*. Raleigh's text follows sixteenth-century usage in printing proper names in italics. I have abandoned this, keeping italics only for words he felt to be foreign, such as *Hamaca*, *Pina*, *Canoa*. This accords with modern usage and explains the unfamiliar form of words which have since been naturalized. The pronunciation of native names should follow normal English rules of pronunciation. To be quite precise, it should follow normal English rules of pronunciation as they held in the sixteenth century and for Raleigh, who was a Devonshire man. It is unlikely that he meant vowels to have their continental value. It is instructive to notice how he anglicizes Spanish names. Berrio is written *Berreo*, Ordaz is *Ordace*, Orellana is *Oreliano*, and Fajardo is *Fashardo*.

PREFACE TO 'THE HISTORY OF THE WORLD'

My text is based upon a copy of the first edition (1614) in the British Museum (C.38.i.10). Its first owner was Prince Henry's sister, Elizabeth, who did not marry into the House of Savoy as Raleigh had heard proposed, but became Queen of Bohemia. In one or two places in the Preface a misprint has been corrected by hand, conceivably by the author perfecting a presentation volume, otherwise in the printing-house, since similar corrections appear in at least one other copy. The book is an enormous folio, carefully printed and liberally illustrated with maps and plans. It is hard to the point of being impossible to bring the punctuation into line with modern practice without destroying some of the rhythmic modulations of the long, meditative sentences.

Raleigh introduces Latin quotations with great freedom, generally following them with his own translations. They would not be as disturbing to a seventeenth-century reader as they are today. When Raleigh himself supplies a translation, I have confined the Latin to footnotes, since for a reader unskilled in the language it breaks the flow and adds an appearance of extra difficulty to a text which is not in any case very easy. Where no translation is given, I supply one in italic type, taking it where possible from Philip Raleigh's *Abridgement of the History of the World*, published in 1700.

The Biblical quotations are not from the Authorized Version, which was published in 1611, by which time Raleigh had most of his work ready for the press. Since he quotes so often in Latin as well as in English, it looks as though he was working with a Latin text before him. Whatever form his private Bible reading took he must, for the sake of the considerable section upon Jewish history, have provided himself with a variety of texts and commentaries.

Raleigh had a good command of French, dating presumably from his service with the Huguenots. If the translations from Spanish are his own, he was well versed in that language, which seems highly probable. We must then think that he talked with Berrio without an interpreter. But very many, probably the great majority of the books he consulted, were in Latin, which was almost a second language to an educated man of his day. He does not seem to have had a similar facility in Greek, and he frankly admits that though he may appear to read Hebrew, a language highly valued at a time when so much scholarship was concentrated on Biblical studies, he had there had the help of 'learned friends'. We know he employed, among others, the Reverend Dr Robert Burhill, a Hebrew scholar. Ben Jonson claims that he contributed 'a piece of the Punic War' which Raleigh used without acknowledgement. It was something to be able to tell one's friends that one had had one's brains picked by no less a man than Sir Walter Raleigh. Jonson admired the *History* and supplied the verses which explain the allegorical frontispiece. Laborious as it must have been, Raleigh had enough time on his hands for the compilation to be largely his own work, and it is plain that such it is.

SELECT BIBLIOGRAPHY

(It will be noted that Raleigh's name is often spelt Ralegh. This is his own fairly constant spelling. The other is the traditionally accepted English spelling of the name.)

EDITIONS

The Works of Sir Walter Ralegh, 8 vols., Oxford, 1829. This is the only complete collection, and the last time *The History of the World* was reprinted in its entirety. Scholars today would query some of the pieces here given to Raleigh, and would add *The Last Fight of the Revenge*, which was omitted, because it was published anonymously.

Arber, E., *The Last Fight of the Revenge*, 1901.

Harlow, V. T., *The Discoverie of Guiana*, 1928.

Latham, A. M. C., *The Poems of Sir Walter Ralegh*, 1951.

Schomburgk, R., *The Discoverie of Guiana*, 1848.

BIOGRAPHIES

Edwards, E., *The Life of Sir Walter Ralegh together with his Letters*, 2 vols., 1868.

Stebbing, W., *Sir Walter Ralegh*, 1899.

Williams, N. L., *Sir Walter Raleigh*, 1962.

COMMENTARY

Bradbrook, M. C., *The School of Night*, 1936.

Bush, D., *English Literature in the Earlier Seventeenth Century*, 1945.

Edwards, P., *Sir Walter Ralegh*, 1953. This is a study of Raleigh as a literary figure.

Firth, C., 'Sir Walter Raleigh's *History of the World*', in *Essays Historical and Literary*, 1938.

Lewis, C. S., *English Literature in the Sixteenth Century*, 1954.

Racin, J., 'The Early Editions of Sir Walter Ralegh's *The History of the World*', in *Studies in Bibliography*, 1964.

Strathmann, E., *Sir Walter Ralegh. A Study in Elizabethan Skepticism*, 1951.
Wilson, J. D., Introduction to *Love's Labour's Lost*, New Cambridge Edition (revised), 1961.

HISTORICAL BACKGROUND

Anderson, R. and R. C., *The Sailing Ship*, 1926.
Benham, F. and Holley, H. A., *A Short Introduction to the Economy of Latin America*, 1961.
Callender, G., 'The Battle of Flores', in *History*, 1919.
Fawcett, B., *Ruins in the Sky*, 1958.
Gardiner, S. R., *The History of England from the Accession of James I*, vols. i–iii, 1883.
Hakluyt, R., *The Principal Navigations of the English Nation*, Everyman Library.
Haring, L. C., *The Spanish Empire in America*, 1947.
Harlow, V. T., *Ralegh's Last Voyage*, 1932.
Laughton, L. G. C., 'The Navy: Ships and Sailors', in *Shakespeare's England*, vol. i, 1917.
Marcus, C. J., *A Naval History of England*, vol. i, 1961.
Merriman, R. B., *The Rise of the Spanish Empire*, 1936.
Oppenheim, M. (ed.), *The Naval Tracts of Sir William Monson*, 1902.
Parry, J. H., *The Age of Reconnaissance*, 1963.
Quinn, D. B., *Ralegh and the British Empire*, 1947.
Rowse, A. L., *Sir Richard Grenville of the Revenge*, 1937.
—*The Expansion of England*, 1955.
Taylor, E. G. R., *Late Tudor and Early Stuart Geography*, 1934.
Wernham, R. B., 'Elizabethan War Aims and Strategy', in *Elizabethan Government and Society*, ed. Bindoff, Hurstfield and Williams, 1961.